TWIST

TWIST

SARAH CANNON

Feiwel and Friends

New York

A Feiwel and Friends Book

An imprint of Macmillan Publishing Group, LLC

120 Broadway, New York, NY 10271

Our books may be purchased in bulk for promotional, educational, or
business use. Please contact your local bookseller or the Macmillan Corporate
and Premium Sales Department at (800) 221-7945 ext. 5442 or by email at
MacmillanSpecialMarkets@macmillan.com.

Library of Congress Cataloging-in-Publication Data

Names: Cannon, Sarah, author.

Title: Twist / Sarah Cannon.

Description: First edition. | New York : Feiwel and Friends, 2020. | Summary:
  A group of gifted middle-school students must band together to save their
  town, as well as a fantasy world, from monsters.

Identifiers: LCCN 2019018599 | ISBN 978-1-250-12330-5 (hardcover) | ISBN
  978-1-250-12331-2 (ebook)

Subjects: | CYAC: Adventure and adventurers—Fiction. | Monsters—Fiction. |
  Ability—Fiction. | Friendship—Fiction. | Supernatural—Fiction.

Classification: LCC PZ7.1.C37 Twi 2020 | DDC [Fic]—dc23

LC record available at https://lccn.loc.gov/2019018599

Book design by Liz Dresner

Feiwel and Friends logo designed by Filomena Tuosto

First edition, 2020

10 9 8 7 6 5 4 3 2 1

mackids.com

*To Bill, because after half a lifetime there's still
no one I'd rather have adventures with than you.*

1

Bushwhacked

It was a green and stormy night. Tornado season in Oklahoma was like that.

People with common sense had already gotten where they were supposed to be—a closet or a bathtub—any room with no windows was good, unless you lived in a trailer, and then it was better to leave completely. Just another day in Tornado Alley.

But tonight the weather had caught Michelle at the worst possible time. She was already riding her banana-seat bike home from Dana's when she realized the sky wasn't just darkening, it was going green. That was a bad sign. Then she realized the clouds had dropped down to form a long wall across the sky. That was even worse.

She still could have been okay, except she took the back way home.

The path cut across a field, but kids had been using it for years, so there was a smooth, dusty track worn by the ghosts of other bike tires. Someone had been on it just a few minutes ago, because in the glow of her bike light Michelle could see dust floating above the path ahead of her. Even though she had glasses on, she blinked, like the particles were going to get in her eyes.

The sudden howl of an animal shocked her, and she swerved. Her bike light flickered as she hit a chuckhole, a big one that hadn't been there last time she'd taken this path. The beaded hair ties at the ends of her long red braids bounced against her back.

"Whoa!" she said out loud to no one, squeezing her brakes. Then she hit another hole and almost flipped her bike. She rode right off the path, wading to a stop in the tall grass. She wheeled her bike around so she could use her light to see.

Right in the middle of the path was a huge pawprint. Something growled, much closer than the howl had been.

Lightning flashed, and thunder rumbled way too quickly for comfort. On the other side of the path, something enormous moved through the grass. It was louder than the rush of the storm, and Michelle thought she saw the tips of bristling fur before the glare of lightning washed across her glasses and blinded her.

Back on her bike, pedaling as fast as she could, Michelle tried to quiet her breathing so she could listen to the thing that was following her. She could hear the panting of the beast and the crashing of its body through the grass as it chased her. Then it was on the path, and its paws were silent but its breathing was getting closer.

Above them, the storm clouds rolled across the Oklahoma sky.

Michelle was in the home stretch now. She could see the lights of her street in the distance. But she was also on a downhill slope. Pedaling couldn't help her anymore. All she could do was hold on and steer. She jumped a bump in the path, then another. She bounced on her seat, and her glasses bounced on her nose.

Then she fell.

The bike skidded out from under her on the dusty path. The handlebar hit her on the knee, hard, and her glasses flew off. There *wasn't any time to look for them. There wasn't even time to scream. With an echoing howl, the creature sprang.*

She lived, but only because the storm had confused the view enough that the monster attacked her bicycle and not her. She pulled herself backward into the sea of grass, her hurt leg dragging on the ground.

On the path, she could hear the squeal of metal and the snarls of the creature as it found a machine instead of meat. Then she heard a snort as its head swung up, fixed on her location. Quick as the lightning overhead, she rolled over and dragged herself to her feet. She limped down the hill toward a drainage ditch as enormous rain drops began to splatter all around her. Lightning flashed, and the thunder was deafening.

She slipped and fell again, this time tumbling downhill into the water at the bottom of the ditch. The rain was blinding. She got up onto her hands and knees as best she could. She started to head up the hill toward the tall wooden fence that enclosed her yard. There was no gate on the back, but she could scream for help, and maybe someone would hear her.

Then an enormous, dark shadow crossed in front of her.

Michelle made for the concrete arch that separated the ditch from the cow pasture. The water in the ditch was rising as the rain ran downhill across the hard-baked summer dirt instead of soaking in. Water got up her nose, and she choked but kept going. She didn't look behind her. She could hear splashing, panting, grunting, but she was too afraid to look, or think, or stop. She half swam across the archway, no longer afraid of the water moccasins her parents had told her a million times were in here and could kill her. Then she hit the other side . . . and her fingers found wire instead of freedom.

The farmer had run fence across the arch.

She turned to go out the way she'd come in, but it was already too late. The creature loomed across the entry. A flash of lightning illuminated its hairy bulk, and she realized it had one great paw up on top of the arch and was leaning down to look in at her, its posture like a person's. Lightning flashed, and its sharp teeth gleamed. Without her glasses she couldn't be sure, but she thought it smiled.

Then it moved. She dodged, but she was a mouse in a trap. There was nowhere to go. Outside the arch, every animal in earshot made itself smaller as the monster pounced. Michelle screamed and screamed. And then she didn't.

The monster's howl echoed across the neighborhood, amplified by the concrete arch. Michelle's neighbors cowered in their closets, fearing tornadoes more than anything, and being completely wrong.

As Eli Goodman finished reading, his teacher, Mrs. Benton, clutched her heart. He guessed she hadn't expected him to be quite so bloodthirsty. Maybe she didn't read a lot of scary stories. The first character who saw the monster never got to live. Everybody knew that.

A few kids said "Whoa" softly. One or two even clapped. It would have been enough to make him want to try that new moonwalk move of Michael Jackson's, except that Scott Gabler was looking around like he smelled something his dog had delivered. He smirked at Eli as his crony, Brandon, muttered in his ear. Eli looked away, but he could still hear them laugh.

"So," said Mrs. Benton, widening her eyes at the class as if to say *Wasn't that something*, "who has questions about 'The Howler'?"

Adriana raised her hand.

"Do you write stories like that a lot?"

"I write screenplays, too."

"You mean movies, like *E.T.*?"

"More like the *Twilight Zone* movie, but yeah."

"So you want to work in Hollywood when you grow up?" asked Scott. It might've been a reasonable question without the smirk.

"That's the idea."

"That's, like, a lofty goal. Not that many people get to work in Hollywood, right?"

Eli'd heard enough.

"So you're saying if something is difficult, I should give up?" he asked.

Scott wasn't used to being challenged. He twitched. Eli thought Scott looked just like a jackrabbit, but if he wrote that into a story it would sound made-up, a fact he found annoyingly unfair.

"I'm just saying, maybe you need a backup plan."

Mrs. Benton didn't generally meddle in arguments unless someone was using fighting words. She liked to say tough questions built brain plasticity, whatever that was. Eli didn't care. He was mad.

"Backup plans are for people who don't believe in what they're doing."

"Or people who aren't any good at it."

"What's the career outlook for people who are obsessed with computer games?"

Eli knew that was a direct hit. Lately all Scott could talk about was *Zork*.

Just as a collective "Oooooooooh" began to rise, Mrs. Benton cut in.

"You know," she said, "you two have given me an interesting idea."

The class, smelling trouble, got quiet fast.

"Let's discuss a new topic. A project."

"Project?" said Jay through blue lips. The boy had a bad habit of putting markers in his mouth when he was thinking. Eli would've paid good money to get him to stop, because at first glance he always thought Jay had been poisoned. It was, he guessed, the downside of being a horror writer.

"Yes, but the good news is that you don't have to go it alone. You'll have help."

"This is a group project?" asked Neha Prasad, looking up from her sketchbook.

It sounded more like an ambush to Eli, and from the look on Neha's face, she agreed.

"Yes," said Mrs. Benton. "Let's call this . . . the Venn diagram project."

Eli knew what a Venn diagram was. It was a chart made out of circles. It was supposed to show where different subjects overlapped—and where they didn't.

"I'm going to break you into teams. Your first step will be to sit down and discuss your various interests. Then I want you to figure out where those subjects connect."

"What if they don't?" asked Scott with a scowl. Eli pictured his and Scott's Venn diagram circles repelling each other like magnetic opposites, same as they did in real life.

"They will," said Mrs. Benton with a smile designed to have the same effect as a firm hand on Scott's shoulder. "In fact, I'm so confident about this that if you can't come up with any commonalities yourselves, I'll sit down with your team over a lunch period and we'll brainstorm. I personally guarantee you we'll find one."

Scott shut his mouth. Nobody wanted to give up a lunch period, even for Mrs. B.

Court Castle's hand went up next. She was leaning back in her chair like it was a rocker, her long blond braid dangling over the back. This naturally made Eli picture her whacking her head on the floor. If he wrote it into a story, though, the floor wouldn't be carpeted. That way the thud would be louder.

"So, after we have this little meeting of the minds," Court drawled, "what do we do next?"

"I'll come up with a list of activities to help you explore your shared interest as a group," said Mrs. Benton. "You'll complete one, document it, and present your results to the class."

"I hate group projects," muttered Kelly. Eli, who was still awkwardly standing by Mrs. B's desk, would have to remember how much she could hear from the front of the room.

Not that he disagreed. Kelly's disgust for group projects was pretty much universal. One kid always ended up doing most of the work, and since this was the pull-out program for gifted students, everybody in Mrs. Benton's class had been that kid.

"Have a little faith," said Mrs. Benton, smiling at Kelly. "Now, to choose the groups. You can sit down, Eli."

She put her hands on her hips and gave the class a good once-over. Then she started rattling off names. Eli waited, and sure enough . . .

"Group five will be Neha, Eli, Court, and Scott."

Eli rubbed one dark-skinned hand across his close-cropped hair, then shook his head. Like he'd figured, it was an ambush. A setup to make him and Scott appreciate each other.

Scott was like a piece of gum on hot Oklahoma pavement, and somehow Eli had gone and stepped in him. Everywhere he went he dragged a long trail of Scott behind him. For other folks it was free entertainment, but Eli wasn't laughing. He was sick of being stuck with that kid.

2

Ripped Off

Eli's story had made Court's hair stand on end, and that took some doing, because her braid was long enough to sit on. It wasn't just that his writing was good, though it was. It was that Court knew exactly how it felt to be that kid biking home at night, speeding up at the thought of claws reaching for her in the dark. Court was new to the Academic Resource Center, but she'd been in the same regular class as Eli for two years, and yet somehow it felt like this was the first time she'd gotten a good look at him.

"Michelle screamed and screamed. And then she didn't," read Eli, and when the monster howled, Court got goose bumps.

She was still wondering if it was okay to clap when Scott started in on Eli, and then Mrs. B got that crafty look in her eye. Court was just cottoning on to how diabolical this project was when the bell rang. There was a rush as kids started shoving their stuff into their bags, but all Court wanted to do was talk to Eli. She abandoned her belongings and made a beeline in his direction, but Mrs. Benton got to him first. She started bending his ear about submitting his story to a kids' magazine.

Court dawdled at his elbow, but before long she started to fidget. Being the last kid on the bus was no fun. She could end up next to someone who picked their nose. She grabbed her books and bagged them up on the run. She'd catch him later. After all, they both rode bus thirty-five.

You could have knocked Court over with a feather when she'd ended up in the gifted class. Schoolwork had never been topmost in her mind. School was fine, it just took too long and happened indoors. When it came to buildings, her head, and rules, Court had always liked outside much better than in. Then her fourth-grade teacher ran a contest to see who could find the most moth and butterfly specimens, a challenge that was right up Court's alley. The second-place kid found forty-seven.

Court found seventy-six.

Miss Tavish could maybe be forgiven for suspecting Court had help, but to her credit she didn't come right out and say so. Instead, she asked Court to tell her more about her collection.

When you know a lot about something, it's nice to be asked. Court started talking and couldn't stop. She explained how she'd snuck into three different yards to check grapevines for the Mournful Thyris moth. She recounted her narrow escape when one fella sicced his dog on her and laughed as she ran. She described the hag moth's caterpillar, a critter so covered with hairy tentacles that people called it a monkey slug. She confided that keeping a bucket of rotting fruit in the garage for moth traps put a strain on things between her and her mama.

Miss Tavish listened until Court ran out of things to say. Then she gave Court an A+, mini-golf tickets, and gifted testing. Now Court went to the ARC three times a week and felt like a fish out of water most of the time. But Eli's story raised a new possibility. What if ARC class wasn't the daytime version of an awkward school dance that refused to end? What if it was actually a paradise of unexplored territory? Court loved to explore.

"Hey, Dwight," said Court to the bus driver as she hauled her stuff up the steps. The radio was turned down low, but Court knew from experience he'd blast it as soon as the bus pulled away from the school.

"Court Castle, heeeey!" said Dwight, and put his hand up for a high five. Court smacked it.

"Hi, Joshie," she said, ruffling her little brother's sun-bleached hair. He and two of his friends were in a seat about halfway back, shoving each other and hollering.

"Hello, buttface!" said Joshie, pulling Court's braid.

Court scoped out the bus and chose a seat right behind Neha Prasad, who already had her sketchbook out and had tucked her dark, shoulder-length hair behind her ears. Court didn't usually pay much attention to her. Neha was a draws-on-the-bus kid, and Court was an argues-on-the-bus kid from way back. Now it hit Court that Neha could've been doing amazing things all along, right under her nose. Court turned sideways and draped her arms across the seat backs, and what do you know? Suddenly she had a killer view.

Eli climbed the bus steps in the nick of time and out of breath. He slumped into the last seat, next to Jay, which Court felt proved her point. Jay was a nice enough kid, but there was no sugarcoating it: a blue mouth was distracting.

As Dwight cranked up Z 104.5 and swung the bus out of the lot, Court craned her neck to see what Neha was doing.

She really has been creating something amazing, Court thought.

Neha was sketching storybook houses. Unlike the boring brick ranches in their neighborhood, all of them hunkered down low in case of tornadoes, Neha's homes were every color under the sun, and they practically sprang out of the ground. They had clapboard siding, big old windows with window seats inside, and little tiny wooden shingles on their roofs.

Houses like that would have twisty staircases and hidden rooms, places Court itched to poke her nose into. She wanted to open one of the big front doors, prowl through hallways lit by stained glass, and skulk her way upstairs, doing her best to avoid the creaks.

Which one of those doors would she try first? To her eyes they were as different as fingerprints. There were doors that had two halves that opened separately, top and bottom. There were paneled doors, and doors with rounded tops. Court had never considered whether doors might have personalities before.

She was still debating between a yellow split door with the top already swung open and a red one with curved moldings when it happened.

The red door winked at her. Blinked an honest-to-goodness eye she hadn't even known it had, right exactly where the peephole ought to be. She blinked back at it, surprised.

Court leaned closer to Neha, who was coloring a brick walkway and didn't notice Court hanging over the back of her seat. The bus swerved, and Court had to hang on tight to keep from landing in Neha's lap. Dwight was trying to open a carton of milk from the cafeteria while he was driving.

Bless his heart, thought Court. It was something her mama liked to say, though she generally meant the opposite.

Maybe the wink hadn't really happened. The way Dwight was driving, maybe he'd hit a pothole and Court had blinked. But if it happened again? That would not be a coincidence. So Court eyed the red door some more.

It blinked right at her.

It was too much for one day. Court sat back and stared at nothing for a minute to get her bearings.

Right about then she noticed Scott smirking over the seat back in front of Neha.

"Hey, Court! When are you finally going to present something in ARC?" he asked. Scott's buddy Brandon turned to watch.

Court's parents ran a pizza parlor, and she knew how to handle a tough customer. She cracked a wide, friendly grin and laughed.

"I had a project all set to go," she said, "but I turned off my light and it got eaten by a grue!"

Grues were monsters in that *Zork* computer game all the ARC kids were playing lately. Court had never seen a game quite like it before. There weren't any little eight-bit aliens, just a black screen with white text describing where you were. You typed in what you wanted to do, and the game told you what happened next. Court thought it was pretty cool, and they were allowed to play it during ARC class, which was even cooler. But Scott and Brandon had a tendency to backseat drive whenever anyone else was playing, so she rarely did.

"Ha ha," said Scott. "I hope you present something with merit. Anything but unicorns and fairies."

Caught between them, Neha hunched her shoulders and leaned over her work. She'd given a presentation about mythical creatures the week before. Court's sister, Amy, ran Dungeons & Dragons campaigns around the Castles' kitchen table, so Court heard a lot of that stuff at home. She'd tuned Neha out, instead hatching a plan to reach the garage rafters from the top of her mama's van. It was a surefire hiding spot. Neha's talk couldn't have been *that* bad, though. Court had nearly fallen asleep during Kelly's lecture on whether plants could think.

"Good grief, Scott," she said, "why do you care what other kids like?"

"We're supposed to use ARC class to develop our talents. Liking unicorns isn't a talent."

Court spotted a flaw in Scott's reasoning.

"Liking *Zork* is a talent?" she asked.

"Programming in BASIC is a talent," he countered, and Brandon high-fived him. Court couldn't disagree, and she had to allow that most of the *Zork* fans in ARC did spend part of the day hunched over the classroom's two Commodore 64 computers writing code in the hopes that someday, they'd be the ones making games. Even so . . .

"Act like you got some sense," she said. "If playing *Zork* got you into code, then why can't liking unicorns get you into something else, like art?"

Neha turned around suddenly to look up at Court. "Stop talking, can't you?" she said.

"Why?" asked Court, feeling a little bit miffed. Didn't Neha appreciate someone sticking up for her?

"You won't convince him. The sooner you ignore him, the sooner he goes away."

Scott leaned over and grabbed Neha's sketchpad right off her lap.

"What are you scribbling in here all the time?" he asked. "I want to see."

"Give it back!" demanded Neha, lurching to her feet as the bus swerved around the corner into their neighborhood. She lunged for her sketchbook, but Scott held it high out of reach.

This sort of thing happened on the bus pretty regularly. Ordinarily Court ignored it, but she saw things differently this time. Neha and Eli had whole worlds in their notebooks.

"Scott, that's mine!" said Neha.

"What, this?" he asked. He tossed the sketchbook up in the air, and Neha made another grab for it, but Brandon whipped it away before she could touch it. He started flipping through it, and Scott turned to laugh at Neha's drawings.

"Awww," said Brandon. "Ain't it sweet?"

"Ooh!" said Scott, putting a hand to his chest and batting his eyes. "It's adorable!"

Neha was hanging over the seat, frantic and flailing, and the whole bus was watching. Scott and Brandon started holding pictures up for people to see. Then Scott snapped the sketchbook shut.

"Jay!" he called, and chucked it across the aisle. Naturally it smacked into Eli, who was making notes on his story.

"Hey!" he hollered. "Would you two knock it off?"

Jay scrambled for Neha's sketchbook, shoving a whole stack of stuff off Eli's lap in the process. When he fished it out of the mess on the floor, he waved it around like a flag. Then he chucked it back to Scott, who elbowed Neha out of the way when she tried to grab it. She was just about in tears.

Court figured she'd better step in.

The bus slowed to a stop to let kids off, and Court moved out into the aisle, cornering Brandon and Scott.

Ornery little weasels, she thought.

Court could whup either one of them, and she figured they knew it. They might scorn her *Zork*-playing skills, but she bet they'd never tied their sheets to their beds and rappelled down the sides of their houses. (Court fell when she was halfway down and landed in the bushes, but she didn't think that undermined her point any.)

It wasn't like she had to touch them anyway. She winked over their shoulders.

"Yoink!" shouted her little brother, Joshie, as he snatched the sketchbook from behind.

Those boys didn't know what hit them. Court couldn't help it. She put her hands on her hips and laughed out loud, along with the rest of the bus. It was their stop, too, so there wasn't much Brandon and Scott could do but get off, slapping the backs of the seats as they went and glaring all the way. Court sure hoped their faces would freeze like that.

"Outta the aisle!" ordered Dwight, and bus law was bus law, so Court sat down. Joshie handed Neha the sketchbook.

"Thank you," she said, and shoved it deep in her backpack.

It wasn't until Neha got off at the next stop that the breeze coming in through the windows blew something against Court's feet. She reached down and picked it up.

It was the drawing with the red, winking door, and it had a long, jagged tear along one side. Court knew an honorable kid ought to give it back, but she couldn't pass up the chance. That eye was shut at the moment, but she wouldn't rest until she saw it again.

3

Monster Problem

When Neha got home, she ran up the stairs and slammed the door to her room.

"Homework first, please!" called her mother from downstairs.

"Okay!" she yelled back.

She chucked her bag toward the corner without looking to see where it landed and leaped onto her bed. Then she opened her sketchbook and laid it out flat on her yellow-and-magenta bedspread, anxiously riffling through the pages. She passed a sketch of the row of shops on Main Street, which was safe and undamaged. The purple Victorian house with the turret and the apple orchard was fine, too. She kept flipping.

In Neha's experience, being terrible was what the Scotts of the world did best. Her parents, like parents everywhere, told her to ignore it. Soon, they said, Daddy would finish up his PhD in engineering, and they'd leave Scott and his nonsense behind. The thing adults didn't seem to understand was that there was a Scott in every town.

That was why Neha had started drawing Forest Creeks in the first place—it was her escape. Forest Creeks was exactly the kind of place she'd always wanted to live in . . . rainbow houses, wild gardens to explore, friendly little art supply shops and ice cream parlors to spend her allowance in, and not a Scott to be seen.

Her hurrying fingers flipped past the frog pond with its little boathouse, the giant treehouse with its many swings, and the arched bridge over the creek for which the whole town was named. There was furtive motion in each picture as she passed, but Neha didn't stop. She wouldn't feel safe until she'd checked every page. Still, even as she worried, she found Forest Creeks wonderful.

Neha's drawings had been the beginning of something huge. She'd woken up one morning to find her sketchbook mysteriously inhabited, like the flower in *Horton Hears a Who*. And just like that, what had started as a hobby had become the center of her world.

Now she not only had to keep Scott off her back, she also had to keep him away from her sketchbook. He'd always had an irritating habit of looking over her shoulder, but this was the first time he'd gone so far as to risk destroying her art. Neha didn't plan on ever having such a close call again.

She flipped to the next page, and her heart stopped.

This wasn't a close call at all, she realized. *It was a disaster*.

The drawing she'd been working on when Scott grabbed the sketchbook was gone. All that remained was a ragged edge of paper clinging to the spiral.

"Oh no," she breathed. She flushed with panicky heat, then went clammy.

Someone very special had been keeping her company on that page.

She quickly flipped to a picture of a gray house with a bright yellow door, surrounded by a field of wildflowers. A dusty red country road led back toward the main part of town.

"Swiz!" she said, tapping urgently on the paper with the eraser end of her pencil. It wasn't quite like knocking on a door, but it worked. "Open up!"

"Neha?" called a familiar, tinny voice from inside the house. Swiz always reminded Neha of an old-timey radio announcer.

"It's me! Hurry!" she called.

The yellow door opened, and the owner of the radio voice emerged from the house. He was wearing a white collared shirt, trousers, and a vest, which officially made him the most dapper stick bug Neha had ever come across. He strode right down the steps of the wooden front porch and waved up at her.

"Hey there, kiddo!" he said. "What's the fuss?"

Neha was awfully relieved to see her friend.

"Are you all right?" she asked.

She tucked her hair behind her ears and leaned in closer.

"Just swell," said Swiz. "What was all that racket?"

Neha's face grew hot with shame.

"Some boys on the bus," she said. "They tore out a page. Sleekit was on it."

If I was bold like Court, she thought, *maybe I could've stopped this from happening.*

Then again, Court had grown up here. She'd probably known Scott when he was in diapers.

Swiz wiped a hand across his antennae, flattening them against his head. His expression was serious.

"That's a pickle and no mistake," said Swiz. "Poor fuzzy gal. How do you aim to get her back?"

"I don't know yet, but I know who has her," said Neha grimly.

"He's not going to get away with it. Can you check around and make sure no one else is missing?"

"Will do," he assured her.

Then she remembered Swiz's houseguest.

"How's Swallowtail?" she asked. Lately her three eggs were the talk of Forest Creeks, and they were due to hatch anytime.

"The old girl's all cozied up inside by the fire," said Swiz, his face relaxing into a smile again. "Seems like she's getting close. She won't get off the nest for anything. Had to close the shop today to look after her."

Swiz ran Swizzlestick's Drugstore and Soda Fountain, where he mixed up all kinds of unusual creations, both delicious and healing. He was the best nursemaid anyone could ask for, but Sleekit's kidnapping had Neha panicked. She wished she could dive headfirst into the world she'd made and check on every single resident.

"If I sleep with the sketchbook open, will you shout when it happens? Maybe it will wake me up!"

Before Swiz could answer, a snarl echoed through the drawing that made the cross-hatched pencil sky shiver. Swiz's smile vanished so fast you'd think his face was a ghost town.

"Oh no," said Neha.

That was another tough lesson she'd learned recently. A world could be Scottless and still be dangerous. At first Forest Creeks had been peaceful, but lately she'd started opening the sketchbook in the morning to find nervous clusters of residents whispering about howls in the night, doors that had been smashed in, and neighbors who'd gone missing. Something was going hunting in her art.

"It's never come in the daytime before!" she said.

"Our luck's run out today, and no mistake," said Swiz, pulling the front door shut. Just before it closed, a long black snake with yellow butterfly wings zipped through the crack. Neha guessed Swallowtail *would* get off the nest after all, if her eggs were in danger. The winged serpent ribboned up into the air to look for the source of the snarl. Neha heard the lock click and watched Swiz tuck the key into his pocket.

"I think it's time to ratchet things up a bit. What do you say, Mayor?" asked Swiz, craning his neck to look at Neha.

There hadn't been any election; sometimes you got drafted. Neha didn't have what you might call "mayoring experience," but she was all the creatures of Forest Creeks had.

"Do it," she told Swiz. "We have to protect the eggs."

Swiz yanked on a lever, and quick as a wink a long fence of defensive spikes swung up out of the grass and locked into place with a thunk. Then he sprang for the porch and rang the big dinner bell that hung there as if he were trying to wake the dead.

In the far corner of the drawing, the grass began to ripple like water as something enormous rushed through it. Chills ran down Neha's spine. She leaned close to the picture, then pushed her hair back behind her ears as if something might climb up out of the drawing and grab it. She snatched a pencil off her bedside table and started to sketch.

"Swiz!" she said, pointing to her new creation. "Get that rope!"

He abandoned the bell and leaped to the task without question, though the rope hadn't been there a minute ago. Neha peered down the road toward Main Street, but it was too far to tell if more help was coming. She drew a baseball bat to go with the rope, and Swiz grabbed that, too. What time she had left she used to conceal the other thing she'd drawn, the thing the rope was connected to.

Swallowtail, undulating above Swiz's head, hissed at the

approaching threat. Swiz started backing away from the spikes. Neha could hear the rhythm of something's pounding feet as it came closer, but between the spikes and the long grass, she couldn't get a look at it.

It slammed against the defenses. They groaned and creaked, but they held.

Swiz gave a quick "Whew" of relief.

Then the thing hit the wall so hard the spikes went flying like bowling pins, and out burst four bona fide nightmares.

4

Missing Beastie

The biggest monster was a tortured arch of gray skin and bone. Its shoulder blades were so pointed and sharp, they seemed about to burst through its skin. To Neha it looked like a giant, hairless, skeletal jackrabbit. Swiz was a beanpole, but the monster towered over him. It screeched, and Neha covered her ears in spite of herself. Swiz was shaking so hard his antennae chattered. He slowly backed away, still holding the rope.

As the monster followed him, three more came strolling, bouncing, and oozing out of the grass, bold as you please. One looked like a cross between a slug and a porcupine. At the ends of its quills tiny mouths opened and closed. They made noise, too, the happy little humming sounds babies make when they see the spoon and figure out applesauce is coming. The third monster was a pool of darkness—but if you looked at it right, something was moving inside. As a ruckus started on the road from town, it whirled in that direction and snarled, and Neha saw way too many sharp claws in that inky cloud.

The last one was the smallest, but it didn't turn her stomach any less. It was round, and its fur was the soft brown of a tabby kitten, but otherwise it was mostly teeth—the type of critter Neha pictured anytime she had to reach under her bed for something. It was already clicking its teeth together, almost absentmindedly, as if whatever it was about to do amounted to one item on a long list of chores.

Neha was shivering, and she wasn't even in the picture. Then Swiz did something that shocked Neha so much you could've knocked her over with a feather.

"I don't know this for a fact," he said in his steady, tinny voice, "but rumor is monsters aren't too bright. If you came here to start trouble, I guess I heard right."

He danced backward as the skeletal jackrabbit monster lunged in response to his smart-alecky taunt, and in an instant, three things happened.

A huge silver dog named Bay came racing into view, responding to Swiz's alarm bell. The shadow creature rushed her, and a spitting, snarling brawl erupted.

The rabbit monster put a foot down, and the ground beneath it creaked.

And Swiz yanked the rope he was holding, springing a trapdoor in the ground and dumping the remaining three monsters into a pit.

Neha held her breath.

The porcupine-slug got out first, humming cheerily as it oozed its way up the wall. It headed straight for Swiz, who used his bat to fend it off. Then the bony rabbit monster and the toothy puffball launched themselves out. The rabbit monster landed in front of Swiz with a grin meant to show off its yellow, chisel-like teeth.

The dark thing attacking Bay was slashing at her, and Neha

flinched when she heard the dog yelp. Her pencil darted back and forth in the air as she tried to think of something to draw that would help without getting in the way.

Swiz pulled a big white marshmallow out of his pocket and threw it at the porcupine-slug. As soon as it touched one of the creepy little mouths, it expanded with a poof. Neha crossed her fingers anxiously. She and Swiz had been working together to cook up special defenses like this. The marshmallow oozed down over the mouthy little quills, and the porcupine-slug's eyes, too. Blinded, it took to turning in circles.

"YES!" cried Neha.

"What was that, beta?" asked her mother from downstairs.

"Nothing!" she shouted, glancing at the door.

When she returned her gaze to the sketchbook, Swiz was backing toward the house. As if being a ball full of teeth wasn't enough, it turned out the puffball could jump, and it began bouncing higher and higher, getting closer to Swiz with each hop. The jackrabbit monster capered as if it were a cute little bunny rabbit, and Neha shuddered.

The next time the puffball came down, it went for Swiz's leg. The stick bug hollered and swung at it with the bat, trying to get it off, remembering just in time about the rabbit monster. It sprang, but Swiz swung the bat as hard as Casey in that poem from school, and caught the monster right in its twitching nose.

Swallowtail streaked in and tangled with the puffball, but it caught hold of her and worried her with its sharp teeth. Neha cried out, her pencil darting in the air as if she could stab the little monster. Swallowtail struck once, twice with her glistening fangs, then wriggled free. Neha could see deep wounds marring Swallowtail's beautiful ebony scales. As the puffball sprang at the snake again, more help arrived. A girl Neha's age with short, dark hair swooped down from the sky in a cloud of black, red, and yellow wings, and snatched the little monster right out of the air.

"Redwing!" cried Neha, then clapped a hand over her mouth, hoping her mother hadn't heard. The fuzzball twisted, trying to sink its teeth into Redwing's hands. Her black high-tops swung forward as her cloud of wings swirled around her. Neha could hear the fuzzball's teeth clacking as Redwing struggled with it. The flying girl twirled in midair, soared out high over the field, and let go. The fuzzball plummeted to earth with a screech and a thud. There was more empty space in the sky, and Neha quickly sketched a boulder to follow the puffball down. That would stop it from hurting Swallowtail or anyone else ever, ever again.

Then the porcupine-slug, which had been randomly circling all this time, ran smack into the rabbit monster. At least a few of the tiny mouths must have cleared themselves of marshmallow, because the way that monster jumped it had definitely been bitten. It turned and attacked, crunching down on the slug with its chisel-like teeth. This turned out to be a very bad idea. The rabbit monster howled in pain and rage. Flinging itself backward, it smacked Swiz with one flailing paw and sent him flying.

Bay was still locked in a desperate battle with the shadow creature, but now Neha had a stroke of inspiration. She started drawing a huge tangle of string: on the ground behind the creature, in the air above it . . . everyplace she could think of. As it got all fouled up in her mess, it stumbled, and Bay rammed right into the center of the shadows and knocked it to the ground. There was a snap. The creature yowled, and when it dragged itself to its feet, it was limping.

The monsters had obviously had enough. The rabbit thing left a cloud of dust in its wake as it bounded down the red dirt road in the opposite direction from town with the shadow beast limping along behind.

"Is everyone all right?" Neha asked. Swiz picked himself up out of the dirt. He brushed off his fancy clothes, but one leg of his pants was soaked with blood. He was limping. So was Bay. The poor old girl had claw marks on her neck.

Redwing's sneakers hit the ground lightly, raising a puff of dust. She brushed off her jeans with her palms.

"Where's that round one with the teeth?" asked Swiz, looking around sharply.

"Dead," said Neha fiercely. She started to say that Redwing had killed it, but that wasn't true, was it? Neha was the one who'd dropped a boulder on its head. When she thought of what it had done to Swallowtail, she was glad.

"Swallowtail!" she exclaimed suddenly, remembering. She leaned closer, scanning the drawing.

"She was right there," she said, touching the tip of her finger to the page.

Swiz, Bay, and Redwing ran to the spot, and Bay immediately put her nose to a narrow trail in the dust. It led into the tall grass. Neha held her breath as they searched.

Redwing's heartbroken cry told Neha the news was bad. Swiz pushed through the grass to reach her and Bay.

"Oh," he said. "Oh no. Poor old girl."

When they emerged, Swiz had Swallowtail's limp form cradled in his arms. Neha's eyes welled with tears. She wiped them away just in time to keep any from splashing on the page.

Inside the house, the three unhatched eggs were already orphans.

Neha and her friends looked at one another in silence, and Neha made a vow. She didn't know where the monsters had come from, but she wasn't going to let them turn the refuge she'd created into a trap. She was going to stop them. But first, she was going to get Sleekit back.

5

Wrench

Reading his story in Mrs. Benton's class had gone better than Eli had dared to hope. He'd darn near missed the bus, so many kids had tried to talk to him about it. By the time he got home, he was fired up. All he wanted to do was pound the keys on his most prized possession: a sleek blue Smith Corona Super Sterling typewriter. He was feeling like Stephen King.

Then again, he bet Stephen King didn't have to write in front of an audience.

"Where'd he get a wrench?" demanded Lisa, then stuffed her mouth full of fluffernutter sandwich. Eli made 'em for her every day, and every day he hoped they'd stick her mouth shut, but it never worked. Even if it had, she still would've read over his shoulder. Little sisters. He shook his head.

"I can't understand you when your mouth is full," he told her.

"I said where'd he get a wrench at? You don't just get wrenches in arcades." Her two little buns resembled perked-up ears.

"They have to fix the machines sometimes, or how come stuff

has a DOWN FOR REPAIR sign on it? Dang, Lisa. You can't just ask me 'Where'd he get a wrench?' when I'm in the middle of something."

"How are you going to write the rest of the story if this part is messed up? The whole thing will be about what he did with an impossible wrench."

"Listen, don't you have something else to do?"

"I'm just offering 'structive criticism."

"You only know what that is because I told you. And it's not constructive when you tear down something I'm still building. Go play, Lisa!"

She was sitting on his bunk bed, so the look of scorn she gave him down her round little nose was even more effective than usual.

"I don't need to play like *some* people, but I guess I could check my traps." She slid down, her sneakers crunching on the balled-up drafts spilling out of Eli's wastebasket. Then she reached over and broke Eli's Twinkie into two pieces. She snatched up half and made a run for it.

"Stay in the yard!" he hollered after her, but if he was being honest he could admit that he was so glad for a break she could go to the moon if she wanted.

Eli had been known to try to get some writing done at school, but when his math grades started slipping even though his math book was conspicuously propped open on his desk, Ms. Garlett, his regular teacher, cottoned on. Nowadays if she saw him writing in class, she'd take his stuff away.

In Mrs. Benton's class his writing was encouraged, but sometimes Eli couldn't hear himself think over Scott's ego.

The front door slammed, and Lisa went by his window toting a long pole with a croquet ball screwed onto the end. The man at the garage sale where she'd bought the croquet set had even drilled a hole in the ball for her so the pole would go into it. She called this invention the Whacker! She made Eli and their momma practice saying it until she could hear the exclamation point.

The big air conditioning unit outside Eli's window kicked on with a roar. He bit into what was left of his Twinkie, ignoring the Lisa germs all over it. Then he leaned over his typewriter and got back to his script.

To his irritation, Lisa was right about the wrench. He went back over that part with the correction tape and took it out. He was working on the part right after Michelle vanished, and the arcade at the mall was full of whispers as her classmates spread wild rumors about what had happened to her. Things were going bump in the night. Pretty soon, Eli knew he'd have to kill off somebody else.

He shut his eyes and pictured the kids he knew, looking for weaknesses that would make them good monster bait. He found plenty, especially when it came to the clothes girls were favoring lately—lace headbands, plastic hoop earrings, lots of bracelets—things claws could catch on. He wrote a scene at a school dance, where people were sure to be wearing all three of these things. He was just working on the part where one girl made the fatal decision to go outside alone and wait for her ride, when:

"Eli!"

He jumped, knocking his pencil cup off his desk.

"What?" He spun around in his chair to find his momma framed in the doorway of his room. She was wearing her scrubs, and she had her nurse face on. Nobody messed with Eli's momma's nurse face.

"It's like your head is actually inside the typewriter, I swear! Where is your sister?"

"In the yard?"

"In the yard."

Eli realized a second too late that the look on her face meant she already knew exactly what he'd say, which meant he was 180 degrees wrong.

"She's not?"

"Right this second she is out front, rinsing her legs off with the hose."

He didn't want to ask, but the raised eyebrow he was facing didn't leave him much choice. "What's on her legs?"

His momma chucked his answer right back at him. "What. Is on. Her legs?"

She began to count off the possibilities on her fingers.

"Could it be suntan lotion? Bug spray? Sidewalk chalk? Let's see. What else could my precious baby have on her legs at five thirty on a school night when I am away from home?"

"It's five thirty?" demanded Eli, realizing his mistake before he'd even gotten his mouth shut. He cut his eyes to the right and immediately knew the sun was way lower than it had been. Slanting through the blinds, in point of fact.

"She was knee-deep in the drainage ditch, way down by South Eighty-Seventh Street. If she didn't have her red backpack on, I wouldn't have seen her at all."

That was bad. She could've ended up being one of those milk carton kids. Eli rubbed a hand across his face.

"Momma, I'm sorry, I just got busy . . ."

"There is no such thing as being too busy to know where your sister is!"

Eli knew that ought to be true, but somehow when he was working on a story, it wasn't. He didn't even remember real people existed when his writing was going good.

"What was she even doing back there?" he asked.

"What do you think she was doing? She was hunting monsters!"

No question, Eli was on the hook for that, too. When he'd first started writing, Lisa had nagged and nagged to find out what he was doing. In the end he'd caved and read her a script he'd written for their daddy. Eli was hoping she'd run screaming and stop pestering him with questions. He could admit it was not his best big brother moment, and he probably deserved how badly it had backfired. Lisa hung on every word of every story, and instead of jumping at shadows the way Eli'd expected, she'd made monster preparedness her hobby like she was a hunter living in a shack out in the woods. The traps were impressive, but she mostly caught cats and possums. Occasionally Eli.

"Eli, I know it's not easy to have to watch your little sister. But I also know you realize my job's at stake. I cannot have something terrible happen to Lisa because your mind is wandering."

Eli hung his head. He wanted to tell her his mind wasn't wandering. He was too focused, that was the problem. He also wanted to tell her that he wouldn't have to be in charge every afternoon if Daddy wasn't out in California trying to make a go of it as an actor. When Momma was in nursing school, one or the other of their parents had always been home in the afternoon. But Momma said nursing school had been her turn to do something big, and this was Daddy's, even if it meant money was tight.

She'd still managed to get him the Super Sterling for his birthday.

I should've paid better attention, he thought. There were copperhead snakes around those drainage ditches, and water moccasins, and Lisa was so busy looking for imaginary monsters she might overlook the real ones.

"I'm sorry, Momma."

Her hands slid from her hips. Her shoulders slumped, and she sighed. Her scrubs looked like they'd seen some things, he thought.

He stood up.

"I'll check on Lisa and make grilled cheese. It's okay, Momma. You can take a shower."

She shook her head a little. "Thank you."

She walked out into the hall, and Eli heard her door close.

Outside, Lisa had finished hosing off and was dunking her toys in a puddle she'd made where the sidewalk curved and the yard got low. Her brown plastic cassette player with the handle, the one she'd had since she was a baby, was blasting "Wanna Be Startin' Somethin'."

"*It's too high to get over,*" she sang to a toy lion. "*Too low to get under . . .* You should've took swimming lessons. You're in trouble now."

"No, I'm in trouble," said Eli. "What were you thinking?"

"I wasn't thinking," she said. "I was strategizing. You want to catch a monster, you have to go where they go."

"Monsters go where their brothers tell them," he said. "Which is what you should do. Didn't I say stay in the yard?"

"You said go outside. You didn't say where."

She started singing along with the music again.

"Mama say, mama saw, ma sock you sauce—"

"That's not how it goes," he objected, watching her squish a Little Person into the mud with her toes.

"It is today," she said.

"Quit getting all muddy again. Come here, let me rinse you off." She cooperated for a change, and as Eli hosed off her toes, he said, "I'll make you a grilled cheese."

"With ketchup."

"Yeah."

"What about the wrench?"

It took him a second. Then he frowned.

"Never mind about the wrench."

She stomped with glee on the warm concrete. "I told you!" Then she ran inside the house in her wet feet, leaving Eli to pick up her sneakers.

6

Sleekit

Court was sitting on her bed gawking at Neha's drawing when Joshie came slamming into her room. She flipped the edge of her Star Wars sheets to cover the torn piece of paper as he grabbed her soccer ball.

"Bye!" he said.

"Whoa, whoa, whoa! Where do you think you're going with that?"

Joshie looked offended, and he chest passed the ball off the wall a few times to vent his feelings. "Outside!"

"Where's yours?"

"Mine was Nerf. Bert's dog ate it."

Bert's dog ate stuff no dog should be able to chow down on and live. Frisbees. Entire pizzas including the box. Shoes—lots of shoes.

"And where are you taking my ball?"

"To Bert's."

"Of course you are. Give me that."

"Why? You never use it!"

Court weighed her options. She did like that ball, but the last thing she needed was Joshie hanging around getting in her hair.

"Fine," she said. "You can take it. But if you lose it, you buy it. I don't want to hear about its new home on the Laughrans' roof."

He was already gone. She heard the front door slam.

Carefully, Court uncovered Neha's drawing and went back to eyeballing it. Down in the corner, Neha had drawn a little sign. It was smeared, but it appeared to say: FOREST CREEPS. Now that she could examine it without sneaking, Court saw all sorts of little details she hadn't noticed before. The rough texture of the brick path Neha had been drawing. Hinges on the doors and shutters of the nearby houses. Antique doorknobs that were oval instead of round. Teeny little ladybugs on the teeny little plants.

She stared at it, willing something, anything, to move. But even though she had this sneaking suspicion she'd seen curtains move out of the corner of her eye, nothing out and out proved what happened on the bus was real. Still, there was something about Neha's drawing that made her want to look at it for hours, the way she'd watch frogs, or dragonflies, or a red-tailed hawk. It had that same kind of quiet to it. Life in the Castle household was like living by well-traveled train tracks, so Court wasn't opposed to quiet.

Downstairs, Amy was getting her long-running Dungeons & Dragons game rolling. Most of the players also delivered pizza for the Castles. Court could hear both of the Mikes (who'd been nicknamed Shorty and Wig for everyone's convenience), and Amy's boyfriend, Ian, too. He was one of their most reliable drivers, so he'd practically be family even if he weren't dating Amy.

"In our latest adventure," said Amy, "we'll attempt to recover three powerful weapons, stolen by the wizard Keraptis, from White. Plume. Mountain."

Everyone cheered.

"You got it?" cried Ian. "Awesome!"

Amy was the Dungeon Master, the one who spun the elaborate choose-your-own-adventure tales they battled their way through together. She tortured them, and they loved her and hated her for it in equal amounts. Court thought of them as the Lost Boys to Amy's Wendy.

Court sat quiet, watching the paper and listening to the game downstairs, until the light outside started to fade and she got a crick in her neck. Finally, she got her reward.

The eye in the door opened and looked around real slow. It blinked. She jumped a little but caught herself before it noticed her. Then the door swung open, though Court didn't know if it did it on its own or if someone inside turned the knob. A moment later, an animal poked its head out. It resembled a weasel, or maybe an otter. It had rounded ears and a long, ringed tail. Its fur was silvery purple, and the colors shifted when it moved.

Finally, thought Court.

She figured anything that could understand how to work a doorknob could communicate if it wanted to, so she waved a little bit.

"Hey there," she said.

The door shut so fast it just about took off the critter's tail. The otter-weasel chittered, scolding the door, then whipped around to search for the source of the noise. To Court's surprise, when it spotted her, it relaxed.

"Hello, Court," it said.

Court near about fell off the bed.

"I don't exactly recall being introduced," she said.

"I'm Sleekit," said the creature. "I know you by reputation. You stopped that Brandon boy from gleeping."

It took Court a titch to wrap her head around this. Then she understood. The critter was talking about *gleeking*, a recent fad on the bus that raised the bar for gross, in Court's opinion. Kids had figured out how to shoot jet-propelled streams of spit at people from a gland under their tongues. Brandon had made some little kids cry one day doing this, and it was possible Court had bent his fingers back when diplomacy failed. (Amy said that in D&D diplomacy generally meant "I hit it with my axe," and in Court's experience this was often true in the real world, as well.)

"'Scuse me for asking, but I'm not sure why gleeking interests you," said Court, hoping she wasn't going to tick off the otter thing and waste all her hours of waiting.

"You stopped him from doing it. That's what interests me."

Sleekit whisked up onto the porch railing to get closer to Court's eye level.

"We need help, and you're a helper, Court Castle."

Court's heart jumped in the air and clicked its heels together. If movies and books were anything to go by, she was long overdue for an adventure like this.

Then she paused. After all, this wasn't her drawing.

"Why aren't you asking Neha? And if you did already and she wants my help, too, why wouldn't she ask me herself? We see each other every day."

Court had a horrible thought.

"Wait. Is *Neha* doing something bad?"

That didn't fit at all.

To Court's relief, Sleekit about fell off the railing laughing. Court couldn't help grinning back, even though she felt somewhat abashed.

"I had to ask," she said.

Sleekit rolled over, which made her fur sparkle in the moonlight in the most glorious way.

"Neha is wonderful. She's the reason we have this place. But we could all use some advice from someone more . . . rough-and-tumble. Neha included. Will you help us?"

If Court had learned one thing from being a big sister, it was to get the details before you said yes.

"Help with what, exactly?"

Before she could answer, something in the drawing howled. It was so loud and so close that Court jumped.

Sleekit vanished. Just swirled right down the railing and took off into the house. The door shut behind her as quick and as quiet as it could, and the eye squinched shut as if it was afraid Court would poke it. Court heard the deadbolt engage.

Then a nightmare lurched out of the dark borders of the drawing and shambled across the page.

It was gorilla strong and wolverine fierce, and being small on the page didn't stop it from being huge compared to everything around it. It was sniffing around as though it was looking for Sleekit, and Court's gut told her they weren't exactly friends. The scene played out like a scary movie, and she had no idea what to do. As she watched, Sleekit appeared in the window of the house's turret. She pressed against the glass, peering down at the monster.

Then Court noticed something small outside the house, sneaking through the dimness. It was some kind of bird, but darned if she'd seen anything like it before. It was soft and dusk colored. The only reason she could see it at all was because its edges glowed faintly. It had dark eyes and a long beak, not unlike a kiwi bird. So maybe it couldn't fly away. Instead, it hid in the bushes.

The little bird was all alone. Its body language made Court look where it was looking, and she spotted a little burrow under the looping root of a tree. The creature would have to pass right under the feet of the hunting beast to get there. It stirred anyway, and Court thought it might be just desperate enough to make a run for it. But even that tiny flash of activity pricked the ears and flared the nostrils of the monster, and Court knew the little bird was about to get caught.

She reached for the paper, figuring she'd pick it up and shake it, or something. Anything to cause a distraction. What happened next shocked Court so much she just about peed her pants. The monster whipped its head around as she touched the paper. It looked straight at her. They locked stares.

Then it howled, and Court could hear it as if it were standing on her ugly pink rug. It ran at her. She scooted back, which was never going to work while she was holding the picture, and only missed falling off the bed because her free hand found empty air before her backside did. The monster's snarling face grew larger and larger as it rushed toward her. Then, when it filled the margins of the page, it hit some invisible boundary that stopped it—barely. The paper bulged and rippled, like it was struggling to contain the world inside.

She hollered in shock.

"Are you watching Mama and Daddy's TV?" Amy called up the stairs.

Court looked over her shoulder.

"It's the radio!" she hollered back.

When she set eyes on the drawing again, the monster was gone. She leaned over, searching every corner for some sign of it, but found nothing. Then the door that had first gotten Court's attention in the first place eased back open, and Sleekit slipped cautiously out. Her whiskers were drooping, her eyes soft and scared.

"Will you help us?" she asked.

Court figured she'd have to have a heart of stone to say no.

"I'll do what I can," she promised.

Now she had to figure out what that was.

7

Bigger Problems

Neha was doing her level best to stay calm, but she was losing the war. On top of being worried sick about Sleekit (maybe even because of it), she was having one of those days. The ones where you have to run for the bus with your jacket half on. The ones where you raise your hand in math class and you're wrong. The ones where you shove a book into the rack under your desk and accidentally shove everything that's already in there out the other side and onto the floor.

At least in ARC she could look at her sketchbook. She had to be careful in her regular class, because Mrs. Miller did not take kindly to distracted students. She was the kind of adult who'd say, "What's so interesting, Nee-ha?" (Mrs. Miller always said Nee-ha instead of Nay-ha no matter how many times the other kids corrected her.) She was liable to take the sketchbook right out of Neha's hands and keep it until the end of the day. Mrs. Benton always got her name right, and students were encouraged to work on their own projects during class.

But being able to look didn't mean there was anything good to see. Like every other time Neha had peeked, the residents of Forest Creeks shrugged their shoulders at her if they had shoulders, and hung their heads and tails if they didn't. There was no sign of Sleekit—and no telling when the monsters might come back.

Most of the residents were out working on traps they'd built or Neha had sketched. Neha had been doing her best in spare moments to draw a tricky little pulley system that could drop rocks on the monsters' heads from between houses, but she couldn't get the rope to lie quite right.

"Draw it coiled on the ground, gal," urged Swiz, who was hiding behind a tree in case one of her classmates glanced over. "I can run it through that doodad for you, lickety-split."

"What did you say?" asked Adriana.

"I asked if you know what's for lunch," said Neha.

"Why?" asked Adriana. "You never buy."

This was true.

"Just curious," said Neha.

She gave up the rope as a bad job and let Swiz handle it. He took care of it in a flash, as promised, but all that did was make her feel clumsy, then ungrateful, then ashamed for being ungrateful.

"Whoa, what's that?" said a voice behind her. She went to slam the sketchbook shut, but a hand landed with a smack on the left-hand page before she could.

"Stop that!" she said, alarmed to realize how close she was to shouting. Heads turned.

Naturally, the hand was Scott's.

"What is all that?" he asked.

"My business," she snapped back. "Didn't you see enough of it yesterday?"

"I didn't see *that*," he said, and she was relieved to realize he was pointing at her pulley system and not Swiz, whose antennae were sticking out of the bushes.

"That would work in real life, you know."

She sure hoped so.

"That's kind of the point," she told Scott.

"Why the heck are you reporting on unicorns when you understand mechanical engineering?"

"I reported on the Pegasus, not unicorns," she said. "But it doesn't matter. I can like what I want."

"I know," said Scott mildly, and suddenly Neha was stuck half-way between rolling her eyes and staring in shock.

"But not everybody can do that," Scott persisted. "Don't you get it?"

Neha had opinions about who was going to get it, and it wasn't her.

"All I'm saying is if you applied that skill to our group project, we'd blow everyone else out of the water," he said.

Neha hit her boiling point.

"Do you have my drawing, or not?" she demanded, standing up.

"What drawing?" he asked.

"Neha!" called Court suddenly. Neha glanced at her. She was standing by Mrs. Benton and waving. Neha decided to ignore her, then rounded on Scott.

"The torn-out one!" she said. "What did you do with it?"

"Neha!" said Court again, louder.

"Nothing! I don't have it." Scott started edging away.

"Really? Because I remember you playing keep-away with my art on the bus, and now Slee—"

Before Neha could finish the foolhardy act of saying Sleekit's name out loud in front of everybody, yet another hand descended on her poor abused sketchbook. This one flipped it shut and picked it up, and then the hand's mate grabbed Neha's arm and started to steer.

"Don't argue—walk," muttered Court in her ear, and only the memory of Court's help the day before stopped Neha from digging in her heels and shouting that nobody had better touch her sketchbook ever again.

Mrs. Benton smiled and waved as they went by. To Neha's shock, Court steered her right out of the classroom and kicked the door shut behind them.

"Where are we going?" asked Neha.

"The atrium. To weed. I told Mrs. Benton you looked like you needed a break. Here."

Court shoved Neha's sketchbook and backpack at her. She was already wearing her own. She led the way down the hall.

The atrium was one of Mrs. Benton's pet projects—a garden in the center of the school, open to the sky but walled in on three sides with glass, and on the fourth by a wall of the school.

"She never lets anybody come in here without her," said Neha as they slipped through the door into the warm, humid space.

"Mrs. B knows I can tell weeds from plants. That's the kind of thing that landed me in ARC in the first place," said Court.

"Well . . . that's good," said Neha. "It was nice of you to bring me."

Kids generally picked their best friends to do things like this, and Neha, who hadn't lived in Tulsa as long as her classmates, tended to be forgotten.

"Let's hope you still think I'm nice ten minutes from now," said Court, and led the way toward the back of the garden, leaving Neha wondering what had gotten into her. Court was usually so sunny-side up. Could weeding be that bad?

Weeding, it turned out, meant hiding between the tallest plants and the only nonglass wall.

"If Mrs. Benton checks on us, she'll think we're truant," said Neha.

"Nobody says truant," said Court, who was busy pulling her Trapper Keeper binder out of her bag.

"I bet you can still get in trouble for it, though," said Neha.

"Mrs. Benton will be thrilled. Nobody ever weeds back here. Anyway, I think you and me got bigger problems," said Court. "You want to tell me more about this whole creatures-that-live-in-your-sketchbooks phenomenon?"

Neha knew she was blinking too much, but it seemed to be a byproduct of trying to think of the right thing to say. She settled on, "It's nice that you like my drawings, but it makes me uncomfortable when people look over my shoulder. My art is private."

"It's hard to keep something private when it's howling so loud."

That got her attention. "What?"

"One of your drawings tried to attack me. Well, something in it did. I mean, first it was attacking other stuff in the drawing, then me. It's what Mrs. Benton would call pugnacious, I guess."

Mrs. Benton was a fan of Latin roots.

Neha got over her shock quickly, and on its heels came anger. "What would you be doing with one of my drawings?"

"Pull those up while you holler at me," said Court, motioning toward some tiny plants. Then she ripped open the Velcro flap of her Trapper Keeper and flipped the binder open. Sitting on top of the folders inside was Neha's missing sketch, with a big rip down one side.

"There it is!" cried Neha, dropping a weed and snatching the paper. "Where did you find it?"

Court turned so red her freckles looked like powdered sugar. "On the floor of the bus."

Neha eyed her suspiciously.

"Yesterday," Court admitted.

Neha's face got hot. Wasn't there one kid in this whole school she could trust? She opened her mouth to lay into Court for going almost a whole day without telling her the truth, but before she could, the drawing itself demanded her attention. The front door of the house with the tower opened with a bang, and out came Sleekit. She rushed right into the foreground of the paper, making her seem larger, or at least closer.

Neha had never been so glad to see anyone in her life. Sleekit was the picture of health—excuse the pun. Her fur was soft and glistening, her whiskers were long, and her eyes were dark and bright.

Once Neha knew Sleekit was safe and sound, she was furious.

"Where have you been?" she shouted, her voice echoing off the glass of the atrium.

"It couldn't be helped. The page got torn out," said Sleekit, and reached up to innocently groom her whiskers.

"Did you even try to get back to the rest of Forest Creeks?" Neha demanded.

"Forest *Creeks*," said Court, as if her own personal light bulb had just lit up. Neha frowned at her in confusion, then turned back to Sleekit, clearly waiting for an explanation.

"It all worked out. I'm fine, and besides, I told you, we need this one!" Sleekit waved a paw at Court.

"No, we don't!" said Neha, who had not forgotten about Court keeping the drawing for a day.

"Do what?" Court asked in apparent disbelief.

"I hate that phrase," said Neha, frowning at her. "I've never heard it anywhere but here. Just say, 'Are you kidding?' like a normal person."

But Neha didn't wait for Court to amend her question. Instead, she pointed at Sleekit, who pretended to bite her dirt-covered finger. Court stifled a grin. Neha saw it and turned on her.

"*She* wanted me to tell you the truth and ask you for help, and I wouldn't. I've spent a whole day going out of my head looking for her, and she was exactly where she wanted to be the whole time."

"That's not quite fair," said Court mildly. "She got attacked, after all."

Neha's scowl faded. She looked at Sleekit, who was running in a circle to make it clear that of course she hadn't been pretending to bite anyone. Who had the time?

"You're really okay?" Neha asked.

Sleekit held still long enough to say, "Right as rain. But it was big. And hungry."

Neha's anger vanished as quickly as if someone had poured a bucket of water over her head and put it out.

"There were monsters in the sketchbook last night, too," she said. She took a deep breath. "Sleekit . . . Swallowtail died."

Sleekit froze. As Neha's words sank in, her whiskers dropped. Her ears drooped. The sparkle in her eyes vanished. If Neha was the mayor of Forest Creeks, Sleekit was the next-door neighbor who knew everything about everyone, and she and Swallowtail had been particular friends.

"Her poor eggs," Sleekit said.

Neha nodded, then rested her head tiredly on her knee.

Court reached over and put a hand on Neha's arm, gently this time.

"None of this is your fault, y'all," she said. "That thing me and Sleekit saw was huge. You're not in a fair fight."

She told Neha what had happened, giving the best description she could of the monster.

"I wish I understood where they were coming from," said Neha in frustration, balling her fists.

"Are you gals weeding way back there? Bless your hearts!" said Mrs. Benton from the doorway, and both girls jumped like startled prairie dogs. Neha pulled out another handful of weeds, just to be safe.

"You two are going to miss your bus if you don't skedaddle! Doesn't Eli ride thirty-five? He's long gone."

Neha jumped up and grabbed her backpack, the drawing fluttering in her other hand. She carefully stowed it inside. She was halfway to the door, which Mrs. B was holding open, when she realized Court wasn't following her. She turned to find Court still sitting with a thunderstruck look on her face. Had Neha been that rude? She didn't think so. And while she still wasn't sure she wanted Court's help, she was at least convinced Court was genuinely offering.

"Come on, Court," she said. The other girl looked up at her, and a ready-for-anything glint sparked in her eyes. She leaped to her feet, and the two of them rushed out the door.

"Here, don't forget your fund-raiser flyers," said Mrs. Benton, handing each of them a sheet of bright yellow paper. "I'm looking forward to checking out your parents' new place, Court!"

"They're excited, too, ma'am," said Court politely, but she was already dragging Neha by the arm.

"Bye, Mrs. B!" Neha called over her shoulder, but she didn't hear her teacher's reply. For the second time that day, Court hustled her down the hall.

"Court, I know how to walk," said Neha.

"Do you know how to run? Because we've got places to be," said Court.

"Dwight will wait," said Neha. At least, he would if he noticed.

"I ain't talking about the bus," said Court. "We got bigger fish to fry. That giant monster? It's that thing from Eli's story. The Howler."

Neha tried to stop so she could look at Court, who kept them both moving without missing a beat. "How can it be? He doesn't draw."

"I don't know. But I remember how he described it, and I'm telling you, that's what it is."

"I'm going to murder Eli," says Neha.

"Well, you can't murder him on the bus. But don't worry about that. I know where he lives."

8

Believe It or Not

It was a good thing Court hadn't said anything about the Howler sooner, because the way Neha was scowling there was about an 80 percent chance she would have launched herself at Eli if he'd been standing in front of her.

Instead, they were the last kids on the bus and had to cram onto the ends of seats next to kids they barely knew. Court got off at her regular stop and made Neha swear to do the same. The second Court got home, she dumped her stuff and made a beeline for Neha's.

When she got there, Neha was already half a block away.

"You don't even know where his house is," said Court, catching up. She hurried alongside, trying to catch her breath.

"I know it's in this general direction," Neha said. She was still steaming, but Court noticed she took the time to step over a fuzzy woolly bear caterpillar as it crossed the road.

"Try to simmer down, okay?" Court asked, but the set of Neha's chin didn't give her much hope.

Eli lived on Mrs. Harvey's cul-de-sac, and Court viewed it with new interest. The big circle of asphalt would be good for games, she figured, but in the evening all the adults would come home and park on the street, and she'd have to worry about busting out car windows by mistake. More than normal, that was. On the whole she preferred living by the vacant lot.

The moment it took her to reach this conclusion was long enough for Neha to storm up Eli's sidewalk and start banging on his door.

"Whoa, wait for me," said Court, chasing after her. Fortunately, it took Eli a minute to answer. When he did, he was barefoot. He had a Twinkie in one hand and a disgruntled look on his face.

"Monsters!" said Neha, without so much as a hello. "You just had to write about monsters!"

"Why do you care?" asked Eli. He looked down at his Twinkie, then shoved it in his mouth to get rid of it.

"Your monsters are eating Neha's Creeps," said Court.

Eli and Neha both stared at her.

"What?" said Eli through a mouthful of Twinkie.

Yet again, Court found herself blushing. She looked at Neha when she answered. "I thought the label on your drawing said *Forest Creeps*, so that's what I've been calling them in my head."

Eli swallowed the Twinkie.

"Drawing? I never touched your drawings. That was Scott," he said.

"Apparently *you* don't have to touch my drawings to ruin them," said Neha. "All you have to do is write horrible things."

"Hey," objected Eli, "some people enjoy my writing."

Court held up her hands in a peacemaking gesture.

"Your writing's not the problem; it's your characters."

They both looked at her again.

"What's the difference?" said Eli.

"Aren't they the same thing?" said Neha.

Court shook her head with amusement. These kids were two peas in a pod. Maybe she should have waited by the mailbox. Eli turned back to Neha.

"Look, not everyone likes horror," he said. "I get that. But—"

"This isn't about what I read for fun. I drew a town in my sketchbook and—" Neha stopped for a second. Court didn't blame her. The whole thing sounded made-up.

But Neha took a deep breath and kept going.

"The . . . Creeps . . . moved in. I didn't draw them. They showed up in my sketchbook, and they're alive. Now your monsters are hunting them. Which is a problem, because then they'll be the opposite of alive."

Before Eli could answer, there was a loud wolf whistle down the street. Court turned to see Brandon and Jay slowly biking past the entrance to the cul-de-sac.

"What's up, nerds?" yelled Brandon, who was holding a giant Styrofoam Slurpee cup in one hand.

"You're in ARC, too!" Neha began, but Eli shook his head at her.

"Don't bother," he said.

"Why not?"

Court answered, "My mama says there's no point confusing some people with the facts. It won't matter to those two what you say."

Eli nodded.

Jay and Brandon were already moving off anyway, laughing loudly.

Neha shook her head in disgust, then turned her frown on Eli again.

"You have to fix this," she said.

"Listen," said Eli. "You draw; I write. That's cool. But pretending the stuff we make up is alive? As games go, this is pretty weird."

"It's not a game!" said Neha. "It's real!"

Eli winced. He glanced over his shoulder, then stepped outside and pulled the door shut behind him. He lowered his voice, but his tone was fierce.

"Look, I don't care if you're playing around or not," he said. "You've got to cut it out. My little sister believes my stories. She sets monster traps all over the house. Yesterday I got electrocuted by my own Operation game. Not buzzed, seriously shocked. Do you know how bad that hurts? If she hears you she'll be even more obsessed than she already is."

"Wait," said Court. "Your sister's here right now?"

Eli frowned at her. "Yeah. You saw her on the bus."

Court tossed her braid over her shoulder and shrugged.

"I know my family's real rowdy, but at my house when things are this quiet it means somebody's up to no good."

Eli's eyes widened.

"Oh, crud," he said. He lunged for the door and disappeared inside.

"Lisa!" he shouted. "Lisa!"

Court and Neha glanced at each other, then followed him in. They could hear him hollering from the back of the house. Court turned to peek into the coat closet.

"You can't just go through people's things!" said Neha, appalled.

"Coat closet's on the top-ten list of most popular hiding places," said Court, and reached inside to move the coats. There was a snapping noise.

"Ow!" hollered Court. Her hand emerged with a mousetrap clamped on her fingers.

Neha helped her pry it open.

"At least it was one of the small ones," said Court, flexing her fingers. She couldn't help but be a little impressed with Lisa, though.

Eli returned, hopping on one foot as he put on his Adidas.

"She's gone," he said. "I have to go find her."

"She do this a lot?" asked Court.

Eli groaned. "You have no idea."

He hustled the girls out of the house and locked the door behind them, shoving the key in his pocket.

"Look, what can I do so you won't be mad at me anymore?" he asked Neha. "I got enough people mad at me as it is."

"You can burn all your stories," suggested Neha.

Eli looked at Court as if maybe she could explain Neha to him. Instead, Court said, "That would do it."

"Funny," said Eli. "I guess I'll see you later."

Court had an intuition that Eli was planning to avoid them as much as possible from now on. This conversation couldn't be allowed to end here.

"You'll find Lisa a lot faster with some help," she said.

Eli stared. "You'd help me look?"

Court glanced at Neha. She was still spitting mad, but she was also the kind of kid who wouldn't step on a caterpillar. Court raised her eyebrows in what she hoped was a meaningful way, and after a moment, Neha nodded.

"Where should we start?" she asked.

9

Bowl of NO

Eli couldn't believe Lisa had taken off on him again. His momma was going to kill him. Or maybe these girls would do it first. They seemed to have an unhealthy predisposition to burn things.

"All I mean is that if you light your stories on fire, the monsters might vanish. The source material will be gone," said Neha.

"I've spent years writing that source material, and I'm not destroying it for you or anybody," said Eli. "Can you stop talking? I'm trying to listen for Lisa."

Neha was always so quiet in class.

Eli headed straight for the ditch where his momma had found Lisa yesterday, the one he had put in his story. He got there just in time to see the flash of one of Lisa's beaded hair ties as she passed under a willow that was probably bigger than any tree was supposed to be down there.

Why couldn't she just play in her playhouse like a normal kid? Then again, Eli'd seen a rattlesnake behind the playhouse once.

He guessed the yard could be dangerous, too. But he'd told her to stay put, and he was going to give her a piece of his mind when he caught her.

By the time he got to where he'd seen her last, she was already over a fence she had zero business climbing. It guarded a pasture that backed up to the drainage ditch. Tall trees marked a watering hole Eli, Lisa, and every other kid in their neighborhood were absolutely forbidden to go near. The whole thing was a great big bowl of NO.

Eli squished his way across the hummocky grass of the drainage ditch with the girls following behind him. As he got close to the stream that ran down the center, a frog squeaked and plunged into the water so loudly Eli could've sworn it was a muskrat. He stumbled, and one of his Adidas plunged right into the water, which was scummy and orange around the edges.

He cussed out loud, then cringed. Good thing his momma couldn't hear him. He started to apologize to the girls, then stopped. Truth was, he didn't know if he wanted them to stay or go. Neha was taking this yarn she was spinning a little bit too seriously. Still, looking for a missing sister was lonely and, if he was being honest, scary. Lisa was always getting herself into heart-stopping trouble.

In the end, he said nothing. They squelched up the far side of the ditch, only to discover the fence had a line of what his grandpa called bob wire at the top.

"I'm not allowed to go in there," said Neha.

"Me either," said Eli, and started to climb up where he'd seen Lisa go over.

He was balanced, his palm on top of a fencepost and one foot in the mesh of the fence, and was easing his other leg over the top, when a bluebird came busting out of a hole in the post like there was some kind of interdimensional bird portal in there. Eli just about landed on the bob wire and did himself some serious damage, but in the end he managed to fall off the fence instead. On the wrong side. In front of Court and Neha. He waited for them to laugh.

Instead, Court put her hands on her hips and gave the fence a once-over.

"Could be worse," she said. "At least it's not electrified. Here."

She laced her fingers together to make a cradle out of her hands.

"Let's try this again. I'll give you a boost."

"Thanks."

Eli made it over the top the second time and was there to help Neha down. She looked as nervous about fence-climbing as he was, which made him feel a little better. It wasn't until Court was swinging to the ground without any help at all that Eli felt a draft on the back of his leg.

He twisted around to look. On top of everything else, he'd torn up his jeans. He'd be in trouble for that, too, but if he found Lisa first, he might survive.

He looked around. "Where the heck would she go?"

"I've got a pretty good idea," said Court. "Follow me."

Eli had noticed the old barn plenty of times. You could see it from the road around their neighborhood. It just hadn't occurred to him that they could walk there. It loomed ahead of them, as dilapidated as a moth-eaten mammoth in a museum. Did Lisa have the guts to go strolling right up to it—maybe even inside?

Of course she did.

"There could be anything in there!" he said. "Rusty tools, or animals, or—"

"Lisa," said Court. "That's totally where I'd go."

"You've been inside?"

"Nope," said Court. "Always wanted to, though. Your baby sister's something else."

"You keep an eye on her, then!" he grumbled. He wasn't about to confess he admired her, too.

As it happened, Lisa wasn't inside . . . yet. They found her setting up a net outside the barn doors.

"What are you doing?" demanded Eli.

"Covering the exits," said Lisa. She started flinging her rope into the air, trying to get it over the hayloft pulley.

"You need a weight on the end of that," said Court.

"Good idea," said Lisa, and ran to pull a rock out of the crumbling foundation.

Eli rounded on Court. "Could you not help, please?" he asked.

"Perfect," said Lisa, securing the rope. She chucked the rock into the air. It missed the pulley, but it would have scored a direct hit to Eli's head if he hadn't jumped out of the way.

"Lisa, stop that!" he hollered.

She stared at him.

"Just move," she said. "Up there in the smart-kid class, and you don't even know how gravity works."

She paid out the line on her rope and tried swinging the rock in a circle.

"Eli," said Neha, "we found her, and she's safe. Now can we please talk about lighting your monsters on fire?"

"What? No!" said Eli. "Stop saying that!"

"I'll stop saying it when your monsters stop hurting the Creeps!" said Neha.

"Neha, you have to cut it out," said Eli. "You sound like you believe this stuff. You're the poster child for how everybody thinks ARC kids actually are."

"I'm pretty sure Jay and his purple tongue have that covered," said Court, "so why don't we focus on fixing this problem?"

Eli couldn't believe what he was hearing.

"Why are you humoring her?" he demanded. "Monsters are not real!"

Neha made a furious noise.

Court raised her eyebrows.

"Oh, really?" she said, reaching over to unzip Neha's backpack and pull out the sketchbook. "Including these monsters?"

She opened the sketchbook with a flourish, right in Eli's face.

If Eli'd had time to expect anything, he'd have anticipated the little town he'd noticed Neha working on once or twice. He was not prepared to be confronted by a purple creature that was maybe an otter or possibly a weasel. Its silvery-purple face took up the entire paper, as if it had pressed itself as close to him as it could.

"Boo!" it said, then chattered loudly.

Eli pinwheeled backward and landed on his butt in the red Oklahoma dirt.

"What the heck is that?" he shouted.

"It's a her, and she has a name!" said Neha. "You call her Sleekit!"

"You drew that thing?"

Sleekit chuttered ominously. The rock-thunking stopped.

"Of course not. She just . . . showed up. Like the rest of the Creeps."

"So how did that thing get in your drawings?"

"I don't know! How did your monsters get in there?"

That got Eli back up on his feet.

"Where?" he asked, peering cautiously at the page.

It was a good question. All three of them huddled around the sketchbook to look. Sleekit had backed off. She was busy washing her round ears on the front lawn of one of the houses. Other Creeps were chatting and putting away tools. Court and Neha waved with the tips of their fingers, like all of this was normal. Some of the Creeps waved back.

"How do you make them move?" asked Lisa, who had ducked under Court's arm when Eli wasn't looking. She tapped the drawing with one finger.

"Don't smudge it!" warned Neha. "I don't make them do anything. I drew their neighborhood, that's all."

"So you woke up one day and these . . . Creeps were living in your notebook?" asked Eli. "How many are there?"

"I lose count," said Neha. "Sleekit?"

In the drawing, Sleekit puzzled. She held up her front paws. Then she balanced on those and held up her back paws. Frustrated, she stood on her head and held out all four paws. Then she gave up.

"Lots," she said.

Deep down, Eli was still afraid the girls were going to laugh at him, that they'd been hoodwinking him all along. But the purple otter-weasel, the tall stick-bug man who was toting a ladder under his arm, even a floppy-looking thing that was rolling around in the dirt and looked as though it was made out of socks . . . they were real in a way Eli couldn't shake. They had texture and personality and motivations of their own.

So when Eli had another question, he asked the otter-weasel directly.

"Where'd you come from?"

She appeared to be frustrated by the question. Eli guessed that was fair. Life with Lisa had taught him that "Where'd you come from?" was a conversation that got awkward fast.

"What I mean is, did you travel here? From somewhere far away?"

"We started here," she said, which both did and didn't answer his question, because it sounded as if it could be an old-fashioned way of talking, like "We started off to this place," which really means, "We ended up here." That was what he got for reading about hobbits, he guessed.

"You were born here?"

"No. We started here. Every story has a beginning, and all our beginnings were here."

"So you all came from stories?"

"We're the hearts of them, yes. Like you're the heart of your won story."

"You mean your own story?"

"No. Stories are earned. You're the heart of your won story."

Eli mulled that over.

"If you won," he asked, "how come you live in a notebook?"

Sleekit showed her tiny white fangs. Lightning fast, she streaked closer.

"It's not our fault," she said. "Stories have tellers. All of ours quit."

As a storyteller himself, this seized Eli's interest.

"What do you mean, they quit?"

"They quit telling our stories. Once, we were so interesting that our stories had to be told. And then"—she looked quickly away, turning her sinuous neck this way and that to avoid his gaze—"then we weren't."

So . . . Neha's notebooks were like Mos Eisley spaceport. A slew of different creatures with no place to go, all jumbled together.

"Those can't be my monsters, then," he said, shaking his head. "I never quit."

That was when he heard it. It was faint, as if it was far away inside the drawing, but there was no mistaking it or pretending he didn't recognize it. The howl.

A panic broke out inside the sketchbook. Creeps of all sizes and colors came shambling and bouncing and racing across the pages, away from the sound. One of them was a giant green spider as tall as a tree. Something that big couldn't get inside a house to hide. It was stuck outdoors. Another treelike thing, this one a huge evergreen, disintegrated before Eli's eyes, and he realized it was actually dozens of smaller clockwork trees balanced in formation like circus acrobats. They were all desperate to get away.

His monsters were coming.

10

Electric Avenue

Eli might have been reeling, but this wasn't Neha's first rodeo.

"Put it on the ground!" she said to Court, then frantically dug in her pockets. "I need a pencil!"

She turned them inside out. She slapped her back pockets. Nothing.

"Lisa!" said Court. "You got anything to scribble with in that pack of yours?"

"Yeah!" Lisa scrambled for it and came back with a grubby handful of pencils and crayons. Neha whipped one out of her hand so fast it barely had time to arrive. She hovered over the page, shoving her hair behind her ears.

All across Forest Creeks, Creeps were scrambling. They wound every winch, set every trap, and hoisted every weapon.

And while they did, Neha touched pencil to paper.

"A wall?" she asked, hesitating.

"Try a maze," said Court.

A cloud of dust was looming on the horizon. Time was short. Neha staggered several tall, stout posts on both sides of the road, then began stringing wire between them as fast as she could go. Just as the first monsters came into view, she drew an electrical box with a switch at the base of the post closest to the defensive line of Creeps.

"Mixface!" she said. "Flip that on!" A stocky little person with a portable cassette player where his face should have been jumped to obey, and a low hum rose from the wires.

Sleekit was bristling, every last tiny white tooth bared. Swiz had a stout stick in his hand and was guarding the porch of the house where he'd stashed poor Swallowtail's eggs.

Some of the more timid Creeps were cowering behind the fortifications, or going door-to-door collecting others. But most were wide eyed and ready. They stared down the country lane that ran past Swiz's house and waited.

Above the drawing, Eli, Neha, Court, and Lisa sat, tense and silent.

Almost silent.

"Eli," said Lisa, "it's them."

Eli put his palms on the ground for balance and leaned as close to the paper as he could get. Neha could see his gaze flickering as he took in every detail.

"This can't be happening," he said at last.

"Yeah, we know the feeling," said Court.

On the other side of the wire barrier, nightmares prowled, snarling and hooting and laughing. A hyena-shaped creature with smiling red eyes and more teeth than face lunged at the wires, sending smaller Creeps flailing backward. Neha couldn't understand how it laughed that way without cutting its own face to ribbons. The inky cloud-beast was there, too, lashing its tail in a pool of blackness.

A tall, angular creature with skin stretched too tight over its bones extended one long finger from a hand that had too many of them. It touched the wire. The other monsters roared with laughter as it shook from the electrical shock, its teeth chattering. Then another monster stepped up beside it. And another. And another. They reached out with hands and paws and stranger things Neha could not name, and as one they gripped the wire. Little Lisa gasped.

Some monsters hollered or squealed from the pain. Smoke rose from the maze of wire, and Neha could have sworn she smelled it.

Then the little box at the base of the post spat sparks. There was a sizzling noise, and the hum of the fence was silenced.

Every monster with a mouth smiled.

Then they charged.

Some of the monsters attacked the wires directly, ripping them down. Others went after the posts, slamming into them until the wood began to crack under the strain. Plenty more streamed off into the trees on either side of the road and worked their way in from there—not that this was easy to do. The Creeps had prepared, and their work was causing the monsters ten kinds of heck. Neha and the others couldn't see through the trees, but they couldn't miss the monsters who were flying up in the air and hitting every branch on their way back down.

That didn't change the fact that there were more enemies than traps. Creeps turned to fight as the first monsters broke through into the town. Neha's pencil flicked back and forth helplessly, but the monsters and the Creeps were too close to each other, and she wasn't sure what would happen if she scribbled over a Creep by mistake. She settled for drawing nets in the air, waiting to draw the last line until a monster was directly underneath. Creeps were dodging in and out between the houses, triggering defenses whenever they could. Buckets of Swiz's special small-batch slime upended themselves on monsters' heads. Catapults launched. But the Creeps were being driven back.

"Turn the page!" said Neha, and Court flipped it. The monsters weren't just attacking the Creeps, they were wrecking the town as they came through. Swiz smacked a horned, hairy purple monster with his stout pole, but though he succeeded in driving it back, it hefted a rock and smashed out the plate-glass window of Swizzlestick's Drugstore and Soda Fountain.

"You sack of hair, leave my poor soda fountain alone!" hollered Swiz, and bashed it again before it could go inside and do more damage.

Sleekit was whizzing around the page so quickly that all any of them could see was a snarling purple blur. Monster after monster grabbed at some suddenly bleeding part of itself as she passed.

But the Creeps were being overwhelmed. Neha could hear their panicked cries. And over it all, she heard the wicked laughter of the Howler.

Redwing soared by, lugging a heavy rock, and dropped it on the nearest monster.

"Neha, help us!" she shouted.

"You've got to get the Creeps out of there," said Court. "They're about to get stomped."

Trouble was, Neha didn't know what to do. She'd tried to connect Forest Creeks to the real world before, but it never worked, and she didn't know why. The Creeps were no help. They didn't have the faintest idea how they'd gotten there in the first place, and since they liked their new home, they'd been disinclined to leave.

This time, their lives might depend on it.

"Retreat!" said Neha. "Everyone retreat!" Then she flipped back one more page and began to scrawl the help that Forest Creeks needed.

"Neha," Eli asked, "where will that door go?"

"Hold on," she said. Creeps began to spill onto the page as the door took clearer shape. The howling monsters rampaged behind the Creeps, practically under Neha's wrist. She didn't think they could hurt her, or she'd have been able to touch Sleekit one of the thousand times she'd tried. But she arched her wrist a tiny bit anyway, trying to keep it off the paper.

Sleekit was calling to all the Creeps in her shrill little voice, and the ones who'd been hiding instead of fighting came pouring out of the hidden spaces of the neighborhood, rushing toward Neha's latest work. Swiz hopped from roof to roof, something cradled in his vest. He slid down a drainpipe and ran for the door.

"What's the plan, gal?" he shouted.

"Open it!" Neha cried, and Sleekit dangled from the latch, letting her weight drag the wide, heavy door open. There was a stampede so dense that Neha could hardly tell one creature from another. She was still scribbling away.

Behind her, Eli asked again, "Neha! Where does that door *go*?" She ignored him.

"Frog Boy!" she cried to one of the stragglers, who was lugging a sloshing bucket, "lock it behind you!"

On the inside of the open door she'd drawn as many locks as she could fit, and heavy brackets for a bar. Frog Boy's hand reached back through the opening. As he pulled the door shut, the Howler arrived in the midst of a pack of nightmare creatures so dense it looked like a cloud. There was one monster that looked like the skeleton of a horse. There were galloping amphibians with glistening skin and teeth they had no business having. And the nasty rabbit creature was back.

The Howler drew up short before the door, scenting the air. Then it reared back and slammed into the door with all its strength. The door shook, and all four children flinched. The Howler backed up, but only to make room so its minions could take their turn, flailing against the stout wooden surface, ramming into it and one another, landing on the ground and trampling one another without rhyme or reason.

That was when the Howler noticed it had an audience. Neha, Eli, Court, and Lisa all scrambled backward, shouting in alarm as it lunged, filling the page with its snarling maw, and this time its roar was so loud that cows mooed in alarm on the other side of the field. It rushed them again, and this time, the paper seemed to actually stretch from the force of its rage.

Neha screamed.

Lisa scrambled to her feet with a rock in one hand.

Court jumped in front of her.

Eli reached over and slammed the sketchbook shut.

And suddenly it was silent as the grave.

11

Never Put Your Rock Down

Slowly, the four of them began to pick themselves up out of the dirt.

"Lisa," said Eli, "put the rock down."

"Uh-uh," said Lisa. She backed toward the barn, never taking her eyes off the sketchbook.

Neha was none too happy to realize she knew exactly how Lisa felt. She'd held that sketchbook in her hands a thousand times. She'd even fallen asleep on it from time to time. And yet right now, she didn't want anything to do with it. It had become a hot potato—or maybe the blackbird pie from the old nursery rhyme, only full of monsters instead of blackbirds.

This was why Neha was facing in the exact wrong direction when the barn door started to rattle.

Court and Eli had been slapping red dirt from their clothes, but when the latch started shaking in its catch, Court jumped, catlike, to face the new threat. Lisa was already reversing direction, too.

"I told you!" she said. "Never put your rock down!"

Neha crouched and picked up the closest rock she could reach. Out of the corner of her eye, she could see Eli doing the same.

Court, on the other hand, had cocked her head and was listening. Neha strained her ears, trying to hear what Court heard. That was when she recognized an impatient chattering noise emanating from inside the dilapidated barn. She smiled in spite of herself and took a step closer. Court grinned, too. She grabbed the door handle and flipped the latch.

"Ready?" she said.

Neha could feel a laugh tugging at her mouth, begging to be set free. "Yes."

Court looked down her freckled nose at Neha.

"Okay," she said. She opened the barn door with a flourish, and what happened next was impossible and perfect all at once.

Out of the barn erupted figures so familiar to Neha that she might as well have created them herself. But she hadn't. They were real all by themselves, and here was the proof, because they came leaping into the outdoors like unicorns rushing headlong out of the sea. Sleekit led the charge. Sinuous and shining, she sprang from the doorway, twisting in midair as the Oklahoma breeze ruffled her fur. She landed on perfect, flexing toes and circled Neha.

Behind her came so many other familiar friends. The Spider Plant extended its impossibly long legs through the doorway one by one, expanding as it emerged. A herd of little round Snorkelchorts rushed, meeping, out of the shadows, and Redwing burst skyward like a phoenix. Then Swiz stepped out, still cradling something nestled in his vest.

Silver, oscillating creatures swept from the barn, their endless rows of legs rippling so that they operated more like wings, or oars in an old-timey galley ship. They undulated away across the pasture, with schools of smaller creatures among them, darting between clumps of grass. Those were Cootie Catchers, she knew, the paper fortune-tellers kids made at school. Only the ones from the notebook were alive, and they flew through the air, opening and closing their little portals as if they were mouths.

Neha watched them go, feeling a bit alarmed. Were they coming back? Shouldn't they all stick together?

That was when everything went dark. Not dark as if she'd been knocked unconscious, but as if something had climbed her like a spiral staircase to use her head as a lookout. Then there was light again as Sleekit turned upside down in front of Neha's face and locked gazes with her. Her eyes, it turned out, were amazing.

Neha had always thought of Sleekit's eyes as dark, and they were, but there was so much more sparkle and light than could ever be properly rendered on paper. Neha thought she could devote the rest of her life to her art and still never get them right.

And Sleekit's fur. She reached up to touch it. She couldn't even help herself. It was every silver-purple-plum-violet color you could ever imagine, with long, fine guard hairs on top and a thick coat of shorter fur beneath it that put an otter's to shame. For a split second, all Neha wanted in the world was to meet the kid who had dreamed Sleekit up.

"Hello," said Sleekit, touching her nose to Neha's.

"Hello," Neha said in return. And then the paws on her shoulders and the paws on top of her head both vanished as Sleekit raced down to twine around her waist and squirm up into her arms. They looked at each other the right way around this time. Then Neha buried her face in Sleekit's fur.

"I'm so glad you're all right," she said.

One little paw patted her head.

"Uh, Neha?" said Court.

Neha looked up. The Spider Plant was standing over Court. Literally. It usually camouflaged itself as a willow tree, but right now it was in full spider mode. It was taller than a giraffe and had twice as many legs, and they were all shifting around Court as it cocked its strange compound eyes to stare at her, whirring and clicking.

"Yes, hello," said Court, clearly trying to behave in a manner that was socially acceptable to enormous plant-based insectoid things. It buzzed with curiosity and bumped her with one enormous leg. She stumbled a little and ended up braced against the opposite leg. The Spider Plant lifted another leg to explore her hair.

"This is fine," Court said.

In Neha's arms, Sleekit gave the little churr that meant she was laughing.

A piece of sky morphed from blue to black, red and yellow facets flashing. It folded itself in complex fashion and landed at Neha's left elbow.

"There's so much space," said Redwing. Her ever-plexing wings blew Neha's hair into her face, but Redwing's short dark hair just rustled in the breeze.

There was no point putting Sleekit down to hug Redwing. Neha wasn't sure either of them knew how to hug each other. Redwing was nice, she was just . . . to herself. Not someone who needed to touch or be touched. Neha looked at the barn door. The trickle of creatures had almost completely stopped, and Lisa was peering in around the edge of the frame.

Eli looked over her shoulder.

"It's just a barn," he reported.

Court shook her head in wonder.

"How did this happen?" she asked.

"Your door had to lead somewhere," said Redwing. "What was your plan?"

That made Neha stop and think for a minute.

"I wanted to get you out of there."

"Well, it worked."

Redwing looked at her, her eyes reflecting blue water and green cattails that weren't there.

Suddenly, Neha remembered all the stories she'd read about wishes. Because that was what she'd gone and done. She'd wished for her friends to be safe.

Everyone knew that wishes weren't free.

She let out a slow breath.

"Is this everybody?" asked Court.

"It's enough," said Eli, looking at her in horror. "Lisa, stop that!" he added, lifting his sister down from one of the Spider Plant's knees, for lack of a better word.

Neha and Court laughed.

But Swiz's next words sobered everyone right up.

"We've got a bit of an emergency on our hands. You see . . ." He leaned over and folded down the edge of his vest. Nestled inside were three long, pale eggs.

Court nodded at once.

"They need to be kept warm," she said.

"Sorry to say, that's not my forte," said Swiz. "Being a bug and all."

Court immediately unzipped her hoodie.

"Here," she said. "I'll take them."

Swiz transferred them over. "Careful, gal," he said, but there was no need. Court handled the eggs as though they were made of glass.

Lisa slipped closer to peek.

"Can you save them?" she asked, and she didn't sound like a monster hunter now, only a worried little kid.

"I'll do my best," Court assured her.

"So," said Swiz, "looks like we're stuck here. That is, unless you can send us back when all the hubbub dies down."

"I don't know how to do it again," Neha admitted. "I don't know how I did it the first time."

"If you tried, you might let the Howler out," said Redwing. "It isn't safe."

"We can at least see what's happening in the sketchbook," said Court.

They weren't ready for what they found.

Monsters were swarming around the door Neha had drawn. They rammed it. They clawed at it. Neha held her breath. So far, nothing the monsters tried seemed to be working. But what happened if they busted down the door? Neha thought about that old saying, the one that meant it was too late: *The horse is out of the barn.*

Whoever had come up with that didn't know the half of it.

Neha glanced uneasily toward the barn, and that was when she noticed Eli's expression. He looked as though he'd swallowed a frog, and his fingers were trembling against the leg of his jeans. She followed his gaze to the page full of monsters roaming Forest Creeks.

"You do recognize them," she said softly.

Eli nodded.

12

Did You Lose Your Weasel?

Eli longed to turn back the clock half an hour to when Court and Neha had been playing an annoyingly earnest game, and he'd thought it was total hogwash.

There was no denying it now. He knew those monsters by name, and he knew exactly what kind of devilry they could accomplish—he'd spent most of his free time over the past few years making them do their worst.

Neha wasn't the only person worried about the open barn door. It creaked as it swung on its hinges, and the writer in Eli could picture wickedly long claws slowly wrapping themselves around the door frame as clearly as if they were already there.

When he'd gotten hold of himself enough to pay attention again, he found Lisa crouched nose to nose with that three-foot-long purple weasel.

"Lisa!" he said sharply. Not only did his sister not jump back like an intelligent person, she turned to give him her most scornful look.

"Oh, is your pity party over?" she asked.

"Get away from that thing!" he said.

She glanced around, past the weasel, as if she had no clue what he was talking about.

"What thing?"

"That caterpillar weasel that's about to eat your face!"

The weasel in question pulled herself up taller than should've been possible, given that some portion of her had to stay on the ground holding up the rest of her.

"Her face is safe, but I might eat yours!" she said.

Lisa scoffed.

"He's harmless; he's just got no common sense," said the double-crossing little kid. Both the weasel and Lisa dismissed him and went back to checking each other out. Lisa showed the weasel her monster-catching net. The weasel seemed impressed.

Eli looked around at the crowd of Creeps around them. Some of them looked human, or at least like recognizable animals. Others, not so much.

Silver creatures the size of manta rays undulated through the tops of the grass. They each had a pair of black eyes, like praying mantises. Their long, eel-like bodies had two rows of rippling silver legs, and they were swimming through the air as if that was a natural thing to do. The giant spider-tree chittered directly above him.

"Whoa!" he said, backing away. He stumbled, and it scooped him up with one leafy leg and dropped him on his feet.

"Eli, look!" shouted Lisa.

She and Sleekit were chasing the weird, silver swim-flying creatures through the tall Oklahoma grass. The pasture even made ocean sounds when the wind blew. But suddenly all Eli could think about was what might be hiding beneath the depths.

The Creeps he'd seen so far seemed friendly enough, but that didn't mean they all were. And there might be other things, maybe even things he'd made up, out there ready to grab his sister. There was no real mystery when it came to creatures like the Howler. It hunted when it was hungry—and it was always hungry.

"Lisa!" he said. "Don't go too far!"

She didn't listen in the slightest. Eli tried to remember what weasels ate, then decided it didn't matter, because purple weasels were unlikely to eat ordinary weasel cuisine. He bet they ate something ridiculous, like marshmallows.

Neha was looking a little bit irritated, which made him feel better. He guessed when you were used to having your purple buddy all to yourself, it was annoying when it glommed onto someone's baby sister instead.

"What's the matter?" he asked Neha. "Did you lose your weasel?"

She looked at him as if he'd said tornadoes were fun distractions.

"Sleekit's not a weasel!" she said.

"What is she, then?"

Neha opened her mouth, then closed it. She glared at him.

"Special!" she finally said.

"Well, she can stop messing around with my sister," he said, unable to think of a good reason but also unable to stop being mad.

"Hey, be nice to Sleekit. That big monster of yours just about ate her!" said Court.

"When did you start getting all chummy with other people's weasels?"

"Stop calling her that!" said Neha.

"What do I call her, then?"

"You call me Sleekit!" said the creature, weaseling her way up his leg without warning. Eli yelled and fell over backward. Not his finest moment. She barreled right up his chest and put her nose to his. She smelled good, but not like marshmallows. Like pine needles and fresh air.

"If you unleashed that beast, you're the only one who can fix it," she said.

That was exactly what he didn't want to hear.

"I didn't unleash it!" he said. "I just wrote about it."

"Same thing."

"It's not! How can it be? That would mean that everything anyone ever wrote is out there walking around. That can't possibly be true."

"It doesn't matter what everyone does," said Neha. "It matters what *you* did."

"Why would my characters be running around and not anyone else's? Besides, somebody came up with the Creeps. Whose are those if they're not Neha's?"

He looked at Sleekit.

"Whose are you?"

Her nose twitched.

"I'm mine," she said. "Are those yours?"

She flicked an ear in the direction of Neha's sketchbook.

He gulped. "I guess so."

Then her head swiveled so suddenly his neck got sympathy pains.

"What about that one?"

Eli followed her gaze, and what he saw turned him even more upside down than he already was. Sliming its way out of the barn was one last creature, but it wasn't a Creep. It was a slug the size of a collie, with a whirling vortex of blades inside its mouth. He'd put a bunch of them into a story right after his daddy left, when he'd started helping out with the cooking for the first time—he'd had an uneasy relationship with the garbage disposal.

Now he was face-to-snoot with one of his own monsters, in Tulsa, Oklahoma, on a normal afternoon.

Eli was pretty sure this was the slug he'd named Blatt, but before he made up his mind whether to try to get a better look, the other Creeps noticed it. Court shouted a warning, and everyone scrambled back away from it except . . .

"Lisa!" he yelled.

She brandished her net like she was some kind of Jedi.

"I got this!"

"You do not," he said, scrambling up and starting for her. "Get back here!"

He grabbed Lisa's shirt as she squirmed and struggled. Half the Creeps were panicking, and the other half were attacking. In all the ruckus, Eli couldn't see where the slug had gotten to. He dragged Lisa backward as the dust from the scuffle rose, making it even harder to see.

When it cleared, Blatt had vanished.

"Where did it go?" he demanded.

But nobody knew.

13

Creeped Out

Court figured it was best to take the back way home, which led them partly through fields and partly through yards with no fences. For her, it was a familiar route. The other kids looked nervous, but no adults came out to confront them for trespassing, and no one's dogs tried to eat them.

She was still half expecting the police to converge on them at any moment. That seemed like the predictable reaction to panicked 911 calls about giant spiders. But a postal worker walked right by and didn't pay them the slightest attention. Cars passed within view, and none of them screeched to a halt (though there were openmouthed children glued to the windows in some of them). Court was becoming cautiously optimistic that adults couldn't see the Creeps.

Even if they could, Court knew her house was excellent camouflage. The Castles' yard and the lot next door were a maze of toys, bicycles, and unmowed grass, so there were lots of places to hide.

"Y'all stay out here and try to act casual, okay?" she said to the small army of Creeps, then led the other kids through the garage and into the big, messy kitchen.

"Can I have one of those?" asked Lisa, pointing at a domed cake plate piled with golden-brown donuts.

"Lisa," Eli scolded, "you don't ask for food at somebody's house!"

"It's fine," said Court. She lifted the lid off the dome and handed Lisa an apple fritter.

Lisa chowed down, making happy humming noises. Court replaced the lid and watched Eli and Neha trying not to ask for their own. Neha broke first.

"I am kind of hungry," she said.

Court laughed and turned to get more, only to find the entire dome filled with purple fur and two dark, innocently blinking eyes. At the same moment, the swinging door between the kitchen and the family room opened, and Swiz poked his head in.

"Oh, is there grub?" he asked.

"How did you get in here?" asked Neha. "We told you to wait outside!"

Swiz hooked a thumb over his shoulder.

"Door was open," he said.

They peered through the gap.

Sure enough, Creeps were ambling in through the family room's sliding-glass door—Joshie must have left it open. He tended to think of the vacant lot as an extension of the living room.

"Swiz, can you take these upstairs? There's an old Easter basket in my closet you can use for a nest. I'll be right up."

Court carefully handed Swiz Swallowtail's eggs, one at a time. Then she ducked under his arm and went to the sliding-glass door.

"You have a pool!" said Neha behind her, right as Court realized the sky swimmers were amphibious. Two of them trailed slowly through the deep end of the water as a third undulated into the house, its cilia brushing her hair as it passed.

The Spider Plant had already set up shop in the vacant lot. It was right next to the only other tree in sight, which helped, but the kids who played baseball out there every day had noticed it. The kids and the Spider Plant were looking each other over, equally keen.

"What does that thing eat?" asked Eli.

"Not baseball players," said Neha, but to Court's ears she didn't sound as confident as she should have.

As a couple of kids wandered over to look at the new "tree," more Creeps brushed past Court's legs and into the house. Meeping attracted her attention, and she turned to find a procession of little round creatures with snorkels sticking out of the tops of their heads hopping up the stairs toward the bedrooms as other, faster Creeps streaked by on either side.

"Now, hang on a minute," Court began as something lumpy bounded across the room and stuffed itself headfirst between the couch cushions until it disappeared. "Yum!" it said, and loud crunching noises followed. Court made a mental note: there shouldn't be that much evidence that they ate on the couch when their parents weren't home.

There wasn't any time to fuss over it. Two roadrunners the size of Bert's dog came streaking in. One was blue with yellow around its eyes and at the tip of its tail. It had something round and white clamped in its beak, and the other bird, rusty orange with startling flashes of red, was in hot pursuit. Joshie came piling in after them.

"Hey!" he hollered. "What the heck are those things? They took our baseball!"

The birds paused and cocked their heads, eyeing Joshie.

"BRAAAAK!" said the orange one. The blue one chuckled through its beakful of ball. They looked at each other, then at the stairs.

"Stay out of my room!" shouted Joshie, which only seemed to confirm their intentions. Both birds bolted. Joshie raced after them. He was fast, but they were faster, so the next thing Court heard was a door slamming and Joshie pounding on the wrong side of it.

"Lemme in! Court!" Joshie hollered again. "What are these things?"

Court looked to Neha for an explanation.

"Their names are Pell and Mell," Neha called up to Joshie, "but they call themselves the Rogue Runners."

"Well, somebody get them out of my room!" said Joshie, kicking his door in frustration.

Court couldn't help laughing.

"You always said you wanted a pet!" she told him. To Neha, she said, "He's gonna be steamed if they eat his ball, though."

"They'll drop it soon," said Neha. "And let him in, too. They mostly want what other people have, but they get bored fast."

Mixface stuck his head in through the swinging door. The play button on top of his blocky head engaged with a click.

"News flash," he said. "Sleekit ate all the donuts, and we're gonna need more snacks."

Court mourned the donuts briefly. Apple fritters were her favorite.

Lisa had been lifting the couch cushions, trying to get a peek at the crunching thing. Now she stared at Mixface's cassette-player mouth.

"What kind of food do you even like?" she asked.

"Hot eats and fat beats," said Mixface with a wink.

"What about pizza?" asked Court.

"Yum!" said Mixface.

That was a relief.

"Pizza we can do," she said. "And there's soda in the fridge." Mixface, satisfied, let the door swing shut between them.

Eli was at the slider watching a horse that appeared to be made out of grass, which was grazing on the Castles' shaggy lawn.

"Isn't that cannibalism?" he asked.

"Is the grass screaming?" asked Neha, a bit tartly.

"At this point I don't even know," said Eli.

"We got bigger problems anyway," said Court as Lisa tried to show Sleekit how the TV worked, and Sleekit completely blocked the screen by sitting on top and hanging upside down to look.

A burp echoed from the depths of the couch. The kids elected to sit on the floor.

"We can't fit all the Creeps here," said Court. "We're going to have to split them up."

Eli wore an expression of horror.

"I can*not* take any of these things home with me," he said.

"Why not?" Neha demanded.

"Whoa!" shouted someone outside.

They looked.

One of the baseball players had gotten too close to the Spider Plant, who had picked him up to have a better look and was now dangling him in the air by one foot.

Neha jumped up and went to the door.

"Drop that!" she ordered. Startled, the Spider Plant turned its head to look at her, letting go as it did.

The boy fell with a thud.

"Hey, Baker, you okay?" called another player from a safe distance.

"Ow," came the muffled reply.

Eli bugged his eyes out at Neha and Court in an I-told-you-so fashion, but they were having none of it.

"The Creeps wouldn't even be in this situation if it weren't for you, Dr. Frankenstein," said Neha. "Helping is the least you can do!"

He opened his mouth to argue, but before he could say anything, the front door opened with a bang.

"Hey, kids!" said Court's sister. Both Court and Amy had the same long blond hair, but Amy wore hers down. She had an armful of pizza boxes, and behind her came a tall, dark-haired boy wearing a Showplace Pizza uniform and carrying another stack. They headed for the kitchen.

Court held her breath.

"What the heck were you kids doing in here?" called Amy. "It's a mess!"

The fridge rattled as it opened.

"Did y'all drink all the soda? Good thing the Mikes are bringing more."

Court had to see this for herself. She went out to the kitchen with Eli and Neha trailing cautiously behind. Mixface was sitting on the counter. Swiz had returned from upstairs when Court wasn't looking, and he and a tall Creep who seemed to be mostly made of hair were quietly rummaging in the pantry. Three snorkel things were hiding under the bottom shelf, drinking all the Capri Suns. Amy, who was clearing off the kitchen table, didn't seem to notice any of it.

"Ian," she said to her boyfriend, "can you bring in the extra chairs?"

The pizzas were piled on the kitchen counter, and Mixface was slowly easing a slice out of the top box. Court saw opportunity knocking.

"We get four," she said, seizing the top half of the stack. Mixface jumped down from the counter and took off with his piece.

"Two!" countered Amy.

"Three!"

"Done!"

Court headed for the stairs with her prize.

"Come on!" she said to the others. "And Neha, for Pete's sake, shut the back door."

Upstairs was chaos. Swimmers floated up and down the hallway. Joshie had finally gotten into his bedroom and was in the middle of a Nerf war with the Rogue Runners. The three of them just about knocked the pizza out of Court's hands on their way past.

Court upended a milk crate in the middle of her floor and set the pizza boxes on it.

She went to the closet to check the eggs while Neha began passing out pizza. It wasn't Court's first time bringing home something small and helpless. She positioned the lamp she kept there for that purpose, then turned it on. Satisfied, she returned to her friends. As soon as she sat down, one of the snorkel things clambered into her lap.

"What is this?" she asked.

"They're called Snorkelchorts," said Neha.

"Story?" it said hopefully.

"Maybe later?" Court said. There was an awkward pause while the Snorkelchort sulked, which involved scrunching up its snorkel and making a series of annoyed puffing sounds.

Some of the Creeps wandered off to eat in other rooms as Pell and Mell ran past again, this time being ridden by Sleekit and a vaguely doglike Creep made of argyle socks.

"And stay out!" said Joshie from the direction of his room. Court figured that would last for about five minutes.

Eli turned to Neha.

"What did Sleekit mean about being her own?" he asked. "Where did the Creeps come from if you didn't make them up?"

Neha frowned and fiddled with her shoelaces.

"I asked a few times. Other kids made them up, but they said none of those kids are around anymore."

"Like they left?" asked Court.

"Or grew up, I guess," said Neha.

"I can't imagine anyone forgetting the Creeps," said Court just as the Snorkelchort in her lap blew a bead out of its snorkel that hit her in the nose.

"It's going to be dark soon," said Eli. "If we're going to divide them up, we'd better do it."

"You can come home with me," said Neha to Sleekit as the Creep prowled back into the room.

"I know," said Sleekit, leaning on Neha's knee. Neha rubbed her rounded ears.

"We're only just now deciding," pointed out Court, who wouldn't have minded having Sleekit at her place.

"You didn't need to bother," said Sleekit. "Everything's already sorted out."

Neha jumped to her feet, dislodging Sleekit, with the dread of someone who'd been through this before.

"Sleekit," she said, "where are the rest of the Creeps?"

"On their way to your house. And Eli's house," she added, daintily picking pepperoni off Court's pizza slice.

"What?" demanded Eli as Lisa cheered and Neha groaned.

They dashed from the room with Court trailing behind.

"How long are we gonna be running hotels out of our houses, exactly?" she asked, but nobody answered. The door to the garage banged shut behind Court's friends, leaving her alone in the laundry room. She shook her head.

"Ahem," said an imperious voice near her ankles.

She looked down to find Sleekit waiting.

"You'll keep the eggs warm?" asked Sleekit as Court opened the door for her.

"I will," Court promised.

As she stood pondering how much money she had hidden in her sock drawer and whether it was enough to bribe Joshie to keep his mouth shut about the Creeps, a more familiar argument broke out behind her at the kitchen table.

"What do you mean, super tetanus?" asked Shorty, who was one of the drivers, and also one of the Mikes. "There's no such thing."

"There is today," said Amy, "and you've got it. Unless somebody casts 'Cure Disease,' you're dead."

"How many turns have I got?" he demanded.

Court went back through the kitchen. As she expected, Amy was stroking her chin thoughtfully, and Shorty was buckling under the stress.

"Best case scenario? Five," she said.

"Worst?" he asked.

She grinned. "Two."

"No way, man. No way!"

Court wandered back upstairs, musing about whether Creeps could give you super tetanus. She shooed the sky swimmers out of the bathroom so she could use it, realizing she also needed money to patch her window screen, a Nerf-related casualty that was going to make it tough to keep the swimmers outside. 'Course, first she was going to have to find the screen. It was down in the bushes somewhere.

As she shut the bathroom door, she saw a long, inky tentacle extend from the sink drain, grab Amy's toothbrush, and start scrubbing the sink with it.

She decided to use the downstairs bathroom instead. She took her toothbrush with her.

14

Trashmouth

Sometimes little sisters didn't know when to shush.

Eli couldn't help but notice how Lisa had latched on to Sleekit, so all the way home he'd reminded her that the best way to help her new buddy was to keep her lips zipped.

He'd thought that would buy him at least a day of silence.

He'd thought wrong.

They were on thin ice the minute they got home, because the streetlights were already on. Eli was supposed to have Lisa home before that happened. Even worse, although the glass storm door was shut, the wooden door behind it was open. That meant Momma had beaten them home. And Eli realized with a groan that in his hurry to find Lisa he'd forgotten to leave a note, breaking another iron-clad rule.

In other words, if Eli didn't play his cards just right, it was sarlacc-feeding time. And that would be true even if they didn't have a house full of Creeps, which they did. The argyle-dog thing was sitting in the foyer wagging his sock-tail like he owned the place, and the tall Creep who was basically a stack of brownish hair waved shyly behind him.

So when Lisa busted through the front door into the dinner-scented air and the first words out of her mouth were "We went to the old barn and almost got chewed up by a slug!" Eli had to shove his hands in his pockets so he wouldn't put them over her mouth.

Kids in stories knew how to keep a secret. He needed to teach his sister some tropes.

Their momma pulled her head out of the refrigerator and cocked it like a predatory bird. On top of the fridge, a Snorkelchort swung its stubby arms, gauging the distance between itself and her back.

Don't, mouthed Eli.

"You went to the where?" asked his momma.

Eli could've tried to laugh it off, but Momma was sharp, so instead he aimed for the perfect amount of irritation.

"You know better than to say things like that! Why you wanna stress Momma out when you know that's not true?"

Their momma had one hand on the open refrigerator door and her eyebrows up by her hairline, proof that she was not buying what Eli was selling. If his writing ever did make him famous, Eli planned to say he owed it all to his momma—he'd hear about it if he didn't. But it wasn't a lie. He really did up his game trying to stay off her radar. Like he was doing now, even as the Snorkelchort jumped down onto the fridge door, and from there to the floor. He lost sight of it after that.

"So you didn't go to the old barn?" their momma asked.

"I know better than to take Lisa over there!" said Eli. "You know how she likes to pretend."

He was pretty sure she was about to ask more questions, but then Lisa put her foot in it.

"Momma, you're wasting energy," she said, looking at the open fridge door.

It couldn't have worked any better if she'd done it on purpose.

"Little girl," said their momma, and Lisa slowly took one step backward. "Who pays the electricity bill in this house?"

"You do," said Lisa, so quick their momma almost didn't have time to finish her sentence.

"And who buys all the groceries?"

"You do."

"And who works long, hard hours making sure I can keep paying for the electric bill and the groceries?"

"You do." Lisa was trying to get behind Eli, but he wasn't having it. If it looked like he disagreed, he'd be next.

"So if I, driven to distraction by my children, forget one single time to shut the refrigerator, do I have any need to hear about it from an eight-year-old?"

"No, Momma."

"No, I do not. I will tell you what I need. I need my children to show up at home on time. I need them to wash their hands. And I need them to set the table before dinner goes to waste."

Eli hadn't even gotten around to considering what was for dinner, but now that he stopped to smell, his eyes lit up.

"You made lasagna," said Eli in a voice some people reserved for church on Christmas.

"I made lasagna," agreed his momma.

"And garlic bread," breathed Lisa behind him.

"And I rented *Star Wars*. So grateful children would—"

That was as far as she got, because Eli launched across the room in his muddy Adidas and hugged her around the middle like she *was* the garlic bread.

"Momma, you're the best!" he said. They'd been eating so

much tuna salad lately Eli had been checking himself in the mirror for gills. He was pretty sure he could demolish half that pan all by himself. And he was way overdue to watch *Star Wars* again.

"You're welcome," she said, but she turned him toward the bathroom as she said it. All that wandering around cow fields and being licked by Creeps must have left its mark.

Eli had just lathered up his hands when a kid hollered outside. Yelling kids weren't out of the ordinary on their street, but the tone of panic definitely was. Loud crashing noises followed. There wasn't any time for Eli to wipe his hands. He could already hear Lisa's feet pounding toward the door.

"Lisa Shirley Goodman, you get back here!" shouted their momma from the kitchen, but Lisa had been primed to fight monsters for months, and Eli knew she wouldn't stop. He took off after her, still covered in soap.

Outside, he found their trash cans upended and rolling across the pavement. On the other side of the street, a kid was using a garbage can lid as a shield. Lisa was attacking him with the Whacker!

"Come out from there, you coward!" she shouted.

"Lisa!" said Eli.

"Knocking over our trash cans and scaring my momma. I'll show you!" said Lisa.

Eli finally caught up to her. He reached over her from behind and grabbed the Whacker!, holding it still.

"Lisa, that's Eddie!" he said.

"Eddie?" asked Lisa with a ferocious frown. She peered at the garbage lid–brandisher, who lowered it slightly.

"It's just me," Eddie said, holding up his free hand in surrender.

Eddie Shotwell was one year older than Eli, and went to the middle school. His arm was scraped from wrist to elbow.

"What were you doing in our trash cans?" asked Eli.

"Nothing, I swear," he said. He put the lid down, scanning the area nervously. "I was bringing in our cans, that's all. There was something moving around by yours. I thought it was a dog or a possum, until I saw it."

Lisa yanked the Whacker! out of Eli's hands and whipped around, looking for the threat.

"What was it? Where did it go?" she demanded.

"I don't know what the heck it was," he said, his voice higher than normal. "It came right at me, and I tripped on one of the lids and fell. Look what it did to my shoe!" He lifted one foot. The entire sole of his sneaker was gone.

"What are you kids doing out there?" demanded their momma from the doorway. The hairstack Creep was behind her, peering over her shoulder and looking a bit jittery, but she was oblivious. Eli had a sudden horrible vision of her being attacked by a monster she couldn't even see. Fortunately, Eddie was checking to make sure all his toes were there and didn't notice their guest.

"It's all right, Momma! A possum got into the trash cans! Eddie chased it off, though."

Their momma relaxed a little.

"Thank you, Eddie. You be careful, though! Those things can carry disease."

"Yes, ma'am!" he said.

"Put the trash cans away and come inside," said their momma. "Daddy's going to call in half an hour!" She shut the door.

"It wasn't a possum, man," said Eddie in a low voice, letting go of his foot. "I don't know what it was. It was slimy, and its teeth were . . . *spinning*."

"That's messed up," said Eli, like this was all news to him. But inside he was shuddering. He knew exactly what his slugs could do. Eddie was lucky he hadn't lost a foot.

The boys each grabbed their own trash cans and sorted out the lids. When Eli turned to haul his up the driveway, he realized Lisa was prowling along the front of the house, all alone.

"I found something!" she said.

"Get back here!" said Eli. "It's not safe!"

"Look!" said Lisa, and when he joined her he could see the perfect half-moon crescent something had taken out of the bush at the corner of the house. Crossing the yard was a two-foot-wide trail of ooze, shining in the glow from the streetlights. It led in the direction of the drainage ditch.

"Y'all are asking for it, getting near that thing. I'm going in," Eddie said. He hustled up his driveway, can banging against his knees.

"Coward," muttered Lisa.

"We're *all* going in," Eli told her.

"But it's that slug—" started Lisa.

"I know it," he said, watching for movement between them and the ditch. "But it's getting dark out, and that thing's dangerous."

"That's what I'm saying. It could hurt somebody, Eli!"

Eli crouched in front of his little sister.

"You're really brave," he said. "And that's good. But we can't just go running at stuff. What would Momma do if something happened to us, huh?"

"We have to stop that thing," argued Lisa.

"Yeah, we do. But we have to be smart about it. Let's go in and eat, and we'll talk about it tomorrow. Okay?"

"Okay."

Lisa looked down, then frowned.

"Why do you got soap all over your hands?"

"Because *you* weren't there to look after me!" said Eli. "See what happens when you leave me all alone?"

Lisa giggled, and Eli held up his soapy hands and chased her into the house. Inside, a parade of Snorkelchorts joined the chase down the hall toward the bedrooms.

Eli screeched to a halt when they reached his room.

"Hey," he yelled, "who ate all my Halloween candy?"

A trap snapped in Lisa's room, and the Speak & Spell she'd wired to it began to chant "I got you. I got you. I got you" in its robotic voice.

"I'll just go on and eat this lasagna myself," announced their momma from the kitchen, but any kid peeking through the storm door would have seen the argyle-sock-dog nibbling on the edge of Lisa's serving.

Outside, in the drainage ditch, a small animal squealed. Something metallic revved and whirred. There was a wet, squelching burp.

Then there was silence.

15

Do You Really Want to Hurt Me?

Neha and Eli had reached home at almost the same moment. Unlike Eli, however, Neha had managed to return without attracting her mother's attention. She'd had two strokes of luck. First of all, a relative had called from India. Neha hadn't been able to tell who it was, but they'd definitely phoned the Prasad household and not the other way around. Otherwise her mom would have been watching the clock and fussing about the cost of the call.

It had also been someone her mom liked. If she hadn't wanted to talk, she'd have been standing right by the phone, twisting the cord around her finger. Instead, she'd gone to the trouble of untangling the cord so it reached all the way across the kitchen. The receiver had been tucked between her ear and her shoulder. There'd been a frying pan in the sink, and she'd been rolling out balls of kesar peda and sprinkling them with pistachios, which meant that even though Neha had spent the afternoon breaking so many rules her mom hadn't even thought of most of them yet, they'd be having dessert with dinner. Neha's mom had barely glanced over as she passed.

That, however, was where Neha's luck had come to an end. When she opened her bedroom door, her room was full. Not just of Creeps—she'd expected that—but also a complicated and growing maze. Neha knew there'd been string in the shoebox of craft supplies she kept in her closet, but she hadn't known there was quite so much of it. It spread across her room like the world's most elaborate spiderweb, and the Creeps were hard at work making it bigger.

"What is all this?" she asked.

"Countermeasures against the slug monster," said a Treebot, turning to look at her. "Sleekit's orders."

"How did Sleekit give you orders when she was running around Court Castle's yard twenty minutes ago?"

Sleekit, who had dashed upstairs ahead of Neha, erupted from a toy box Neha pretended not to use anymore with a doll head in her mouth.

"Wasn't that attached to something?" Neha asked.

Sleekit's reply was understandably muffled. She moved through the maze of yarn like it wasn't even there. Neha crouched and removed the doll head from between her small, sharp teeth.

"It will be good for holding things," Sleekit said.

Neha was almost afraid to ask. "What things?"

"Tacks. Marbles. Broken glass."

"You can't use any of those things," she said. "Someone could get hurt."

"Exactly," chorused half the Creeps in the room.

"It might be me," Neha pointed out.

"Ohhhh," said someone near the back.

Sleekit considered.

"New plan," she said.

"Where is Redwing?" Neha wanted to know. Maybe the flying girl could apply order to this chaos.

Sleekit shrugged. "Soaring somewhere," she said. "Looking for that slug."

Neha agreed the slug was worrisome, and that some defenses might be a good idea. That didn't change the fact that the Creeps' "countermeasures" were going to be tough to hide.

"Are you sure we need all this?" she asked. "There's only one monster out here."

"It always starts with one," said Sleekit grimly.

A rubber ball flew past Neha's nose and bounced off the wall above her bed. A second later, a Snorkelchort leaped after it. It promptly invented a game in which it shot the ball out of its snorkel and bounced it off the ceiling. Neha winced, then relaxed as her mom started laughing at some story her caller was telling.

"So," said Sleekit decisively, "what we will do is this. We will create countermeasures that are painful, but probably not lethal."

She turned to a Treebot.

"Go look for shaving cream."

Neha supposed that was as good as things were going to get for the moment. She picked her way through the yarn maze and sat on her bed, evicting the bouncing Snorkelchort. Then she opened her desk drawer and pulled out an empty sketchbook. The yarn bomb that had exploded in her room was a problem, but it was also way too cool not to sketch.

A funny thing happened as she detailed the scene. She started adding to the existing mess. It occurred to her that there was a stash of unused toys in the hall closet downstairs. The Treebots would have been all over them if they'd known. She clambered back through the maze and ran down the stairs—but when she returned with her arms full, the door wouldn't budge.

"No, it has to still open wide enough for Neha," directed Sleekit's voice from inside. There was a brief scuffle, and then the door creaked open just far enough for Neha to slide through. When the Creeps saw her, there was a collective "Ohhhh." The smaller ones started to swing over on yarn vines in an effort to snatch things out of her arms.

"Stop!" she said, turning to shield her stash of supplies. "Wait until I tell you what to do with them."

She dumped them in the middle of her bedspread and grabbed her notebook again.

"Okay," she said. She pointed to the nearest Snorkelchort. "You. Come take these."

Then she flipped open her ERECTOR Set box.

▲　▶　▲

"All right," she said when she was satisfied, "let's see if this works!"

"Who's going to test it?" asked Sleekit.

Oops. Neha hadn't quite gotten that far.

"Frog Boy can do it!" shouted a Treebot. This was met with a wave of enthusiasm.

"Frog Boy, Frog Boy, Frog Boy!" chanted the Creeps.

Neha looked at him.

"You don't have to," she said.

"I'm used to it," he said. "Besides, it entertains the tadpoles."

She took a moment to look past the string and found cups with tadpoles in them on multiple surfaces.

"Why aren't they in the bucket?" she asked.

"They were arguing," he said, as if this were the most reasonable thing in the world.

She wondered how he'd figured out who to separate. Then she realized the pitcher on her bedside table was full of tadpoles, too.

"What happens when they turn into frogs?" she asked.

"I'll have to bring in some worms," he said.

She nodded slowly.

"Frog Boy, Frog Boy, Frog Boy!" chanted the tadpoles in their tiny voices.

Which was how Neha ended up staring at her watch, waiting for the second hand to reach the top of the dial.

"Three . . . two . . . one . . . go!"

Frog Boy, who'd been ordered to wait in the hall, opened the door and stepped into Neha's room. A network of string dropped from the ceiling. Too widely spaced to be a net, it was more like a cat's cradle. It settled around his waist, then there was a pause. Frog Boy looked at Neha.

"Aw, I'm sorry," he said. "It didn't wor—"

Pulleys began moving in every corner of the room. The cat's cradle tightened around Frog Boy, pinning his arms to his sides. There was a whirl of strands, and in a flash Frog Boy was trussed up in a makeshift cocoon.

The tadpoles cheered.

"Time!" said Sleekit.

"Thirty-six seconds!" said Neha.

"Excellent. Reset!" said the imperious otter-weasel.

The process reversed, and Frog Boy was left wobbling dizzily in the middle of the room as the cat's cradle whipped upward to blend into the white ceiling.

"Next," said Neha, steadying him.

Frog Boy walked cautiously toward Neha's bed. Before he could get there, two contraptions powered by frantically pedaling Treebots zoomed out from under the bed. The wire strung between them tripped him and he pinwheeled forward, landing facedown on Neha's quilt.

"That's not good," said Neha. "All we did was help the monster get to us faster."

"Maybe it was a fluke," suggested Sleekit. "Let's try it again."

"Again?" asked Frog Boy, his voice muffled by the mattress.

"Again, again!" chanted the tadpoles.

They did it four more times to be sure. Frog Boy hit the bed three times and the floor once. He was starting to look a bit ruffled.

Several of the Treebots climbed up one another to get a better view. They held hands to steady themselves, like leafy water skiers.

"What if we put a second trap on the bed?" asked a Treebot.

"On top of me?" asked Neha.

"Oh yeah. Maybe not."

Sleekit scampered over to trace a line across the floor.

"What if we run a tripwire right here?" she asked. "It'll get him whether he's headed for the bed or the closet."

"Perfect!" agreed Neha.

"You know I'm on your side, right?" asked Frog Boy. Neha patted him on the arm.

"Of course! Now, stand here so the booby trap in the closet doesn't miss you."

The results were satisfyingly dramatic. The shaving cream in particular was a stroke of genius. Neha and the Creeps stopped Frog Boy from falling out the window, but it was a close shave, if you'll pardon the expression. Razor thin.

Neha smuggled some of the finished kesar peda upstairs to appease Frog Boy. She found him in the middle of a cluster of cups full of tadpoles. The mini-amphibians were all telling him how brave he was. It was helping his mood some.

Keeping the rest of the Creeps in the bedroom was proving to be an impossible task, though. Unlike Neha, they weren't the least bit worried about her mom spotting them. Sleekit poked her nose into every pot as Mrs. Prasad made dinner, and narrowly missed lighting her own tail on fire.

Dinner was slower at Neha's house on Fridays. The university didn't have Friday-evening classes, but her father often worked late anyway, grading papers. Neha and her mother usually read the *Filmfare* magazines her aunt sent from India while they ate.

It was a good dinner, warm and spicy and filling, but Neha had to remind herself to chew, because every now and then a hand or paw would reach up and swipe food off the table. Neha's mother didn't so much as glance up from the article she was reading. Sleekit sat on the table and ate off Neha's plate, and Mrs. Prasad never batted an eye.

By dessert, Neha had relaxed enough to enjoy the sweet, soft kesar peda, with their crunchy bits of pistachio on top. She didn't get as many as usual, because she was handing out most of her share under the table, but she didn't mind.

Normally Neha would stay downstairs longer. She and her mother would watch *Webster* together before the more grown-up *Dallas* came on and Neha was banished. Instead, she rinsed her dish in a hurry and rushed back upstairs while her mom was still reading all the gossip about famous Bollywood actresses like Rekha and Hema.

"I'm going to read in bed, Mom!" she called over her shoulder.

"Good night, beta," said Mrs. Prasad.

Neha brushed her teeth, even though the toothpaste erased the taste of dessert. Then she carefully climbed through the maze in her room and into her bed. Downstairs, her mother skipped *Dallas* entirely and slid a videotape that had arrived with the magazines into the VCR. The bright notes of the music from the opening credits spilled up the stairs from the family room, and the door creaked open as most of the Treebots snuck downstairs to watch.

Sleekit curled up against Neha, and for a few minutes Neha stroked her impossibly soft, silvery-purple fur. All around the room, Creeps were settling in for the night—nestling in her dresser drawers, curling up in her dirty laundry basket, clustering at the foot of her bed. The tadpoles were humming, and she found it oddly soothing.

Then Sleekit's ears perked, and she looked pointedly down at Neha's backpack, which was shoved between the bed and the bedside table.

"What?" asked Neha, propping herself up on one elbow.

Sleekit hissed softly.

Neha reached down and pulled out her battered sketchbook. She scooted back to make room on the bed, and Sleekit circled the sketchbook intently when she laid it down and flipped it open.

It hurt to look. When the Creeps had escaped, the monsters had obviously turned their anger on Forest Creeks. Some buildings were burned; others were smashed to ruins. Someone had chucked the big milkshake mixer from Swizzlestick's into the street.

Monsters prowled around the door Neha had drawn. They had piled tree branches and other debris in front of it, and as Neha and Sleekit watched, an inky, octopuslike creature ambled over. It put the tip of one tentacle up to its mouth and coughed into it, and with a pop, fire burst from the end of a completely different tentacle and set the stack ablaze.

Neha flinched as if the whole sketchbook were in danger of igniting. She reached for the tadpole-filled cup on her bedside table in case dousing the notebook would help.

As she moved, she bumped a Snorkelchort who'd crept under her arm to see. It squeaked in alarm.

As one, the monsters looked up at them. A chorus of howls, snarls, and yowls arose. All around Neha's room, Creeps woke with frightened cries. Fortunately, the monsters were better at scaring people than they were at building fires. They were so eager to rush at Neha and Sleekit that some of them stampeded right through the fire, scattering the brush pile and putting it out.

Neha slammed the sketchbook shut. She shoved it back into her backpack and rolled over, and the Creeps settled in around her again. She stroked Sleekit's fur like it was a lucky charm.

Looking at the yarn web, Neha realized the Creeps had one advantage over the monsters: they'd been dreamed up by kids who wanted friends to play with. They loved puzzles, and riddles, and building things. The monsters, on the other hand, existed to hunt and chase. Building fires was not their wheelhouse. For now, that would buy Neha and her friends some time.

She wondered how much.

16

Hatchlings

Court fell asleep to the Snorkelchorts' soft meeping, but it was the rustling that woke her up. Her alarm clock said she'd only gotten an hour of shut-eye. She groaned.

"Shush, y'all," she said sleepily. Then she looked over at the Chorts. In the glow of her nightlight, she could see the soft rise and fall of the still-sleeping pile. The rustling was coming from her closet.

Court jumped down from her bunk bed and flipped the closet light on.

The basket on the floor was filling with a shimmering maze of coils and wet, crumpled wings. Cautiously, Court stroked a scaled back with the tip of one finger. Then she hunkered down by the basket to watch. The hatchlings' wings slowly extended as their veins filled with fluid. One was black with monarch-butterfly wings. The gold one had the pale green wings of a luna moth. But the third was Court's favorite. Its wings were the startling black and white of a zebra swallowtail, with the same red dots along the edges. Its scales were the brilliant blue of an autumn sky.

The baby snakes' eyes were bright and curious. The black one smelled her with its tiny tongue, and when she put her hand down close beside the blue one, it twined around her wrist like a bracelet.

Court knew real butterflies usually dried their wings for hours before they tried to fly, but apparently flying snakes were quicker on the draw, because before she'd had time to give some thought to what she was going to do with them, the front door opened and closed, and all three snakes undulated up into the air and fluttered toward the foyer.

"Get back here!" hissed Court, but it must've been the wrong kind of hissing, because they only turned long enough to swoop behind her and push her forward with their tiny noses. Then they sailed ahead again. She took the stairs two at a time trying to head them off, but when she got a look at her folks they seemed so worn out she got distracted for a minute.

"Hi, Mama. Hi, Daddy!" said Amy, emerging from the kitchen, where she'd been cleaning up after the game. She wiped her hands on the towel she was holding. The luna moth hatchling grabbed the end of the towel in its tiny teeth and tried to fly away with it. Amy looked down at the flapping towel with a frown.

"Almost forgot what the house looked like," said Mr. Castle. His shirt was stained with grease and sauce, and he smelled like pizza.

Their mama patted Court on the shoulder. Court meant to hug her, but she got sidetracked towing the black snake out of a potted palm tree.

"Place looks nice, girls," Mama said. "So far, so good."

Court gulped as another baby snake flew past her mama's head.

The Castle kids were known for getting into hot water

together. Once upon a time, their folks had thought it was funny. Maybe they were even a little bit proud of how ornery their kids were—until they signed a franchise agreement and opened up a Showplace Pizza. Then things got unfunny real fast.

That was when they took to threatening their children with Mrs. Harvey.

Mrs. Harvey didn't babysit at their house—they had to go to hers. She liked to cook, which was a problem because she was bad at it. Her spaghetti recipe was a crime against nature that called for Campbell's vegetable soup. She also smoked like a house on fire.

Court and her siblings had begged for a chance to prove they could mind themselves. Their parents agreed, but they had conditions: no more disasters, no wars, and no extra work for tired parents.

The Castle kids still had sleeping bag races down the stairs. "Catapult This!" was way too much fun to give up. Shaving-cream-water-balloon fights were just tradition. But they followed what you might call "the spirit of the law" by gathering all their antics under the umbrella of one big game. They liked to call it "That Was Close." To win, you got everything neat as a pin before your mama and daddy walked in the door. So far their record was flawless, and Amy had assured Court and Joshie that they were learning practical life skills, like how to get blood out of carpet.

But a houseful of Creeps was bound to complicate matters.

The black snake twined its way up Court's arm and around her neck, turning to touch its nose to hers. Court gently cupped it in her hand and tucked it behind her hair so she could see, trying to make it look like she was waving away a fly. Luckily her parents were already headed into the family room and didn't notice her gesture. Wide orange wings suddenly sprouted on either side of Court's head, and she sighed.

Court's daddy crashed on the couch—which said, "Ouch!"—and draped one arm across his eyes. Her mama nestled against his side. The blue snake circled his head while the gold one investigated the fireplace. It knocked over the hearth tongs with a loud clatter. Court rushed over to fix it.

"Must not've been in there right," she said, shooing the snake away.

"Was it a good day?" asked Amy hopefully. When they'd first opened the doors of Showplace, every day had been a good day, but lately the shine was off the apple.

"It was a long day," said their daddy without moving his arm. Some arcade tokens slid out of his pants pocket, and the couch whispered, "Yum!"

"I'll get you some iced tea," Amy decided, and headed to the kitchen.

"All the days seem long lately," said their mama as Court tried to shoo the snakes back upstairs and failed. The gold one discovered the ceiling fan and coiled the tip of its tail around the stem of one of the fan blades. It dangled, twirling with the fan and looking for all the world like a delighted kid on an inverted merry-go-round. The others immediately floated over to join it. Court did her best to ignore the trio of twirling hatchlings, thanking the heavens that at least snakes were quiet.

"You know what the worst part is?" asked her daddy.

Court's mama shook her head. Both of them had their eyes closed, but it didn't seem to matter.

"The pizza," he said. "Frozen dough, frozen cheese, canned sauce. I know how to make good pizza, Melissa!"

Mama made soothing noises. "The company has rules. You can't help that."

"I wasn't planning on running an arcade instead of a restaurant."

Court's eyes were watering, which was making it tough to keep an eye on the snake-babies. Her parents fed people like it was their job even when they weren't at work. Serving bad pizza must have made them sore.

After they'd sipped the tea Amy brought them, the two girls pulled their parents up by their hands and pushed them up the stairs. The baby snakes thought this was a grand game and used their heads to help, but if Court's parents noticed that Court and Amy seemed to be pushing on them with more than the usual number of hands, they didn't say anything. Court shooed a silver flyer out of her parents' bathroom and filled the tub for her daddy while Amy put clean sheets from the laundry basket on the bed. By the time the tub was full, Amy had finished fluffing their folks' pillows and was on her way to bed herself.

Joshie came wandering in, his eyes half-open. Court shoved the black snake behind her, but that didn't do much good when the blue one flew right past his ear.

He blinked.

"Whoa, where did that one come from?" he asked.

"Which one, honey?" asked their mama.

"My T-shirt, right, Joshie?" asked Court with a warning frown.

"Right," he said, recovering. "It's ugly."

Court rolled her eyes. *Nice save*, she thought. Joshie had been bribed and sworn to secrecy as soon as Eli and Neha left. She'd had to pay extra because the Rogue Runners insisted on living in his room. They'd taken a shine to him and kept trying to feed him lizards.

"Hey," said Joshie, glancing at the TV as their daddy went in to take his bath. "You can watch *Superman II* with me."

Their mama shook her head at him, smiling. "Oh, I can, can I?" she said. "Climb in, kid."

He crawled into the middle of the bed, and she dragged him

under the covers like he was still a baby and not a little muscle man with a supertan, as Amy liked to call him. Lucky for Court he was already half-asleep by the time Superman accidentally busted General Zod and his buddies out of space jail, because the hatchlings were attracted to the screen and kept bumping their tiny noses against it like they were trying to get in. Once she'd finally managed to herd them toward the door, she figured she'd better get out while the getting was good.

"Good night," Court said, blowing her mama a kiss, then grabbing a snake by the tail.

"Night, Coco," her mama murmured. No one on God's green earth was allowed to call her that but her parents.

"Don't bite the bedbugs!" said Court as she left. She shut the baby snakes in her room with her and hoped for the best.

She must have fallen asleep the second her head hit the pillow, because the next thing she knew it was Saturday morning. And she smelled freshly made donuts.

"Yum," said Court, sitting up.

"Yum!" said a Snorkelchort. There were three of them nesting in her beanbag chair. One of them promptly shot a Lego out of its snorkel. It hit her square on the forehead.

"Ow!" she said.

"Ow!" it said.

"This," sighed Court, "is why we need a plan."

17

Bothering People

Goooood morning!" boomed a voice as Court was putting on her jeans. She flailed in surprise, then fell over. Pulling herself up on the bedside table, she reached for her alarm clock, but slapping its buttons did nothing to silence the noise.

"Coooourt Castle! The sun's up, and it's about to go down!"

It was Mixface, and he was pointing at the hall, where a rising commotion demanded her attention. Joshie, it turned out, was using a water pistol to exchange fire with the bathroom sink. His mouth was ringed with toothpaste foam.

"What are you doing?" she asked, bleary eyed.

"The shink won't let me schpit," he said through a mouthful of toothpaste. "Look!"

He took a run at the sink and tried to unload his mouthful of Crest, but before he could, a jet of water shot out of the drain and blasted him in the eye.

"Gaaah!" he said. "Shee?"

He shot at the sink again. It shot back.

"Go spit downstairs!" said Court. When she'd shoved him in that direction, she turned to the sink.

"Knock it off, you, or I'll pour a bottle of shampoo right down your gullet," she threatened, and something squished nervously in the drain.

"Scrubbler will stop," it burbled, and Court nodded grimly.

Court was what was commonly known as a take-charge kind of gal. She also had a bad feeling in her stomach after hearing her parents talk about work, and no earthly idea what to do about it. Put those together, and it was a foregone conclusion that she'd devote all her energy to solving the Creeps' problem instead.

She sat out by the pool, passing chunks of her breakfast donuts to the waiting Creeps, and mulled things over. It was a prickly issue, she thought as the baby snakes did lazy figure eights around her arms and neck. After all, Neha and Eli were the ones whose worlds were colliding. Court was just along for the ride. But Sleekit thought Court could stand up to the monsters, and Court had a bad feeling they weren't going to stay in the sketchbook forever. Even now, that slug thing was roaming around somewhere.

Pell and Mell came blasting out of the house, with Joshie close behind. Both Rogue Runners had several donuts apiece speared on their beaks.

"I said two each, you guys!" said Joshie. "Gimme mine!"

"Who the heck took all the donuts while I was in the shower?" hollered Amy from the kitchen.

The Creeps were entertaining, but they were a heap of trouble, too.

Court knew there was no way she was getting out of the house alone, but since the grown-ups hadn't noticed the Creeps yesterday, she figured they could travel around the neighborhood a bit without drawing too much attention.

Unfortunately, the Spider Plant insisted on following her, and there were few things more obvious than a giant arachnid ambling from yard to yard. The trio of hatchlings (*Serpenteens*, Court thought) were a close second. They spent so much time in her hair she was beginning to wonder if they believed it was traveling grass.

They were pretty little things, though. She'd dubbed the monarch-winged one Archie. The green-and-gold one was Luna, of course. And the blue one, her secret favorite, was Zeb. She'd made an effort to corral them in her closet, but it was like herding cats, so she'd let them come along.

Her bike basket was also stuffed with Snorkelchorts.

As she pedaled up Neha's driveway, she caught a glimpse through the open gate of Mr. Prasad, who was mowing the backyard in a white T-shirt and canvas shorts. Cut grass was a Saturday smell, and it always put her in a good mood. Hopefully Neha was the same way, and even with all these hangers-on, she'd be glad to see Court.

She wasn't.

"What are you doing?" Neha demanded when she answered the door. "You can't let them run around in broad daylight!"

Court was still blinking from the staring contest she'd been having with the eyeball that had started all this for her in the first place, which had apparently taken up residence on Neha's front door.

"Don't get your shorts in a twist," said Court. "We're visiting, that's all."

The Spider Plant reached over and patted Neha on the shoulder. Court thought that was awful sweet. Neha, still frowning, didn't seem to agree. Then Zeb stuck his teeny blue head out of Court's hair and hissed. Archie landed, coiling, on top of Court's head and leaned down to have a closer look at Neha.

"They hatched!" said Neha, her frown relaxing into a smile for a moment. "Oh, Court, thank you!"

She reached over and hugged Court so fast that it was already over by the time Court thought of hugging her back. But Neha's delight was short lived.

"Look," she said. "I have something important to tell you, but I can't do it now. The tadpoles had a water fight, and I have to clean up before my mom gets back from her tutoring job."

That caught Court's interest.

"A water fight? How, exactly?"

"They can spit really far. They're like crabby little water pistols."

Court laughed.

"I can help you clean up," she offered.

"While the Creeps you brought with you make new messes. No, Court. Please just get them out of here for now."

Court figured she might be flustered, too, if her parents were around.

"Well, if you get out later, come look for us. I'm going to Eli's," she said. Then she hopped back on her bike and pedaled that way.

When she got there, Lisa was playing alone out front.

"Hey, kiddo," she said, dropping her bike on the driveway as Chorts bailed in every direction. "What're you doing?"

"Building a trap," she said. She had a bunch of junk laid out, old toys and a milk crate and Court didn't know what all, along with duct tape and tools.

"A trap, huh? How's this doohickey supposed to work?" she asked.

Lisa frowned like she knew Court thought she was cute.

"Y'all don't know how much trouble you're in," she said, snapping shut the top of the Shop-Vac she'd been messing with. "I do. I've heard all my brother's stories. Even helped with some of them. There are a lot of monsters out there."

Court thought about the rush of monsters toward Neha's hastily drawn door.

"It's okay," Court told her. "They're trapped in the sketchbook."

"For now," said Lisa. "But the slug got out. So did the Creeps." She looked up at the very suspicious willow tree that had appeared in her front yard. It blinked its big bug eyes at her.

Court sighed as a snake tongue tickled her ear.

"All right, kiddo. How can I help?"

"See?" Lisa said, showing her a drawing on a piece of notebook paper. "I got the garage door booby-trapped, and the side door to the garage. Then I thought, *Wait! You forgot the dryer vent!* So now I'm working on that."

It was a slick little idea, and there were pulleys involved. If there was one thing Court loved, it was pulleys and rope.

"You think this'll lift a small monster?" asked Lisa.

"Sure! I put my little brother on the roof with less than this," said Court.

"Really? How?" Lisa demanded.

"Oh no you don't!"

Court looked over her shoulder and saw Eli standing on the front porch with his arms folded. She was doing a real nice job of ticking everyone off today.

"Mrs. Benton says it's important to support people's passionate interests," she said. To Lisa she muttered, "I'll be right back, okay? Here, hang on to this for me."

Court handed Archie the Serpenteen to Lisa and went over to Eli.

"She's not supposed to be outside alone in the first place," he told her. "Blatt was hanging around last night. What are you doing here, anyway?"

"Um, this is what most people do on Saturday. They go bother other people. Besides, we need to talk."

"Should those things be outside?" he asked, looking at the Serpenteens, who were looping in and out around the Spider Plant's legs. The Snorkelchorts were digging holes in the yard.

"You having any luck keeping your Creeps inside?"

On the side of his house, a window screen fell out with a crash. The Creep who looked like a pile of hair leaned through the opening. He was soaking wet and smelled very much like wet dog. There was a towel wrapped around his head, and for the first time Court could see his brown eyes.

"Hey, Eli, can I borrow your blow-dryer?" he asked.

It was probably rude to grin, but Court couldn't help it.

"Court!" said Lisa. "Lookit!"

She did. Luna and Zeb were taking a ride on the pulley mechanism she'd made.

Eli sighed.

"Could you keep her company for a little while? I got stuff to work on, too."

"What kind of stuff?"

He frowned.

"I was looking for the folder with the Howler's story in it, and I can't find it. But since I made the monsters, I thought . . . maybe I could write something new. Something that would help stop them."

That grabbed Court's attention.

"Like what?"

She thought he might be blushing.

"An action hero," he said.

"Oh!" said Court, excited. "I can help! Actions flicks are my favorites. I do my own stunts, too. They don't always work, but I learn a lot. We can start with—"

"I already started!" he said. "Dang! What is it with people trying to write my stories for me?"

"I didn't mean—"

"Whatever. Court, can you please just hang with Lisa? It'll keep her from running off so I can get done."

"Where's your mama?"

"She's a nurse, and she's working a twelve. She won't be home until eight."

"Who watches you?"

"We're allowed to watch ourselves, but we have to check in with Mrs. Harvey next door."

Court shuddered. That didn't sound like any fun. And she was pretty sure that when your mama was a nurse, nobody showed up with free pizza.

She'd put her foot in her mouth with Eli, just like she'd done with Neha. But maybe she could fix it. After all, she liked Lisa. Seemed like the Creeps did, too. The Spider Plant was letting her use one of its legs as a swing. Court nodded at Eli and rejoined his little sister.

"Jump to me!" she said, and like most people who wished they had wings, Lisa couldn't resist. She landed in Court's arms like a sack of potatoes. She was heavy for a little thing. But then, her pockets were jingling with tools.

Eli was already vanishing into the house.

"Brothers are dumb," Lisa said when Court set her down.

"He's just worried," she replied. No point talking bad about him to his own sister.

"He wouldn't be so worried if he'd let people help once in a while." Lisa sniffed. "I could write a better hero than him. I bet you could, too."

"Well," Court said, flipping over the piece of paper Lisa had used to plan out her slug trap, "how 'bout we make a list?"

18

Try to Be Cool

Eli was trapped in a weird parallel universe, one where he hated everything he was writing but desperately wanted it to work.

Seeing his monsters in Neha's sketchbook, alive and menacing, had darn near broken his brain. But Blatt's attack on Eddie had been his real wake-up call.

What if he'd complained about bringing in the trash cans, as he tended to do, and Lisa had marched out there in her jelly shoes to prove how big and strong she was?

He couldn't stop thinking about it.

The worst thing about being a writer was the way bad thoughts unspooled like movies in his head. He kept picturing his sister, afraid and in pain. The Howler was his best monster, but Lisa was his only sister. Eli knew what he had to do.

Eli wanted to give the Howler the ending that such a worthy foe deserved. And he had tried. But as he'd written, a horrible thought had occurred to him.

If the Creeps were real, and the monsters were real, how did he know the human characters in his stories weren't real on some level, too? Defeating a really good monster demanded a high price. Usually only one or two characters survived—everyone knew that. He kept trying to finish the story he'd started, but when it came time to kill people off, he froze.

He ripped his latest attempt out of his Super Sterling, crumpled it, and threw it. It bounced off the rim of the basketball hoop above his trash can, then rolled down the mound of failed attempts that spilled out of it.

Hairstack's big, hairy fist plunged into the can, packing down the contents. Then he scooped the rest of the crumpled pages off the floor and dumped them in, too.

"Thanks," said Eli.

"Everything's perfectly all right now," said Hairstack. "Okay if I use the top bunk?"

"Sure."

Hairstack vaulted up there, hair flying, and was snoring in minutes. Eli knew he must be tired; he'd stayed up all night watching *Star Wars* over and over with the volume on low. Eli sure hoped the hairy Creep had returned his momma's hair dryer to her bathroom, but at least he smelled like dry dog now. Still, Eli was jealous that Hairstack had time for a nap. Eli hadn't gotten much sleep, either, which wasn't helping his flow. It had turned out to be the Gargyle who'd eaten his Halloween candy, and the sock-dog had woken him up three times last night, begging to go out. It wasn't the Halloween candy that had disagreed with it so much as the wrappers.

"Stuck!" piped a small voice. "Stuck!"

Eli reached over and fished a Snorkelchort out of his bottom desk drawer by one foot. He tried to go back to writing, but a noise made him look at the window.

The Spider Plant must have climbed over the back fence, because when he turned around, its bug face was plastered against the glass. He shouted in surprise, then reached over and slid the window open.

"Come on, man, try to be cool!"

He slammed it shut again. On the top bunk, Hairstack snorted and rolled over, muttering something about lightsabers. The Spider Plant wandered sadly away.

At least Eli knew Lisa couldn't run off undetected today. He was lucky Court seemed to like little kids. But the Creeps were turning out to be more distracting than Lisa on her worst day. Two of them were having an argument in his closet, which confused him because only one of them could talk: a stubby little guy with long red hair that stood on end. Everyone called him the Crackler, but Eli hadn't figured out why. The other one was a walking flashcube—one of those clear plastic blocks people stuck on top of their cameras that lit up when they were taking a picture. The Creeps called that one Zoop. She was the other reason Eli hadn't slept worth a darn: the closet was crowded, so Creeps kept bumping one another. And when Zoop was surprised, she went off.

Eli rolled a new sheet of paper into the Super Sterling and decided to try something new. If he couldn't risk hurting characters he liked, maybe he should write characters that annoyed him.

The heroes in horror stories were usually young, inexperienced, and scrappy. Lots of them started off with a serious lack of survival skills. That was partly why Eli was having such a hard time killing them off. Characters in horror stories were hapless victims. They never asked for any of it.

That was why he'd hit on the idea of an action hero. Those guys went looking for trouble.

Eli had never tried to write an action hero, but he thought he had a good grasp of the basics—they had tragic backstories that they overcame as they defeated evil, usually in spectacularly improbable ways. They had lots of weapons. They got banged up a lot, but they always won.

Eli wouldn't feel guilty about risking the safety of an action hero. He figured they knew what they'd signed up for.

He decided to name his hero Dolt. He wasn't totally sure he remembered what it meant, but he knew action heroes usually had short, snappy names, and sometimes they sounded like they were from Germany. Eli knew that was kind of predictable, but if he wrote a fresh, new kind of hero, he'd like him too much. Then he'd be right back where he started.

Dolt prowled across the moonlit Oklahoma grasslands, weapon at the ready, he typed. Eli didn't know that much about guns, but it probably didn't matter, as long as Dolt always had one stashed somewhere when he needed it. *Deep within the dark shadows of the abandoned barn, his nemesis gave a low, thunderous growl.*

Eli's words finally started to unspool. He made sure the ensuing battle was epic, with the Howler's minions attacking from both sides in a last-ditch attempt to protect their ruler, then a final showdown with the Howler itself. It culminated in a now-blazing barn collapsing on top of the still-defiant Howler. The suitably grim and wounded Dolt went off to work things out with his dog, who'd left him for a family with kids.

Eli typed *The End* and whipped the last page from the Super Sterling with a flourish. When he looked at his clock, he discovered he'd missed lunch completely. He headed for the kitchen, elated and hungry.

Zoop and the Crackler had gotten there first.

"Hey," said Eli, "are those the last three cans of SpaghettiOs?"

Zoop went off. Eli was briefly blinded. He blinked as his eyes started doing their job again, then looked around for the source of a crunching sound he hadn't noticed before. It was the Rustlehorse. She'd spent the night in their backyard, but Eli hadn't realized she knew how to open the sliding-glass door. She was eating Cheerios out of the box. With a closer look, Eli confirmed she was eating the box, too.

"Will y'all quit getting into stuff without asking?" he said. Startled, the Rustlehorse pranced backward, near about stepping on the Crackler, whose red hair suddenly burst into flames. Eli did the math: grass horse plus flaming hair equaled disaster. He jumped between them.

"Hey, Rustlehorse!" he said. "Whoa, calm down. Crackler, dude, chill out."

No one listened. His house was about to burn down around his ears, he knew it.

Then the front door slammed, and Court and Lisa came in. As soon as Court laid eyes on the scene in the kitchen, she jumped in front of the now-rearing Rustlehorse. She shoved the Crackler aside with her foot and clapped her hands right in front of the Rustlehorse's nose.

"Back up, you!" she said. The Rustlehorse dropped, confused, and backed away. Court walked up on her, crowding her. Before the mare knew it, she was out on the back patio.

Court whipped an apple out of her pocket. "Here, old girl," she said, and the Rustlehorse took it like she was too surprised not to. Court shut the door in her face.

Then she grabbed the Crackler around the middle and dunked his head in the sink. His hair went out with a hiss. Court set him right side up on the counter.

"Sorry about that," said the Crackler.

"It could happen to anybody," Eli managed to say, stomping out a few sparks that had drifted to the floor.

Court fished a sandwich bag out of another pocket.

"I brought some GORP," she said to the Crackler. "You like GORP?"

"What's GORP?" asked Lisa, sticking her head in through the kitchen door. Eli sighed with relief. He'd been about to ask where she was.

"Good Old Raisins and Peanuts," said Court, "but if you know what you're doing you put M&M's in there, too." She split the bag between Lisa and the Crackler.

"Hey, can I have some?" asked Hairstack, entering the kitchen with a mighty yawn that revealed a huge mouthful of flat teeth.

Eli knew he'd done good writing that afternoon, and he was proud of himself for accomplishing his goal even though he didn't like Dolt. But seeing Court perform feats of derring-do reminded him how much fun he'd thought it would be to play around with new kinds of heroes.

Court turned and saw Eli staring. Her smile faded.

"Did I do something wrong again?" she asked.

"No!" said Eli. "That was awesome. But I was writing about an action hero, and—"

"And I busted in and interrupted. I'm sorry, Eli," said Court. And even though he would have had to be a total punk to be mad at her after everything she'd done to help, she really did look sorry.

"You were great," he said, and meant it. "You reminded me I'm not quite done, that's all."

"Good," said Lisa from the doorway, "'cause we've got a list."

19

Blatt

Neha had spent her entire day juggling Creeps. A few had been injured in their escape from the sketchbook, so she'd searched her closet for the first aid kit she made in Girl Scouts. But the Creeps had promptly stolen all the bandages, and the Snorkelchorts and Treebots had been playing "Keep Away from the Mummy" ever since. It involved a lot of screaming and running.

Redwing had spent much of the day flying over their neighborhood, Walnut Hills, on the lookout for the slug. So far, she hadn't found it.

By the time Neha finally got out of her house, she was downright frazzled. She was still charmed by Sleekit's presence in her bike basket, though.

The Spider Plant was alone in Eli's front yard. Neha gave it a hug and sent it to stand in the field at the end of the cul-de-sac, where it would be less obvious to neighborhood kids. She knocked on the door until it was clear she could either open it herself or stand there feeling silly. When she turned the knob and pushed, the noise hit her like a wall.

"You double-crossing varmint!" said Court. "First you aim to rustle my cattle, now you've started a stampede!"

The Gargyle and a wave of Snorkelchorts came galloping through, almost knocking Neha over with their enthusiasm. Most of the Gargyle was flapping. The Chorts were giggling and whooping. Behind them came Hairstack on all fours, Lisa astride his back. She was yelling, "Hyaah, Hyaah!" Court was crouched and waiting in the family room, and they were running right at her. At the last possible second, Court vaulted over the couch.

"You gotta get up pretty early in the morning to put one over on me!" she hollered as Lisa and the smaller Creeps shrieked with excitement. Hairstack pretended to rear.

The sliding-glass door eased open, and the Rustlehorse slipped in. She tiptoed up behind an unsuspecting Court, then shoved the blond girl with her nose and bowled her over.

"Whoa!" Court exclaimed, upending a nearby drink on her way to the floor.

"Uh-oh," said Lisa, freezing as what turned out to be ruby-red Kool-Aid seeped across the carpet.

"Uh-oh what?" asked Eli, coming out of the kitchen with a pot in one hand and a wooden spoon in the other. "Oh, crud!"

He shouldered the Rustlehorse back out of the house again and latched the door.

The Gargyle hid around the corner and peeked in with a whine.

"Nobody panic," said Court. "Lisa, get me a rag."

Court went and retrieved a bowl and put warm water and dish soap in it. She took the rag from Lisa and dampened it, then used it to soak up the Kool-Aid. Eli watched like a hawk, but he was calming down fast because it was working. Neha put a hand under the pot Eli was holding, which was drooping toward the floor. Her stomach rumbled. Her mother had made her lunch, but she'd fed half of it to the Creeps.

Court dabbed at what was left of the mess.

"Learned this one when Joshie and I forgot we had Kool-Aid in our water guns," she said. "We shot 'em off in the house."

"Why would you put Kool-Aid in them in the first—" Neha started to ask, then stopped herself. Court answered anyway.

"Heck," she said, "he was bored, and I figured it was an interesting way to tie-dye our T-shirts."

That was the difference between her and Court, Neha realized. She tried to prevent problems, and Court did what she wanted and then cleaned up. Neha wondered which way was better.

Court's way was definitely more fun.

"Well," said Eli. "Dinner, anyway."

They trooped out to the kitchen, and Neha sat awkwardly at the table, unsure if she was a dinner guest or just a spectator. Then Eli glopped a big serving of macaroni down in front of her and added some peas. She didn't really like peas, but she was so hungry she ate them anyway. Hairstack took a plate and retreated to Eli's bedroom, lamenting the discovery that there was no such thing as Bantha milk.

Once her stomach had registered the presence of food, Neha reached for her backpack and pulled out her sketchbook.

"I have to show you something," she said.

Before she could, there was a clatter from the laundry room. Neha glanced over.

"Is one of the Creeps in there?" she asked.

Court looked around and shrugged.

"You'd think they'd be all tuckered out."

Neha was mentally cataloguing the Creeps at Eli's house when the clatter became a wet, slapping thump, and the thump became a buzz, and suddenly there was a hole being chewed in the bottom of the laundry room door and something terrible oozed its way into the kitchen.

It was the slug thing that had come blasting out of the barn the day before, and it had obviously found something to eat since they saw it last, because it was bigger.

"Creeps!" Neha shouted. "Run!"

Some of them listened. The Gargyle scampered off toward the back of the house. The three baby butterfly snakes fluttered after him. Chorts jumped up on top of anything nearby: the counters, the couch, the hearth.

Sleekit ignored Neha's warning and leaped up onto the table, where she began throwing all the silverware she could reach, chattering furiously at the thing.

Lisa scrambled around the older kids and ran straight toward the slug.

"Lisa!" shouted Eli in a panic, lunging for her. She pulled a trigger Neha hadn't noticed, tucked under the end of the counter. A cupboard door swung open. Inside was a Nerf gun with the Ghostbusters symbol on it. It projected an image of the little green ghost from the movie on the wall across from it, and the slug paused. It seemed confused about what to attack. With a pop of compressed air, the gun fired, but it didn't shoot the big yellow marshmallow-shaped pellet Neha was expecting. Instead it fired a net, which neatly blanketed the slug. It even had weights to hold it down. Neha cheered in spite of her fear, and Lisa grinned.

"Court!" Lisa said. "Behind you!"

Court reached for a brightly colored plastic something half-hidden in the drapes.

The net covering the slug smoked, then began to melt. The vortex of the slug's mouth whirred as it powered through the disintegrating strands.

It turned on Lisa, who was boxed into a corner between the counter and the sliding-glass door. Outside, the Rustlehorse reared, unable to come to her defense without smashing the glass. Lisa started to boost herself up onto the counter, but not fast enough. The slug sped toward her.

Water streamed past Neha's ear as Court fired what turned out to be a water gun . . . the motorized kind. A moment later, Neha realized it wasn't filled with water. The sharp tang of vinegar rose as the slug recoiled from the splatter, and Lisa took the opportunity to jump from one counter to the other. She dropped to the floor and ran from the room.

"Its skin is covered with acid or something," Neha said to Court, putting a chair between herself and the slug.

"I'm aiming for anything that could be an eye," Court said. The slug didn't seem happy, exactly, but it didn't seem hurt, either.

"What other traps has she got in here?" Court asked Eli as the stream from the gun developed a visible curve. Neha knew they were almost out of time.

"There's a spring-loaded closet, but it'll just eat its way out!"

"Can you talk to it?" Neha asked. "You invented it, didn't you?"

"Does it work like that?" he asked, turning to her with panicked eyes.

"Do I look like I know?"

He moved forward cautiously, keeping a tipped-back chair between him and his creation. The water gun ran out of ammo with a last trickle.

"Hey there, Blatt," he said. "Do you know me?"

It wrinkled its snout like it was testing the air. There was a moment of silence, long enough to make Neha feel hopeful.

Then the slug's vortex of a mouth spun like a jet engine at takeoff. It popped forward with a burst of speed and took one of the legs right off the chair.

"Whoa!" yelled Eli as all three of them fell back.

"Seems like maybe it does!" said Court.

Lisa came running back in.

"Heads up!" she hollered, and a small pouch flew through the air. It clinked as Court caught it.

"Ha!" said Court with approval as she opened the bag and dumped jacks into her hand. Using the chairs and table as cover, she threw a few into the path of the oncoming slug. They weren't enough to stop Blatt, but it clearly didn't like them, so she kept tossing jacks between them and it, a few at a time, as they backed around the table.

Lisa slipped something else into Eli's hand.

"This is butane!" he said. "Where did you get this?"

"Garage sale!" she answered proudly. "I warmed it up already."

"Focus, please!" said Neha, who was nervously watching the slug advance.

Blatt lunged around the last of the jacks and tried to come at them through the rest of the half-eaten chair.

"Hold this!" Eli said to Neha, letting go of the chair back.

"What? No!" Neha shouted in a panic, but she did it anyway. He darted around behind Blatt and pressed what Lisa had handed him against its tail. Instantly, it let out a wail and recoiled at both ends, scrunching up in a slimy ball in the middle of the kitchen. For the first time, Neha got a clear look at what Eli was holding—a battery-powered curling iron.

Lisa and Eli were both exposed where they were. Neha pivoted to put the chair in front of Lisa, who was closest to her, but the little girl ducked away.

"I gotta aim!" she said, settling the leather strap of a slingshot on her wrist. She loaded the pouch, but the ammo didn't look like a rock or ball bearing. It was white.

She let fly.

The slug's reaction was better than any of them could have hoped for. It shrieked and began flailing its head and tail, spinning and trying to get away from the pain.

"What the heck are you using?" demanded Court.

"Rock salt from the garage!" said Lisa triumphantly, firing again. The slug howled.

Court whooped.

But as Blatt tried to get away, it started sliding blindly around the kitchen, and its mouth was still going. It shot toward Eli, who yelled and jumped back. Then it whirled and headed straight for the girls.

Neha knew she wasn't scrappy like Court or Lisa, or even Sleekit, but she *was* a nerd, and that had to count for something.

She looked around for anything that would stop the slug.

That was when she spotted it. She lunged around Blatt, and there was a horrible moment when if it had turned its head even a little, it would have chewed her leg right off. Then she shoved the plugged-in toaster off the counter and into its whirring mouth.

Blades ground as the metal appliance stopped them. One of them must have nicked the cord, because suddenly there were sparks playing up and down its metal teeth. Blatt seized up, contracted, made a horrible series of popping noises . . . and exploded.

They ducked, shrieking.

When they dared to open their eyes, Eli's entire kitchen was coated in slug. Hairstack, who'd finally heard the commotion, had arrived just in time for his long, luxurious hair to be covered from head to toe in slug guts.

They cheered.

"Way to go, Neha!" said Court, slapping her on the back. The resulting spray of disgusting liquid made them both wince.

"Lisa," Court added, "those were some high-quality traps!"

Lisa grinned.

Eli couldn't help grinning back. His sister was something else. Then he glanced at the clock on the microwave.

"Oh no," he said.

Neha, who'd gone to examine the sparking toaster cord, looked up. "What?" she asked warily.

"My momma is going to be home in an hour and a half," he said.

A lump of guts fell from the ceiling and hit the floor with a squelch.

20

Slugs Are Malleable

All year long, Court had been feeling out of place around the smart kids. Now, as they watched slug guts drip from every surface, that feeling blew away like a handful of dust.

She knew her moment when she saw it.

She ran for the phone. She had to wipe it off with a towel to lift it up off the hook, then she wiped her fingers on her jeans so she could push the buttons. She let it ring for as long as it took to seriously annoy the person ignoring it on the other end.

Finally, someone answered.

"Hello?"

"Amy, I need help."

Instantly, Amy's voice swung from annoyance to business.

"Did you fall off your bike? Did you get in a fight? Where are you?"

"I'm at Eli's, and we've got a disaster to undo. It's too big to handle by ourselves."

Amy didn't ask where Eli's parents were, or any of the other annoying questions most sisters would ask.

"How long have you got?"

Court glanced at the microwave clock.

"Ninety minutes and counting."

"We'll be right there." Amy hung up.

Court turned to her friends.

"Lisa, Neha, open every window and the sliding-glass door," she said, and they rushed to obey.

"Eli, get out every bucket you have, and some rags. Old towels. All the cleaners."

She headed for the sink. She rinsed it, ran the disposal (*Ew*, she thought), and rinsed it again. Then she plugged and filled it.

Eli dumped three empty buckets on the floor.

"No," Court directed, "fill them in the laundry tub. Do you have any stepladders?"

While he went looking for those, she grabbed two of the towels he'd brought and rolled them up like hot dogs. She lay them down where the kitchen floor met the carpet.

"Neha," she said, "can you do more of these? Every doorway."

She had just convinced Hairstack to spray himself off with the hose outside when she heard a familiar rattling buzz coming up the street. She ran to open the front door. Amy and Ian parked Ian's junker delivery truck on the street and grabbed supplies out of the back.

"Where is it?" Amy asked, all business.

"Kitchen," said Court. "Where's Joshie?"

"Sleeping over at Bert's."

Ian whistled when he saw the kitchen. "What the heck did you guys do?"

Court thought about lying, but honestly, she was tuckered out. "Neha chucked a toaster at a giant slug and it exploded."

Eli, Lisa, and Neha all stared at her. Then they held their breath while Amy and Ian watched slug globs drop from the ceiling.

"Did it shoot acid at you?" Amy asked.

"Nope," said Court.

She nodded thoughtfully. "That's good. They've got a sixty-foot range."

"Well," Court said, not sure whether her sister was pulling her leg, "I'll take that under advisement."

"Good. Now," Amy said, clapping her hands together, "time's a-wastin'."

Ian went back outside to the truck for more supplies.

Amy pulled a plastic shopping bag out of her jeans pocket and shoved it at Lisa. "Do you know how to take that vent cover off?" she asked, pointing at the one by the sliding-glass door.

Lisa nodded. She looked a little bit tongue-tied to have a teenager paying her attention.

"Great. Wrap this bag around it and put it back in nice and tight, okay?" she asked, and Lisa jumped to do it. Then Amy gave Court the nod.

"All right, everyone!" Court hollered. "This here's what we call a top-down operation. We start with the ceiling and cupboards."

She turned on the sink faucet, grabbed the sprayer, and aimed it at the ceiling.

"Whoa, what the heck are you doing?" Eli demanded. He jumped to intercept her, but she dodged him as best she could.

"Trust me," she said. "You try wiping that ceiling, everything's going to smear and stain it up. You'll never get it all."

"But everything else—"

". . . can be mopped," said Ian. He slapped down an industrial mop bucket, the kind with wheels, in the middle of the floor. He had a handful of plastic dustpans, too. Perfect.

Amy showed Neha and Lisa how to use the dustpans to skim the water and slug guts off the linoleum and chuck 'em out the back door. It had to be done more than once, because slug guts were sliding down the walls and cupboards as Court rinsed, but Eli got up on the stepladder he'd found and started wiping. Ian was mopping up any guts they missed. He headed out into the laundry room to get the places where the sprayer wouldn't reach. A minute later, he called Court in.

"Here's your problem," he said when she got there, his voice echoing. He was up to his shoulders in the clothes dryer.

"Is it broken?" Eli asked from the stepladder.

"Naw," said Ian. "But if y'all fought a slug, this is where it got in, I bet. It was standing open. He could've slid in through the vent. It goes straight to the outside."

He was surely playing along, but for the moment Court pretended he was being straight as an arrow.

"That thing was big," she said. "No way in heck could it fit through there."

"Slugs are malleable," said Amy, popping her head over Court's shoulder. "It's in the rules. They count as one size smaller when they're squeezing through tight spaces."

"Huh," said Court. All that D&D stuff was turning out to be useful. She might have to start telling Amy the truth more often.

By the time Eli and Court were done wiping the lower cupboards, Amy was spraying off the patio with the hose. Eli went to put all the dirty towels and rags in the wash, dodging around Ian, who had a screwdriver out and was swapping the laundry-room door with the one on the heater closet in the garage.

Court took the extra towels outside.

"Not much we can do about the chair," said Amy, "but they've got six. I'd hide it while you figure it out. Maybe his mama won't notice."

Court nodded.

"Ready?" Amy asked. Court could hear Ian packing up their stuff and running loads to the truck. She spread her arms, and Amy sprayed her head to toe, washing off the slug guts on Court's clothes and in her hair. Court turned around so Amy could hose her back. Everyone got the same treatment, right down to their shoes. Eli had the nicest sneakers of all of them. They were green-and-white Adidas, and Court could see he was fussing about them.

"Don't worry," she told him. "We'll fix 'em right up."

He frowned at his feet.

"All right," said Amy, chucking a plastic baggie at them. "Cover story."

Water balloons.

"You're a genius!" Court shouted, and ran to hug her. Amy ducked away, laughing. "Whoa! Maybe wait 'til you've had a shower, Courtney Jane! I'd better get out of here."

"Well . . . ," Court began with a grin.

"THAT WAS CLOSE!" they finished together. Amy ducked out the side gate, just in case, but Ian honked when they pulled away, so Court knew they were in the clear for the moment. The truck buzzed away down the street.

"That," said Eli, "was amazing."

"It really was," Neha agreed. "Water balloons?" she added, looking at the packet Amy had left.

"The best lies have a grain of truth in 'em," said Court.

By the time Lisa and Eli's mama got home, they had every fan in the place going. The Rustlehorse was off in a distant corner of the yard, eating grass that wasn't contaminated with slug innards. Eli, Court, Neha, and Lisa were chasing each other around outside, screaming. The sliding-glass door was shut, and Court made sure she hit it hard with at least two water balloons as Eli's mama put down her stuff.

"Eli!" she said as she opened the door. Court thought it was cool to see somebody in real-life hospital scrubs. They had interesting stains on them. She wanted to look closer, but before she could, Mrs. Goodman said, "You know better than to have company over when I'm at work!"

To Court's surprise, Neha jumped right in.

"I'm sorry, ma'am!" she said. "Court and I talked him into it. We're working on a school project, and I hate leaving things until the last minute. Eli said he had to stay home to watch Lisa, so we came here. We're just taking a break."

"Hmm." Mrs. Goodman sized them up. "And why is the kitchen floor wet?"

Court took that one. "We had the screen door pulled instead of the glass one, and I wasn't looking where I was throwing like I should've. My daddy says I've got a pitcher's arm."

This was a bald-faced lie. Joshie was the pitcher in the family, and every window in the Castle house trembled in its frame when he wound up. But Eli's mama didn't know that.

Court could see Mrs. Goodman weakening, so she stuck out her hand. "I'm Court Castle, ma'am, and this is Neha Prasad. My big sister is my sitter, and she checked on us, I promise."

That ought to take care of any nosy neighbors who'd spotted Amy and Ian.

Mrs. Goodman eyed them for another minute, waiting for someone to break.

"Your parents run the Showplace Pizza?" she asked.

"Yes, ma'am. We're used to minding ourselves. I'm sorry if it's a problem."

"Maybe it's not," she said at last. "Sometimes I forget you're all getting bigger. Lisa, did you have fun?"

Lisa hugged Court around the middle, taking her by surprise. Only then did Court realize that Sleekit was perched up on the roof above Mrs. Goodman's head. Impossibly, she hung upside down by her back feet and grinned at them. Lisa, Neha, and Court all got the giggles, and Mrs. Goodman smiled at their foolishness.

"Did y'all eat?" she asked.

"I made macaroni," said Eli, still looking like he might get busted.

"You cleaned up real nice," she said, and went back inside.

Lisa shook her head.

"If I'd finished that slug trap sooner, we wouldn't have had to," she said.

"You did good," said Eli, squeezing her shoulder.

21

What's Your Damage?

Dwight was late picking them up from school on Monday. Eli thought he seemed more distracted than usual, but that might have been because he was separating Oreos and eating the cream out of the middles while he was driving. He kept dropping cookies on the floor and cussing. He tended to underestimate his passengers' hearing. Maybe he was right. Most of the kids were waving a second round of flyers for the fund-raiser at Showplace. Ordinarily, a night of pizza and video games would have Eli's full attention, and he was curious to see Court's family's restaurant.

But today, he did his best to ignore the mayhem on the bus.

Eli, Neha, and Court had tried to talk about the monsters' attacks on the sketchbook door the night Blatt blew up, but his Daddy had phoned, so the girls had left almost immediately. He knew Neha had filled Court in on their way home, and they had tried to call him on Sunday, but when Court called, Joshie picked up in the other room and made fart noises, and when Neha called, her parents picked up to ask who she was calling.

Talking at school had become equally complicated, because although each of them had checked their bags before they'd left the house, they'd completely failed to prevent stowaways. Court's homework was missing. In its place were the carefully coiled Serpenteens. Fortunately, she'd been hunting crickets for them while she waited for the bus, stowing them in a margarine container. She spent the entire school day slipping wriggling bugs to the snakes to keep them quiet.

At lunch, Eli had opened his metal *E.T.* lunch box and slammed it shut quick, coughing to cover the cheery "Heyyyyy!" from the unusually small Snorkelchort inside, who'd already eaten Eli's lunch. Court had slipped Eli one of her leftover pizza slices so he wouldn't go hungry, and Neha had donated one of her Little Debbie cakes.

"I wish Dwight would hurry up for once," said Court now. "I'm almost out of crickets."

Neha shushed Eli's Snorkelchort, which she had transferred to the inside pocket of her jean jacket when it occurred to her that it might suffocate in the lunch box.

"I'm not sure we can afford for him to hurry," she said. "He has enough trouble driving as it is."

Eli snorted his agreement. He was eager to be home. He was feeling pretty queasy, actually, but Dwight wasn't the only reason.

"Neha, can you draw something to reinforce the door somehow?" asked Court.

"It's standing there in the middle of the street," said Neha. "I've been building structures around it, but they tear them down. See?"

She opened the sketchbook with one hand, muffling the Chort in her jacket with the other, so Court and Eli could see the piles of debris around the door. She shut it as soon as they'd gotten a look, then tucked it under her leg with a glare at Scott, who was watching from across the aisle. He smirked.

"Jerk," muttered Eli.

"It's not just him," said Neha. "I don't know how much the monsters can hear. I didn't want to risk saying this where they could listen."

She lowered her voice anyway.

"Between you and me, I'm scared to draw any more counter-measures. What if they start using the scrap to pound on the door?"

They sat quiet for a minute, pondering this. Then Court snapped her fingers.

"Eli was working on an idea on Saturday, weren't you, Eli?" she asked. "An action hero?"

Instead of answering, Eli rubbed the back of his neck and asked, "Neha, when was the last time you saw the Howler in the sketchbook?"

Neha pondered. "The day the Creeps got out," she said.

"But not since Saturday?"

She shook her head, bumping it on the window as the bus swerved.

"Ouch!" she said.

"*Hey!*" yelled Dwight out the window. "Get in your own lane!"

He popped half an Oreo in his mouth.

"I might have killed him," said Eli.

Neha rubbed her head. The Chort reached up and rubbed it, too. She shoved its hand back inside her jacket.

"I feel that way about Dwight a lot," she said.

Eli frowned in confusion.

"Not Dwight," he said. "The Howler."

Court and Neha blinked at him.

"Can you *do* that?" asked Court.

"I don't know," said Eli. "But I tried. I wrote a big death scene and everything."

To his surprise, Neha patted one of his shoulders sympathetically. Court punched the other one, but when he looked, he realized she was pleased.

"Way to go, Eli!" she said.

"That must have been hard," said Neha, "destroying something you made."

This time, when Dwight veered across the parkway, he didn't just whoosh through a yellow light, he flat out ran a red one.

"Dude!" said Brandon, who was sitting right behind Eli, Neha, and Court.

"Oh my gosh," whispered Neha. "What is Dwight thinking?"

That's when the police siren kicked on behind the bus. Instantly, there was a wall of kids pressed against the rear windows.

Dwight pulled over in the turn lane for Walnut Hills.

"Can we get off here?" someone asked.

"No!" commanded Dwight. "Stay in your seats and be quiet!"

"My mom's going to flip out," said Scott.

"Eli?" said Lisa from across the aisle. "Are we in trouble?"

"Naw, it's okay," he said.

"Scoot over, Lisa," said Neha, getting up to shove past Court and Eli. Lisa looked as though she was going to argue for a second, then she grabbed her heart-covered backpack and made room for Neha to sit down.

"The police officer's just checking on us," said Neha. "It'll be okay."

Lisa rolled her eyes a little bit, but Eli could tell she liked getting attention from a big kid who wasn't her brother. And the

Snorkelchort reached out of Neha's jacket to pat her cheek and made her giggle.

He shot Neha a grateful look.

Joshie was plastered to the windows alongside the rest of his friends. He turned and gave Court a complicated, eyebrow-waggling look.

"What?" Eli asked.

"We always know when someone at the restaurant is getting fired," she said. "This feels a lot like that."

The way heads were turning, Eli was pretty positive an officer was walking up toward the front of the bus. Then Dwight cranked the door open and peered out.

"Is there a problem, officer?" asked Dwight, and Eli started coughing in an effort to stifle his laugh.

"Yeah," he whispered to Court. "I think there's a problem."

She shoved her fist in her mouth.

Eli couldn't hear the officer's exact words, but his tone seemed to indicate he agreed with Court and Eli. The next thing they knew, Dwight was stepping down out of the bus. The entire busload of kids intoned the traditional "you're in trouble" sound simultaneously.

"UUUUUUUHM . . ."

But getting pulled over in a school bus turned out to be kind of boring. The cop walked back to his car and did paperwork while Dwight waited on the bus steps like a kid who'd been sent to sit in the hall. Then the cop came back with a ticket. Some of the kids glued to the windows tried to give everyone else updates; the rest hissed at them to shut up so they could hear.

Across the aisle, Neha was peering at her sketchbook again, and all of a sudden she hunched over it, hiding it with her arms.

"What is it?" Eli asked.

Neha tried to explain, but the chatter on the bus was loud, and just when there was a sudden hush and Eli thought he and Court would be able to hear, Dwight reboarded with the ticket in his hand, and the entire bus went wild.

"Dude!"

"You're an outlaw, man!"

"Whoa, I fought the law, am I right?" said Brandon.

"THE LAW WON!" shouted Dwight at the top of his lungs. Instantly, everyone was silent. "Now simmer down. Face the front!" he said, and Eli stopped hanging across the aisle trying to see the sketchbook so he wouldn't get them in trouble.

Right before Court's stop, Dwight hollered at some laughing kids. Neha saw her moment. She whipped the open sketchbook up for Eli and Court to see.

The door was still there. It was still shut. But anyone could see the damage, even from a distance. The monsters were throwing everything they had at it. It wasn't going to hold forever.

22

Backfired

When Neha's dad opened the door of Showplace Pizza later that night for the fund-raiser, the noise hit Neha first, then the smell. The Prasads almost never ordered takeout, and on the one occasion she'd made the mistake of complaining about it, her mathematician mother had sat her down and given her a lesson on how much cheaper it was to buy food at the grocery store than at a restaurant.

A familiar buzzing noise attracted Neha's attention, and she took the door from her dad while she waited for her friend to get out of Ian's weather-beaten pickup truck.

"Thanks, Ian!"

Court came swanning up as Amy leaned through the driver's side window of the truck and kissed her boyfriend good-bye.

"Eeeew!" said Joshie, slamming the passenger side door. "Gross!"

Neha hadn't realized she was watching until Joshie commented. Her face warmed. She hadn't meant to stare, but she couldn't help wondering what it was like to have a sister old enough to have a boyfriend.

Lightning flashed in the distance, and thunder rumbled. Rain began to patter on the pavement.

"Quick, Amy!" called Court. "Run for it!"

Inside, Court sniffed the air, then made a face.

"What's wrong?" asked Neha.

"You know how the cafeteria smells good on spaghetti day?"

Neha wrinkled her nose. It did smell good . . . until you saw the spaghetti, which was served with an ice cream scoop and held its shape on the tray. Whenever she saw it, she was glad her mom's opinion on school lunches matched her opinion on takeout.

"It's not that bad," she said.

"It is to my daddy," said Court, who'd already confided to Neha and Eli that things at Showplace weren't all they were cracked up to be.

Neha breathed in the pizza smell, but the nose-tickling notes of fresh spices and garlic that meant "food" in the Prasads' kitchen were missing. In other words, Showplace sold pizza the way someone with plastic on all their furniture "liked" animals.

Neha understood, but she planned to enjoy her dinner anyway.

They followed Neha's parents to the tables where the ARC class was gathered, then sat down to eat. Court was right, Neha decided as she chewed. The pizza wasn't anything special. But it was still pizza. They each ate two slices, then they got tokens from Neha's parents and Amy, and headed for the games.

Scott Gabler was playing *Dragon Doom*, shouting at the screen with Brandon and Jay. Even Neha, who rarely played arcade games, had heard of it. She stepped closer to see.

Dragon Doom was special. Instead of sixteen-bit pixel art there was an actual cartoon adventure playing out on the screen, same as you'd see on TV. It was one of the biggest reasons kids got fired up about coming to Showplace.

"Do you want to play?" asked Court.

"No," said Neha quickly. Playing a game that popular meant people would be standing behind her watching, and when it came to video games, she didn't know what she was doing. "I'll wait with you if you want to, though."

"Eh." Court shrugged. "Scott was talking all day about beating the high score, and I don't feel like waiting. Let's play Whac-A-Mole, or Skee-Ball, or something."

Maybe we'll get lucky and he'll stay there all night, thought Neha.

Across the room, loud rockabilly music began to play.

Someone grabbed Neha's arm, and she jumped.

It was Eli. She gave a sigh of relief.

"What on earth is that?" Eli asked them, pointing.

"The Calamity Band," said Court.

Eli was staring.

"I swear they get closer if you stare too long," he said.

The "band" playing the music was a quartet of six-foot-tall animatronic animals. But Neha used the term "animal" loosely, because she'd never seen a giant gray squirrel wearing a flannel shirt and overalls before.

"Is that squirrel playing a banjo?" she asked.

"Yeah," said Court. "I've always been a little bit murky about how it belongs in the same band as the panda in the sequined dress."

There was a keyboard-playing tiger, too. Neha thought any self-respecting tiger would eat the other animals and pick its teeth with one of the rooster's drumsticks—though this one would have to choose between the chicken-flavored kind and the drum-playing kind.

The tiger was wearing a football uniform.

"Those," Neha said, "are the scariest things I've ever seen. Including the Howler."

She shifted something under her arm.

"You brought the sketchbook?" asked Court. She was frowning. "What if something happens to it?"

"I'll be careful; I'm not sure it's safe to leave it anywhere anymore," she said.

"The Creeps are here, too," said Eli.

Neha hadn't realized, but looking around she could see he was right. The Spider Plant was skulking behind a bunch of fake trees over by the band. A little kid at the claw machine was trying to catch Sleekit, who had apparently climbed up through the prize chute. The preschooler was about to pitch a fit because instead of being caught like an ordinary stuffed animal, Sleekit was dangling from the claw and twirling like a circus aerialist. She seemed to be enjoying herself. The kid's mama was having a different experience.

"I don't know what you're talking about," she said. "I don't even see a purple one!"

"They should have stayed at our houses," said Neha worriedly, glancing around to see who was watching. Then she looked at the Calamity Band again. Hairstack, who was standing next to the tiger, gave her a small salute.

"Actually," she amended, "this might be the perfect place to hide."

"At least I got the Serpenteens to stay home," said Court. "They're shedding their skins, so they're crabby. Somebody was gonna get bit if they came."

"The Creeps at my house have been jumpy all afternoon," Neha said, though Sleekit seemed to have calmed down now.

Inside the claw machine, the purple stripes on her tail blurred as she spun faster and faster. The way Court was watching, Neha figured she'd be trying to rig something similar for herself any day.

The kid pointed and shrieked, and his mama tried to run her hand through her heavily hair-sprayed bangs and ended up even more frustrated than she already was.

The pocket of Court's hoodie squeaked. Neha took the edge of the pocket between two fingers and peeked inside. A Snorkel poked out and shot a jelly bean at her. It bounced off her forehead. Like the one in Eli's lunch box earlier, the Chort peering out at her seemed smaller than normal.

"Are the Snorkelchorts breeding?" she asked.

Court and Eli looked at her with identical expressions of horror.

"How 'bout we deal with that later," said Court at last.

"Look," said Eli, "if we've got to be here anyway, we might as well play some games."

Court pulled some of her tokens out of her jeans pocket and jingled them in her hand.

"Skee-Ball first?" she suggested with a gleam in her eye.

"Sure," said Neha. She was pretty sure Court had her pegged as being bad at sports, so this was going to be fun.

Neha still ended up with a small crowd around her, in spite of her efforts to avoid it, but since she was winning, she didn't mind so much.

She flicked her wrist, and her lazily moving ball hit the ball-hop and dropped right into the 500-point hole. Again.

"Whoo!" yelled Court, smacking her in the shoulder. "Look at you go!"

Tickets spooled out of the Skee-Ball machine.

Scott must have been done with *Dragon Doom*, because he'd wandered over.

"Don't worry about it, Court!" he said. "You get all the tickets you want even when you lose, right?"

"You know how parents tell you to ignore people and they'll leave you alone?" Court muttered to Eli and Neha.

"Yeah, that never works," said Eli, and Neha laughed.

They played a few more games, then went over to the counter where kids exchanged their tickets for cheap plastic toys. There were enough Lisa Frank stickers in there to cover everyone at Showplace with unicorns and rainbows. The Treebots were methodically sticking them to the inside of the glass in rows, but the guy working the counter couldn't see their handiwork from where he was standing.

"How the heck am I supposed to clean those up without my folks seeing?" muttered Court.

"We'll make the Creeps do it," promised Neha.

Then Sleekit stuck her head out of a fake tree and started giving orders.

"Get the jacks," she said.

Neha's eyes about rolled back in her head. "No. I am not getting the jacks."

"But we're all out of them. We need them. They're pointy."

"Exactly. We're going to end up hurting ourselves."

"Not if more monsters get out," said Sleekit. She climbed down the tree as if it was a barber pole and she was the stripe. She whisked around behind the counter and came out with the jacks.

"That's stealing!" hissed Neha, scandalized. She glanced at Court.

"It's a matter of life or death," said Sleekit. At least, that seemed to be the gist of it. She had the drawstrings of the jacks bag in her mouth.

Court crouched and started looking at the prizes with new eyes.

"She's got a point," she said. "It doesn't pay to rest on our laurels, and some of this stuff could be useful."

After some discussion, Court traded most of her tickets for caps, more jacks, and a Duncan yo-yo.

Eli leaned over to mutter, "I've got a dart set in my garage that I've been hiding from Lisa."

"Well, shoot!" said Court. "Now we're getting somewhere."

Neha picked a small bottle of bubble soap, a whistle, and some marbles. While the counter kid was getting them, she dropped the rest of her tickets and gave Sleekit a dirty look until she put them in the drawer for the jacks she'd taken. Then Sleekit clambered up onto Neha's shoulder to take a gander at her haul. Neha backed behind the fake tree, glancing around.

"I thought I could squirt the soap in a monster's eyes if it got too close," she explained, showing Sleekit her purchases. "The whistle is in case we get separated, and the marbles are for tripping someone."

"You see!" Sleekit said. "You were anti-jacks, but you chose good defenses anyway!"

A few kids were looking their way, trying to figure out if there were more Sleekits available in the store.

Sleekit was oblivious.

"Pretend you're a stuffed animal!" scolded Neha, and Sleekit went limp with a wink.

They went back to the tables to get more pizza. The adults scarcely noticed they were there. Neha's parents and Eli's mom were swapping stories about professors they knew at the university, while Eli's mom played tic-tac-toe with Lisa on the back of a place mat. Sleekit snuck into the booth beside Lisa and started coaching her on her next move. Lisa slipped Sleekit pepperoni when her mom wasn't looking. Across the room, the Rustlehorse was chowing down on the salad bar.

The Calamity Band was playing again, and the Spider Plant had turned to hover over the dancing, singing panda with the claws at the ends of its leafy legs extended.

Neha shook her head as she refilled her cup with watery soda from a pitcher on the table.

"The Creeps are starting to seem normal to me," she said as she sat back down beside Eli. "Should I be worried about that?"

"Heck yeah, we should be worried," said Court. "The Creeps are grand, but there are still a bunch of monsters out there that want to shred us. We can't afford to relax just yet."

"Speaking of which, let's check the door," said Neha. She opened the sketchbook on her lap, hiding it under the table. They put their foreheads down on the edge so they could see under the table, a time-honored strategy known to everyone who had ever played Seven Up—if you were serious about winning, you had to learn a lot about people's shoes.

But shoes were nowhere on their list of interests today, and what they saw would have held their attention even if Pac-Man had shown up and started eating their pizza.

From the minute the Creeps had slammed Neha's door behind them, the monsters had been swarming around it, trying to destroy it.

Now, it appeared they'd finally found a way.

"What on earth happened to it?" asked Court.

The door frame was charred, and the door itself was a smoldering ruin.

"I don't understand," said Court. "There should be ashes everywhere if they made a woodpile, so how did they do it?"

"They tried to burn it before, and it didn't work," said Neha. "I watched."

Suddenly, Eli groaned in horror.

"My story," he said. "The Howler was killed in a burning barn."

"*The* barn?" asked Neha. "The one the Creeps came out of?"

"Not on purpose," he said, "but it was on my mind. I can't believe I did that."

He thumped his head on the table.

"You're not alone," said Court. She turned to Neha. "That door you drew . . . would you say it's about the size and shape of the door on the barn in the cow pasture?"

Neha sat up to stare at Court, and her jaw dropped.

"I didn't mean to!" she said. "It was right in front of us, and I guess I just . . ."

Neha looked around at the Creeps crowding Showplace, who'd been nervous all afternoon for reasons they couldn't explain. How long ago had the monsters come prowling out of the barn?

She looked toward the front doors. Outside, the sun had set.

It was the perfect time to hunt, and Showplace Pizza was one big watering hole.

The glass doors swung open.

23

Party Over

Eli would go to his grave and never tell a soul how amazing it was to watch a herd of monsters he'd created come busting into Showplace Pizza—but he couldn't help basking in the feeling. In that moment he'd have sworn George Lucas couldn't do any better than him, and he wished his daddy could see.

Then he remembered that these monsters were real.

They came loping and sliming and shambling through the doors in a sea of wickedness. He reached over and shoved Lisa off the booth seat and under the table.

"Hey!" she said, then hushed real quick when she saw why he'd done it.

Their parents didn't even seem to notice.

"Eli, stop roughhousing with your sister," said their momma mildly. Then she turned and kept talking to the Prasads.

"Stay down," Eli hissed to Lisa.

Neha cringed low in her seat as she stared at the oncoming horde, some of who had slowed to sniff the air.

Leading the pack was the Howler.

Unlike just about every horror movie ever, Eli's story had left zero doubt that the Howler was thoroughly, permanently dead. A smear in the dirt. A smoking heap of ash. Somehow none of that was enough. Its fur was singed—in fact, it was still smoking. But it was still alive, and it was angry.

Eli worked hard to make his monsters as scary as he could. While writing the Howler he'd made a discovery: the trick wasn't describing the monster to death. Instead, it was a matter of choosing which details would have the most effect at any given moment. The flash of the overhead lights on its crumpled horns as it turned its head. The gleam of saliva dripping between its ivory teeth as it smiled at the scene before it. And the scariest part of all, the realization that the Howler saw exactly what Eli saw: a restaurant. Only this one served Creeps instead of pizza, and maybe a side dish of kids.

Court already had a butter knife in one hand, and when Eli saw that, he almost laughed in spite of the danger. He had questions: Where did she get it? Who ate pizza with a knife? But mostly he was just glad she was on his side.

"You okay?" he asked Neha, touching her shoulder.

She was shaky, but she nodded.

The gibbering creatures were milling around the restaurant, and while the adults might not see them, the kids were all eyes. Some were laughing, like they thought the monsters were Showplace's newest attraction. Others were edging away or grabbing their parents, who reacted with impatience or amusement.

All around the arcade area of the restaurant, monsters gnashed or whirled their teeth, flexed their digits or tentacles, and looked around with a surprising number and variety of eyes.

There was a brief pause.

An antlered creature that walked on two legs caught sight of the Rustlehorse, who had been chowing down on cherry tomatoes but was now stamping one hoof, neck arched, grassy mane rasping, alert to the oncoming danger. The antlered creature snarled, and in the process revealed a really uncomfortable number of long, sharp teeth. Eli had named it the Interloper, and it could fit a lot of prey in that big belly. It headed for the Rustlehorse, stooping to avoid the salad bar lights, already reaching out.

Some of the kids finally started screaming.

Across the room, Eli heard a table flip over with a crash. The parents who were closest hollered at their offspring for being rough with the furniture, but the kids were too busy dragging their parents toward the door to argue.

"We can't just leave, we have to pay the check," said someone's dad. "What the heck's gotten into you?"

All across the restaurant, adults were jumping out of their seats to deal with kids who were reacting to things the adults couldn't see.

"What is going on?" asked Mr. Prasad, noticing the chaos. "Is there a tornado warning?"

"Lisa!" said Eli's momma suddenly. "Where's Lisa?"

Eli side-eyed his sister, who was too far under the table for their momma to see. He shook his head slightly. For a wonder, she stayed quiet. He was just now grasping how vulnerable the adults were. He had to get them out of the way.

"I bet she went to the bathroom," he said, pointing away from the monsters toward the back hallway.

"In all this chaos? We'd better help you look," said Mrs. Prasad. "You kids stay together," she added. "We'll be right back."

The three adults headed off in search of Lisa, away from the rising chaos.

A furry hand landed on Eli's shoulder, and he spun around. It was Hairstack.

"Hey, Eli. I was thinking we should maybe leave," said Hairstack.

So far, Hairstack had been a friendly, somewhat smelly roommate. But he was big.

"Are you brave?" asked Eli.

Hairstack shoved his hair away from his eyes with one big hand.

"I don't know," he admitted.

"Let's find out," said Eli. "See my momma and Neha's parents?" He pointed.

Still holding back his hair, Hairstack looked, then nodded.

"They can't see the monsters. They need protection."

Hairstack looked shocked to be asked.

"What am I supposed to do?"

As the fund-raiser disintegrated into pandemonium, Eli put his hands on Hairstack's shoulders and shook him slightly for emphasis.

"You're big. You're strong. Bash anything that gets too close."

The Creep nodded.

"It's not impossible . . . used to bullseye womp rats," muttered Hairstack under his breath as he followed Eli's and Neha's parents.

Court dragged a table out of its booth indent and tipped it over onto its side. It hit the floor with a crash that made her wince, reminding Eli that everything at Showplace belonged to her family.

"Get behind it!" she ordered them over the braying, squelching, and growling.

Eli grabbed Lisa and did what Court said. He was good at

imagining things, but Court, he knew, was good at reacting to them. They crouched behind the table and took stock.

That was when Eli spotted the guy who was supposed to have prevented this whole mess.

"Dolt!" he yelled.

Neha smacked the back of his head.

"Be quiet!" she hissed.

"Ow!" he said, but he waved his arms anyway.

"Do you want to die?" she demanded. "Stop drawing attention to yourself!"

The person Eli was flagging down headed their way. He was almost bigger than Eli had imagined: huge. A mountain in human form. He was also glistening with sweat. His shirt strained, barely containing his muscles.

Court whistled, amused or impressed, Eli couldn't tell.

"Who's this fella?" she asked.

"My name is Dolt," said the man. "I'm here to save you."

"You came through the door, too?" Neha said.

"I followed the monsters through the burning barn," he agreed. "To save you."

She turned to Eli.

"You burned down the barn for this?"

"I thought I was only burning it down in my story. I didn't know it would burn down the real barn. I'm working out the kinks."

"What were you thinking?" asked Neha as Dolt flexed.

Eli frowned. "I was thinking we needed a strongman. So I wrote one."

Court was smiling. A lot. Too much.

"How strong are you?" she asked Dolt.

Dolt threw a sudden jab at the boxing game to his right. He hit the punching bag so hard it smashed into the roof of the game and stuck there. Sparks drifted down from the point of impact. Court remembered who owned the game and winced.

"That's . . . something," said Neha cautiously.

"Thanks," said Dolt, cracking his knuckles unnecessarily.

Eli smiled at him in what he hoped was a friendly way.

"I was wondering," he said. "Did you maybe notice all the monsters running around?"

The chaos seemed to register with Dolt for the first time. He nodded decisively.

"Let me handle this," he said, then turned and ran into the thick of the monsters with no plan whatsoever.

Neha and Court looked at Eli.

"He's strong," Eli said. "I didn't necessarily make him smart."

Across the room, a galloping creature that looked like a yak crossed with a wolf was chasing some kids from their class. It was grinning, but based on what Eli had written, it wasn't planning to eat anyone, he thought. Just enjoying itself. Another creature, this one sluglike and similar to Blatt, was opening and closing a razor-sharp, irising portal that served as its mouth. It was slowly crunching its way through the corner of *Ms. Pac-Man*. As it reached the internal machinery, another portal on its back end opened and deposited a smoking mass of chewed-up circuit boards on the tile floor.

"Eli," said his momma, returning with Hairstack looming behind her, "I still can't find Lisa!"

Eli instinctively glanced at the spot where he'd left his sister, behind the overturned table. It was empty. His eye was drawn to a disturbance in the ball pit.

Oh no.

Something was swimming through the pit. It was fast, and it

had way more than the normal number of tentacles, all of which were searching through the balls. Clinging to the netting, with a single tentacle wrapped around her shoe, was Lisa. She must have gotten away from Eli while he was talking to Dolt. She didn't have anything to hit the tentacle with. She couldn't even use her hands, both of which were occupied hanging on to the net for dear life.

"Lisa!" called their momma, spotting her. "There you are! Come down from there. It's time to go."

"I can't!" yelled Lisa. "There's a monster in the ball pit!"

Mrs. Goodman gave Eli a look.

"Cute," she said. "This is what happens when you fill her head with nonsense. You go over there and get your sister."

Something small and toothy flew directly at Mrs. Goodman's head. Hairstack punched it out of the air and grinned at Eli.

"Yes, ma'am," said Eli. What else could he do? He ran over, looking frantically for something he could use to help.

"Here!" said Court, who'd come with him. She thrust something into his hand.

It was a metal fork. A cheap, fast-food-restaurant fork, but it would have to do. He looked past her to see she'd given Neha one, too. Court grabbed a pizza off the table and dumped it on the floor, keeping the tray. Staying low, Court led them around the edge of the restaurant, hiding behind arcade machines to take stock.

Lisa managed to reach through the netting and grab a butter knife off the table on the other side, then poked the nearest tentacle like it was dinner. It recoiled, and any sensible person would have used that time to skedaddle. Instead, Lisa turned around in the netting, braced her feet, and jumped down into the center of the ball pit, landing on the tentacle and riding it like it was a bucking bronco.

Just then, another tentacle exploded upward, shedding rainbow-colored balls as it rose. It was coiled around Dolt, who was roaring as if he had the upper hand.

"Stand still and fight me!" he hollered, trying to punch the tentacle. Naturally that didn't work. Thwarted by his own bad idea, he raised one fist in the air and yelled, "TENTACLLLLLLLLE!" even though the darn thing was right there in front of him. Unsurprisingly, three more tentacles rose out of the ball pit to take turns punching him. Eli couldn't help sympathizing with the tentacles a little bit when it came to Dolt, but his sister, tiny compared to the giant tentacles, was another matter.

He circled the ball pit trying to figure out what to stab with his fork.

"Lisa!" he hollered. "Get out of there!"

Her answer was muffled. He panicked, thinking the tentacle was covering her mouth. Then he realized what was actually happening.

She was biting it.

He couldn't help being kind of proud.

The tentacle writhed, trying to get away from her. The other tentacles, the Dolt-punching ones, turned to smack at Lisa in a *get it off, get it off!* kind of way. Eli knew they all belonged to the same big organism, but it couldn't seem to organize itself to actually solve its problem. Still, he didn't think its confusion would last forever.

"Can y'all see Amy?" asked Court. "Or Joshie?"

Eli scanned the room. "Over there!" he pointed. Joshie was up on top of the Skee-Ball ramps. There was a herd of nasty-looking beetle creatures as big as pigs trying to climb up to him. Eli had written those when he was thinking about dangerous things coming at you through a garbage dump. Their legs were short, so climbing wasn't their strong suit, but their mandibles were sharp, and one of them had already hit on the idea of using them to grip the edge and pull itself up.

Joshie was only a year older than Lisa, and as far as Eli knew monster hunting wasn't one of his career goals. He was shouting with fear. But he was also a pitcher, so he was going after the only weapon within reach . . . Skee-Balls. He was fishing them out of the gutter, filling his shirt with them.

"Look out!" Eli shouted.

Joshie jumped backward just in time, keeping his sneakers out of range of the snipping, snapping mandibles. Then he cranked his arm. The ball smacked into the jaws of the closest beetle, tearing through chitin with a terrible cracking noise. It gave a high shriek of pain and dropped from the edge of the ramp, landing on its back on the floor and rocking idly back and forth, as dead as a block of wood.

Court saw an opening and lunged forward to help, but as soon as she moved she caught the attention of the yak beast, which had been stampeding past. It wheeled to face her with a snort. Court grabbed one of the poles that held up the velvet ropes around the prize store and brandished it. She and the creature locked eyes.

Court would do better handling the yak beast than Eli ever would, so he turned his attention back to Lisa, only to find that Dolt might actually be her biggest threat. While the tentacle monster was distracted by Lisa's pearly whites, Dolt had clawed his way out of the ball pit and pulled a gun out of his coat pocket. Eli'd forgotten about the guns. Dolt fired it into the ball pit until it was out of bullets.

"Stop shooting!" Eli cried in a panic, but Dolt threw the gun away and pulled another one out of nowhere. He emptied that into the pit, too, until it started clicking the way they did in the movies.

"You know that's a made-up noise, right?" asked Court, whacking the yak beast between the eyes with the pole.

Darn it, thought Eli in a tiny, writerly corner of his brain.

The sea of balls was undulating, and Lisa was clinging to her tentacle like a ferocious leech. There was no evidence that Dolt had hit the tentacle monster with a single shot.

The Rustlehorse galloped past, neighing in panic. Behind her came the Interloper, drooling as it ran. Just in time, Neha kicked a chair out in front of the monster. It tripped and crashed to the floor.

Unfortunately, this got all its attention focused on Neha and Eli. With a snarl, it staggered to its feet and headed their way.

24

We Should Go

Court clubbed the yak monster one more time, and it staggered away. She checked on her friends.

That nasty-looking stag monster was headed for Neha and Eli. There was no place for either of them to go—they were trapped between the monster and the ball pit.

"Joshie," shouted Court, leaping up onto the Skee-Ball ramps beside her brother. "Aim over there!"

She bent to scoop up Skee-Balls from one of the other lanes.

Joshie wound up and pitched. His ball whizzed through the air and shattered one of the Interloper's antlers. It gave an angry bray and spun to see who was attacking it.

Court's throw smacked it in the gut, and it doubled over with a loud wheeze. Then the Spider Plant plucked the Interloper up off the floor and threw it. It crash landed on one end of the table where their pizzas had been laid out, catapulting the remains of the fund-raising dinner into the air. Dishes clattered to the floor all over the restaurant.

Some of the monsters snarled in response, and the ones that could grip things started chucking anything they could grab at the Spider Plant. Alarmed, it backed up onto the Skee-Ball ramps, which put Court and Joshie right underneath it. Only Court's pizza-tray shields kept them from getting brained by the hail of missiles.

"Joshie!" cried a familiar adult voice, and Court glanced to one side to find her parents standing slack jawed in the doorway to the kitchen. A plastic cup banged her fingers where they were holding the tray.

"Ow!" she hollered. "Doggone it!"

"Get down from there!" their daddy said. Distracted, Joshie opened his mouth to explain, but a spoon hit him upside the head.

"What on earth?" cried their mama. She looked around at the upended tables and chairs, the contents of the salad bar all over the floor, the dishware flying through the air as if by magic. "What is going on?"

"Everybody out!" their daddy roared. "Now!"

There was a general rush for the parking lot.

"Our daughter's still in there!" Court heard Mr. Prasad protest as he was swept along with the panicking diners headed for the doors. Eli's mother was trying to get to them, too, but she couldn't force her way through the crowd. The yak beast had shaken off its concussion and was headed right for her. Fists pinwheeling, Hairstack bashed it until it stumbled, then hustled Mrs. Goodman outside with the rest of the crowd.

Court turned back to the ball pit, where Eli was crouched on the edge.

"I have to jump!" he shouted.

Court agreed. The tentacles could submerge anytime, and

they wouldn't be able to see Lisa anymore, or know if she was safe.

"Where's its head?" she yelled.

"Heck if I know!"

A roar split the air, louder than anything they'd heard so far. Court spun around and spotted the Howler on the other side of the room. It was rearing up, howling so loudly the room reverberated with it. Then it turned and pounded the nearest arcade game with one mighty paw. The screen exploded, and the circuits inside showered orange-yellow sparks across the room, singeing the Howler's fur.

Eli finally saw his chance and leaped into the ball pit. To his credit, he did land on a tentacle, but he wasn't the bull rider his kid sister was. The tentacle flung him off, and he flew up into the air and ended up dangling from the netting overhead.

"My foot is stuck," Eli shouted. He was trying to curl up so he could get a grip on it, but Court knew from PE class that he wasn't a pull-up kind of kid. "Dolt!" Eli ordered, "get my sister!"

It was a calculated risk. Court wasn't sure Dolt understood anything about children, like how to keep them alive, for example. On the other hand, Dolt wasn't dangling from the netting.

"ELI! I WILL AVENGE YOU!" Dolt roared.

"I'm not dead yet!" hollered Eli. "Help Lisa! She's just a little kid!"

Lisa was busy jamming plastic balls into the tentacle's suction cups as hard as she could, but even from a distance Court could see her roll her eyes.

Between the bullets, the biting, and the colorful plastic balls, the tentacle monster'd had enough. The entire writhing mass of tentacles started hustling Court's way, fast.

"Look out!" Eli yelled, falling into the ball pit behind the waving tentacles.

When the monster emerged from the ball pit, Court couldn't believe what she was seeing, though in hindsight she should have guessed.

The enormous array of deadly tentacles was coming from a round, spiraling shell that was about the size of those spinning See 'n Say toys, the ones with the pull cords, that made animal noises.

"What?" she said in disbelief, and suddenly she stopped worrying about keeping everyone safe and got downright mad.

She looked around at her parents' restaurant. Everywhere she turned, tables were upended. The *Ms. Pac-Man* game was spitting sparks. The Interloper was smashing in the front of the claw machine trying to get to Sleekit, who was using pieces of broken glass to fend it off.

All the duct tape on earth wasn't going to pull off "That Was Close" this time. She was so angry she didn't even know what to do with herself.

She'd had it with these monsters. She was done putting up with their bull.

"Somebody has to save our skins," she said.

Eli looked at her in confusion.

"Is that a quote?" he asked. "It sounds like a quote."

"Princess Leia," she said, and smiled an angry and dangerous smile.

Court slid her hand out of her pocket, her Duncan yo-yo from the prize store cupped in her fingers. The curved weight of it felt good in her palm. She moved closer to the tentacled thing, which was sliding across the soda-coated floor on its flat, slimy foot. Its head, which had big, owlish eyes, protruded from the opening of the shell. She rotated her wrist to loosen it up, then she spun the yo-yo out on its string. The floating, whirring blue orb was beautiful as it sailed across the room.

It whacked the monster right in one of its staring yellow eyes.

The squid thing shrieked and recoiled, and suddenly all the tentacles curled inward, dumping Dolt and Lisa onto the floor. Plastic balls popped out of its suction cups as Lisa's tentacle contracted, whacking monsters all across the room. By the time the spinning blue Duncan yo-yo had walked its way back up the string into Court's hand, all that was visible was a round, spiraling shell toppling onto its side on the floor.

The room was silent except for the music of the surviving games and the rhythm of the popcorn maker, which was starting a new batch.

All the monsters were looking their way.

Eli was hanging on to Lisa's shoulder as if she'd vanish if he didn't. Lisa was staring at the Howler, realizing this was the monster she'd been preparing for. Her sworn enemy. Lisa was mighty, but she was also tiny, so she wasn't so much sizing it up as sizing it up . . . and up . . . and up. Joshie's shoes crunched at her side, and, out of the corner of her eye, Court could see him brandishing a Skee-Ball.

"We should go," Court muttered.

"Uh-huh," said Joshie.

But there was no way this room full of nightmares was going to let them get to the door.

Fortunately, Court had one card left to play.

"Hey, Joshie?" she said. "Hit it."

It was an inside joke, and Joshie got it instantly. He wound up and pitched his last Skee-Ball at the one thing in Showplace Pizza they'd been forbidden to touch ever again, for the sake of their parents' sanity. The ball smacked a button on the wall.

At once, the rubbery recorded music of the Calamity Band cycled up to full speed. The robotic critters lifted their awkwardly tilted heads and their flexing hands. Their mouths started to move.

The song they were singing was called "Pete's a Pizza Eater," which by all rights ought to be a silly, Italian sort of song. Instead it sounded like someone had taken rock-and-roll and country music and shaken them up in a thermos. Every time she heard it she wanted to cover her ears, and the Howler clearly felt the same way. It reared back and snorted, loudly this time.

The Howler snarled, then advanced on the creepy, animatronic Calamity Band. It poked the grinning flapper panda with one long, deadly claw, and Court saw a tiny curl of smoke as it snorted again. The panda twirled her beads, and they hit the Howler in the nose. It roared and circled the band, looking for an opportunity to attack that wouldn't end with a saxophone up its nose.

There was a sudden, furtive movement across the room, and then Scott Gabler, of all people, shot out from under a pinball game and made a run for the door. He was braver than she'd thought, weaving between actual monster legs to reach his destination. But there was another monster pursuing him, a pink bloblike thing, and Court didn't see how he was going to outrun it, because it didn't have to run at all; it was just sliming. Monsters started grabbing for him with teeth and claws as he went by, each hoping to beat the blob monster to the punch.

It was the distraction they needed.

"Let's go!" she said. "Now!"

The second she opened her mouth, the Howler's head whipped around. A mechanical arm, beads still dangling from its clenched fingers, was sticking out of its mouth. She could hear the crunching as it slowly chewed. With one bound it was half-way to them. It crouched on the floor, spread its front claws in a come-hither arc, and grinned. The severed robot arm fell to the tile floor with a sad, whirring clank.

There was no escape.

Then a human silhouette dropped from the top of the play structure and landed between them and the Howler.

It was a woman, gray haired and weather-beaten, wearing a T-shirt, brown pants, and seriously well-traveled boots. In her hands, she cradled a stout wooden staff.

Court gasped. Lisa was bouncing on the soles of her sneakers.

"You wrote her?" Lisa asked Eli in a whisper.

"What can I say?" Eli answered. "Your list was cool."

"What was cool?" Neha asked.

"*Our* hero," said Lisa in a fierce whisper.

The woman rose. The three of them were behind her, but Court was dead sure their hero was looking the Howler right in the eye.

The Howler laughed, low and eager.

The woman shrugged.

"If you think this is funny, you're not real bright," she said.

Before anyone could move, she whacked the Howler right upside his evil, grinning face with her staff. The howl of rage he unleashed was so loud Court almost put her hands over her ears. An instant later, the woman and the Howler were locked in combat. He was bigger, but she was tough and fast. She vaulted right up and over tables before he could catch her, then hit him again, whack-whack-whack.

Not all the monsters were watching. Some were examining Court and her friends, and the Creeps who hadn't escaped the building were still in danger, too. Sleekit was in the corner, crouched over something. It was furry and toothy and small, and her pointed teeth were red. Others were hiding, but Court knew where to look.

Then Dolt cartwheeled into view, stopping in front of them. They stared. He was covered with smears of something black, like the greasepaint football players put under their eyes. His shirt was gone. Or most of it was. Some of it was tied around his head. He immediately whipped out two guns, too large to have come from any of his pockets.

"This is no way to spend Christmas," he said.

"It's September," Court pointed out.

"I know," he said. He did something to make both guns emit loud clacking noises, even though Court didn't think they were shotguns.

A handful of monsters charged.

Dolt opened fire.

"Creeps!" Court hollered. "Run for it!"

They stampeded.

A few monsters still moved to attack them. Neha scooped up a fallen pizza pan and used it to smack anything that got too close. She still had her fork, too, and when a star-nosed warthog beast ran by chasing a Treebot, she poked it right in the snout. Sleekit's bared teeth were enough of a warning to keep everything else away.

Which was how they finally stumbled out the front door into the brightly lit parking lot, Creeps fleeing past them on every side, blinking in the flashing strobes of an uncomfortable number of emergency vehicles—and ran right into Court's parents.

"There you are!" said Mr. Castle, who was sweaty and wild eyed.

"Oh, thank goodness," said Mrs. Castle, hugging the stuffing out of Court and Joshie. By the time she let them go, Mrs. Goodman had snatched Lisa up off the ground and was squeezing her, and the Prasads were checking Neha over from head to toe. Haystack gave Eli a big thumbs-up.

"I'm braver than I thought," he said, and Eli shook his head, grinning, and high-fived the Creep when no one was looking.

"Are you all right?" demanded Neha's father, cupping her cheek.

"Yes, Daddy," said Neha. "I'm fine."

"I was safe," insisted Lisa. "Eli was with me the whole time!"

Sleekit whisked past them and took refuge under a nearby fire truck.

"You two should have come straight out here like I told you to!" said Mr. Castle. "What if you'd gotten hurt?"

"It's probably better they didn't," said Mrs. Castle. "If we'd realized what was happening, we'd have stayed in the restaurant with them."

"What was happening?" repeated Court, confused.

"The police think it was the storm," said Mrs. Castle. "Not a tornado, but real bad straight-line winds blowing right through the front door. We're lucky more people weren't hurt."

Court looked around and saw customers being treated for cuts and bumps by medics. Almost all the injured were kids. She spotted Scott, too. He didn't look hurt, only . . . wet. And faintly pink, like he'd been doused in Kool-Aid. His parents were reading him the riot act.

"But I saw it!" he protested. His mother threw up her hands.

"I'm not listenin' to this nonsense anymore. Pipe down and let's go get in the car," said his father. He turned to look at Showplace Pizza and shook his head in disgust.

"What a mess," he said. "This place'll be out of business in a month."

He put a big hand on Scott's shoulder and steered him across the parking lot. Scott glanced around nervously as he went. Court didn't blame him.

The emergency vehicles' lights flashed. The rumble of their engines made it impossible to tell if the battle inside was over. Then the front door opened, and out stepped Court and Lisa's hero.

Court ran toward the gray-haired woman.

"Don't think we've met," said the woman. "Name's Miranda."

They shook hands.

"Are the monsters . . . dead?" asked Court as Neha and Eli joined her.

"Some. Not the big one with the horns. Sent it packing for now, though. They went out the back."

"Where's Dolt?" asked Eli.

She shook her head with amusement. "He ain't the sharpest tool in the shed, is he?"

As one, they shook their heads.

"He declared victory and left. Said something about needing to patch things up with his dog."

Inside the restaurant, something collapsed with a loud crash. Court's daddy rubbed his face with both hands for a second. Her mama patted his back, looking anxiously at Showplace Pizza.

"Court!" called someone. She jumped. It was Amy, who was waving her over.

"Daddy told Ian to take us home," she said. "Come on."

"But we can't just leave Mama and Daddy," said Court, glancing back at her parents.

"Court, come *on*," said Amy, who was manhandling a protesting Joshie into Ian's truck.

Court had time for one last look at the mess the monsters had made.

As she headed for the car, she knew one thing.

She was going to get even.

25

Unstoppable

Eli was about one straw away from his very last one. Once Lisa knew his monsters were roaming the area, it was almost impossible to contain her. As far as she was concerned, it was time to fulfill her destiny and show the monsters who was boss.

Eli knew she'd sneak out the first chance she got, so he rigged an alarm system while his momma was tucking Lisa into bed. He balanced noisy things on the top sills of the windows, inside the curtains where no one would see. He tied last year's jingle bells to the door handles as tightly as he could.

Then he waited until his momma went to bed and Hairstack was talking in his sleep about scruffy-looking nerf herders, and snuck in to sleep on Lisa's floor.

He foiled her first attempt to break out—she stepped on him by accident and woke him up.

"Either you go sleep in your closet, or I yell and wake up Momma," he said, pointing.

She went, dragging her *Super Friends* bedspread behind her.

"There's too many Snorkelchorts in here," she complained, scooting clusters out of her way and causing a chorus of squeaking.

"Don't care," said Eli, and did his best to block the doorway while he dozed.

The next afternoon was worse. He was trying to search his room one last time for the folder with the typewritten original of the Howler's story in it, but the second they'd gotten off the bus, Lisa had started plotting her escape. Eli and Hairstack kept her distracted by helping her do an inventory of all her weapons and traps. Then by testing them. Then Eli unleashed one (a sort of lobster cage made out of Hula-Hoops and twine) while she wasn't looking. He knew it wasn't nice to trap his own sister, but he kept her in there as long as he dared.

For a little while, Eli convinced Lisa that Hairstack's tawny mop might have excellent rope-fiber properties, and tricked her into braiding it. The big Creep was okay with it as long as he and Eli could talk Star Wars. But when Lisa started hiding mousetraps in his pelt and one of them went off, Hairstack let out a half roar that was almost fierce, grabbing for his backside.

"I'm taking a break, man," he said, retreating to Eli's room.

"Traitor," Eli muttered.

He made Lisa a fluffernutter sandwich. He threatened. He bribed. But he was only human.

Eventually, he had to use the bathroom.

"This is gross!" she complained when he made her sit outside the door. She banged on it with her fist. He could hear her playing with some beeping toy, too. He kept a tight grip on his end of a jump rope, which he'd tied around her waist and run under the door.

"I can't go with you making all that racket!" he shouted back. "Hush up!"

She did, but that didn't stop her from thumping the door in a slow, steady rhythm, just to show him how bored she was.

"See?" he said finally as he flushed the toilet and washed his hands. "Doesn't take that long when you leave me alone."

The bumping on the door kept going. Thump. Thump. Thump.

"Lisa, cut it out!" he said, yanking open the door.

He dropped his end of the jump rope.

His Big Trak robotic tank was backing away from him across the empty hallway. As he watched, it rolled up to the doorway, then backed up and rolled toward it again.

Lisa had programmed his tank to thump the bathroom door for her. Not only had she escaped, she had at least a five-minute lead.

His sister was an evil genius.

▲ ▼ ▲

Eli biked to Neha's, hoping against hope that Lisa wanted to see Sleekit more than she wanted to hunt monsters.

"We haven't seen her," said Neha. She and Sleekit looked equally worried, and Eli realized he was becoming a little bit fond of the otter-weasel.

"I'll get my bike and help you look," said Neha. Sleekit zoomed up her leg and into her arms. She sat up alertly, ready to go along.

Redwing came to join them at the door, the red, yellow, and black of her wings plexing.

"You should stay here in case Lisa does come," she said. "I can get a bird's-eye view."

"No way!" said Neha. "I'm going. I know the neighborhood better than you do."

Redwing frowned. "I kept watch over Forest Creeks, and I'll keep watch here, too. But the monsters must be looking for you, and I can't keep track of everyone if you're all spread out. Somebody has to stay in."

Neha was opening her mouth to argue again when Redwing said, "Please, Neha? You gave me a home. I don't want anything bad to happen to you. Let me go this time."

Eli could see from the way Neha's shoulders slowly eased downward that the argument was over.

"Be careful?" said Neha.

"I promise," said Redwing.

She squeezed Neha's arm and gave Eli a nod, then took off with a rush of feathers, the shoelaces of her high-tops fluttering in the wind of her passing.

Eli was glad to have the help but also impatient to leave.

"Call if you see her?" he asked.

Neha agreed.

He stood on one pedal of his bike and coasted down the driveway, then swung his right leg over the seat and took off.

He didn't think Lisa could have made it all the way to the cow pasture yet, so he headed to the one other place he thought she might go. He was rolling up Court's driveway in record time. He didn't even bother to say hi when she opened the door.

"Is Lisa here?"

"She's out back. I tried to call you, but nobody answered."

Court led Eli through the house and out the sliding-glass door. She pointed at the vacant lot. Swiz had set up a camp so he could cook up new countermeasures. Bay, the silver dog, waited nearby to snack on failed experiments.

Not far from Swiz, a drab green tent had sprouted overnight. Miranda the hero and Lisa were sitting in front of it, roasting hot dogs over a small campfire. The Spider Plant hunched over the scene, providing shade and carefully holding aloft a sack of supplies Miranda had tied to one of its legs. It was eyeing the hot dogs.

Eli slumped against the fence in relief.

"How'd she even know Miranda was here?" asked Court.

Eli gave her a hangdog look.

"Lisa hears everything. After you left last night, I asked Miranda to stay with the Creeps who were too big for our cars, and help them get here safe."

The Rustlehorse wandered out from behind the tent, crunching a mouthful of grass.

"Did you get in trouble?" Eli asked Court. "I thought you might be grounded for, you know, standing on the Skee-Ball ramps."

Court sat down on the grass with a sigh.

"Nope," she said. "To be honest, I'd feel better if they did ground me."

"Court," said Eli, "I'm really sorry about what happened at the restaurant."

She looked over at him with surprise.

"It's not your fault."

"I made the monsters. That makes it my fault."

She lay back and stared at the sky.

"The things you make don't always do what you expect, Eli. Heck, Joshie made a rocket last week and it ended up on the roof. A surprising amount of our stuff ends up on the roof, actually."

There was a sudden outbreak of squeaking from the direction of the house. The screen door opened and the Gargyle came slouching out. Someone slid the screen shut behind him, hard.

"What's he even doing here?" asked Eli.

"Lisa brought him. What's the matter, Gargyle?" asked Court.

The Gargyle hung his head.

"I got this," said Eli. "It happens at my house, too."

He raised his voice.

"You guys, let him back in!"

"No!" said a stubborn little voice. "He smells like feet!"

"He's made out of socks! He has to smell like feet," said Eli.

Court sighed and sat up.

"No point arguing with a Snorkelchort," she said.

She lifted the Gargyle up onto her lap.

The Gargyle gave her a grateful look with his button eyes. Court ruffled his floppy sock ears.

"Now your jeans are gonna smell like feet," teased Eli.

The Gargyle whimpered a little bit.

Court switched from petting the Gargyle's ears to covering them.

"You hush!" she said.

Eli leaned over to fiddle with his Adidas. After he'd stepped in the mud, he'd cleaned them with a toothbrush. He'd washed his laces, too. Squeezed all the water out of them and dried them as flat as he could so they'd look fatter. But they still didn't smell quite right.

Joshie banged the sliding screen door as he came out to join them. He sniffed the air.

"Yum!" he said. "Hot dogs!"

He headed for the campfire.

Miranda gave him the last one and stamped out the embers, then strode over to Eli and Court.

"So, you've got a monster problem," she said. She wasn't asking. It occurred to Eli that she might not accept the existence of questions. He was betting she didn't like having her time wasted, either, so he explained.

"And," he said, as he finished outlining their problem, "what we need is—"

Miranda raised a hand, cutting him off.

"Let me stop you right there," said Miranda in a no-nonsense tone. "What you need is to handle this yourselves."

26

Toying with Monsters

Sleekit," said Neha, "can you stop prowling? You're making me nervous."

Sleekit hissed softly under her breath, more at herself than at Neha. She jumped from the windowsill to a nearby chair, where she could still look out the window, and immediately began flicking her long, ringed tail back and forth, back and forth in the fading light.

They'd both been jumpy since the monsters attacked Showplace Pizza, but Eli's knock at the door had made it a thousand times worse. The only thing more horrible than monsters roaming the neighborhood was the idea of Lisa out there alone.

Neha jumped up and went to the kitchen phone again. She dialed Eli's number and let it ring for what felt like forever. She wished they hadn't told the Creeps not to answer the phones.

She held down the disconnect button, then dialed Court's house. It rang busy. Again.

Neha didn't have to report any of this to Sleekit, who had excellent hearing.

"Why isn't Redwing back yet?" asked Sleekit, her whiskers vibrating with irritation and worry.

Frog Boy, who'd been watching from a corner of the family room, came over to put a hand on her shoulder.

"Everything will be all right," he said gently. The tadpoles in the jar he was carrying nodded their agreement.

Neha wasn't so sure, and when she looked across the room at her ferretlike friend, she knew they were on the same page. The idea was the first thing that had made her smile all day.

"Come on. You can ride in my basket," she said.

"Where are you going, Neha?" her mother called from upstairs as Neha pushed the button that opened the garage door.

"To ride bikes," she said.

"Be home by dark, please."

"I will."

Neha and Sleekit biked to Eli's house, where Neha banged on the door. When Sleekit jumped down from Neha's basket and scratched on a window screen, the Crackler opened the window, and Neha and Sleekit had a whispered conversation with him, Hairstack, and Zoop.

"The kids lit out hours ago," the Crackler said. "We haven't seen 'em since."

Neha rubbed Sleekit's ears while she pondered. She didn't want to wait here. The street was quieter than it should have been on a Saturday, as if something was watching and everyone felt it.

"I want all of you to stay inside," Neha told them. "It's safest."

"Is it true what they're saying?" asked the Crackler, his hair shooting nervous sparks. He stamped them out before they singed the carpet he was standing on. "About the monsters?"

Neha nodded seriously. "It's true."

Zoop, who had been listening, went off with a high-pitched whine and a blinding flash. Neha blinked until her vision returned.

"I've got a bad feeling about this," said Hairstack seriously.

"Me, too," said Neha.

"I could punch something, if you want," he offered in an off-hand tone. "I know how to do that sort of thing."

"Not right now," said Neha. "Just be careful, all of you. And stay inside."

She pedaled off toward Court's, watching the road unspool between Sleekit's rounded ears as the daylight faded from the sky and clouds rolled in.

She was halfway between Eli's and Court's houses when the sky opened up. Then she heard screams on a side street.

She stopped and put one foot down so she could get a better look. Sleekit rippled over the edge of the basket and stood with her front paws on Neha's bike fender, craning her neck.

Kelly, the only kid in their grade with more freckles than Court, was out in her front yard, defending herself and her little brother with a Wiffle bat. The monster she was fending off was toying with her, lunging enough to scare her, then backing up even though the cheap plastic bat was no kind of threat. It was the shadow creature that had attacked Swiz in the notebook. Whatever had happened to its leg had obviously healed. It was even faster and more dangerous than Neha remembered, and her body went ice cold as she realized that soon it was going to get bored of playing and truly attack.

That wasn't the worst of it. Lurking around the edges of the surrounding houses were more monsters, some big, some small, waiting for their turn to join in the fun.

Kelly swung the bat again. Behind her, her little brother was crying. Neha could hear their big dog barking frantically inside their house.

"It's okay, Bert," Kelly said, but her voice was shaking. "Get away!" she screamed at the shadow creature as a clawed paw emerged from its clouded form and slyly hooked the edge of her T-shirt. She jammed the bat straight down, but it was only cheap plastic. The claw began to draw Kelly forward, her Keds sliding on the grass. Her eyes were wide with terror. In the gathering darkness, the surrounding ring of monsters drew closer.

"Leave them alone!" shouted Neha.

A dozen deadly heads turned her way.

"Did I say that out loud?" asked Neha.

"Yes," said Sleekit. She rippled back into the basket in a single motion. "Ride away very fast."

The monsters were all prowling her way, grinning and hooting and snarling. Behind them, Kelly and her little brother ran for their house and slammed the door. Neha stood on her top pedal and pushed off on the asphalt with her other foot.

It felt like it took forever for Neha's bike to start moving. Her heart was going to leap from her chest like a panicky maroon butterfly.

Something running on all fours swung out and around her on the left. She pedaled harder and started to outrun it, but it lunged, trying to knock her off her bike.

She swerved, and then the worst thing in the history of bad things happened.

Sleekit fell out of her basket.

Neha screamed as Sleekit rolled right between the feet of the pursuing monsters, stripes flashing in the glow of the nearest streetlight. A creature with a high-pitched hyena laugh turned to attack her, and Neha saw Sleekit launch at it without ever coming to a complete stop. Then she had to turn her head so she didn't fall off her bike or get dragged off by one of the other monsters.

She wasn't about to leave Sleekit.

Without thinking, she took a hard left into the nearest cul-de-sac. She knew she had to get back out there fast. In her panic she tried to stomp on the brake and turn around at the same time.

To her shock, she did a perfect skid, like the kids who rode BMX bikes, and ended up facing the entrance again. A few of the monsters ran past her in surprise, so now she had the enemy on both sides, but she didn't care. Sleekit was trying to fight the hyena thing off and run, but as Neha watched, she broke free, dashed toward Neha, and was dragged down again. Neha blasted out of the cul-de-sac, standing on her pedals.

"Sleekit!" she shouted, and plowed right into the hyena monster as hard as she could. It yelped, and her tires made a terrible double thump as she rode right over it. Feeling brave, she stomped her brakes again and leaned. She almost went over this time, but she still managed to turn tighter and faster than she ever had before. Sleekit was limping, but her jump was true. She landed in the basket with a thump. Neha barreled through the monsters.

Any of them could have stopped her with a swipe of their claws. One tried, and she felt the edge of her shirt get sliced to shreds. Another yanked out one of her ribbon barrettes, and some of her hair went with it, but she barely felt the sting. She headed toward the smallest monster that was blocking her way, a ball of ratty fur with yellow-green eyes and bared teeth, and looked it dead in the eye.

You saw what happened to the last one, she thought.

"Hold on!" she commanded Sleekit.

The smallest monster jumped out of the way with a yowl,

running into that big monster with the antlers, the Interloper. As they went by, she heard the snarls and yelps of the monsters taking out their anger on one another.

She whizzed around the corner, trying to think what to do next even as she stood on the pedals to go faster. She might be able to outrun them, but they didn't have to stay on the road the way she did. They could cut across yards. And as if being chased by monsters weren't enough, it started to rain.

What she wanted, more than anything, was to go home. But how could she, without bringing a storm of monsters down on her parents and the Creeps? The only protection her family had was that the monsters didn't know which house was hers.

That was when it hit her.

Neha had drawn Forest Creeks because she liked the idea of a place where every house was unique, like a thumbprint. Now, for the first time, she felt lucky her neighborhood wasn't that way. When her family had first moved in, they'd gotten lost a bunch of times. She knew right where the most confusing area was: a maze of interconnected side streets filled with almost identical houses.

She headed straight for it, aiming at a house that she knew would have a jumble of toys on the porch. Panting, she stashed her bike in the back, spotting another toy in the side yard that was going to make her job even easier.

"Come on," she said to Sleekit. "I know what to do."

She dashed around to the front porch, Sleekit at her heels. As Neha fumbled through the playthings on the porch, Sleekit put herself between Neha and the street.

Neha chose a caterpillar riding toy, big and green and bouncy. Then she discovered the luckiest find of all: a yarn-haired Rainbow Brite doll.

Neha squeezed the hidden button inside its left hand.

"What's your favorite color?" demanded the toy.

"Perfect!" said Neha.

"Hush!" said Sleekit. "They're almost here."

"Good," she said. She stuffed the doll through the handle of the riding caterpillar. But that wasn't good enough. For this to work, the doll had to keep talking. Neha reached for her remaining barrette, wincing as its ribbon streamers, which were tangled in her hair, yanked free.

She flexed the barrette, and it popped open.

"Get ready to run," she told Sleekit. Then she snapped the barrette shut on the doll's hand and rolled the apparatus down the sidewalk toward the street.

"Hi, I'm Rainbow Brite!" cheered the doll. "Color me happy to be with you!"

Neha was already running for the side yard. She hurled herself down on the Slip 'N Slide she'd discovered there, shooting across the yard on her belly far faster than she could have run.

Thank goodness it's raining, she thought.

Stumbling to her feet, she grabbed her bike and began wheeling it away.

"Can you name the colors of the rainbow?" said Rainbow Brite as the snarls of the pursuing monsters grew louder. "Red, orange, yellow, green, blue, indigo . . ."

The bike jounced across the lawn of the house that backed up to the one she'd just left. She was almost to the street on the other side when she heard the monsters attack the riding toy.

"Did you know rainbows are good luck?" the doll asked as plastic scraped against the pavement and the monsters began to tear the contraption apart. Neha threw herself astride her bike as Sleekit leaped up into the basket, and she raced for Court's house in the pouring rain.

27

It's Guys Like You

Um, what? No," Eli said to Miranda, like there'd been some kind of misunderstanding. "We need your help."

Fat raindrops began to spatter all around them, causing tiny puffs of dust to rise. Normally Court loved this phenomenon, but she was too distracted by her hero's defection to enjoy it.

"You'd *like* my help," said Miranda. "You don't *need* it." She headed back to her tent, which Joshie and Lisa had abandoned in favor of sword fighting with the hot dog roasting sticks.

Dismayed, Court followed Miranda, with Eli close behind.

"Shouldn't you wait 'til it stops raining?" asked Eli.

"I'm not sugar. I won't melt."

The gray-haired adventurer quickly broke down the tent, stowing all her loose belongings in her pack. Then she swung the bag up onto her shoulder.

"Where are you going?" Court asked. She could tell she sounded a little bit lost, and it annoyed her.

Miranda looked Court dead in the eye.

"I have a question for you," she said, pointing at the Castles' split-level. "If monsters attacked your house right now, what would you do?"

Court thought about this.

"Are they coming in through the front, the back, or the garage?" she asked.

"Exactly." Miranda clapped her on the shoulder with one strong, callused hand. "Kid, you may be young, but you and I are cut from the same cloth. Monsters, stories in a notebook . . . no offense, but this is child's play. And children are the most qualified people to handle it. I'm supposed to find expeditions that have been lost in uncharted territory, or foil airplane hijackings. So I'm going to go look for people who need me to do those things, and you are going to handle this little infestation so you can tell me about it over drinks someday."

"Kids can't drink," Court pointed out.

"Well, I'll have worked up quite a thirst by the time you can," said Miranda. "Better make it a good story."

Neha pulled up on her bike, panting, just as Miranda walked away.

"Where is she going?" she asked.

"Wait!" said Lisa, dropping her hot dog skewer. "You need a sidekick! I'll run home and get my stuff."

"Give it a few years," called Miranda over her shoulder.

Lisa chased after her, and Eli chased after Lisa.

When he caught up to them, Lisa was pressing an orange Duncan yo-yo into Miranda's hand.

"It could be useful," she said. Miranda pocketed it, nodded, then strode off into the Oklahoma evening. They watched until she was out of sight.

"Well, that didn't go how I expected," said Court.

"Hmm," said Eli, looking thoughtfully after Miranda. Then he turned to Neha. "You couldn't stay home, huh?"

"No. Neither could the monsters. I barely got away. We should go inside. Now."

They dripped their way through the laundry room, accompanied by assorted Creeps.

"What are we going to do?" asked Eli. "We can't bike home."

"Let me handle it," said Court. She approached the kitchen table. The D&D group was taking a break, which mostly consisted of eating pizza and pretending their soda straws were blow guns.

"Ames," said Court. Her sister had just been killed by a pretend blow dart, so she was lolling over the chair back, and her ear was easy to reach.

"Go away, Court, I'm dead," said Amy without opening her eyes.

"Okeydoke," said Court. "You guys, Amy says you can stay over. Eli, grab a pizza!"

"Whoa, hold on a second," said Amy, sitting up suddenly. "Nobody approved that."

"I know," said Court, "but the Goodmans and Neha need a ride home, and you're dead, so . . ."

"I'm getting better," said Amy. "But the Dungeon Master can't bail on the game, so I'm going to have to send somebody else on this particular quest."

Wig, Amy, and Ian immediately touched their pointer fingers to their noses. Shorty looked wildly around at them.

"No! We are not doing 'Nose Goes'!"

Amy shrugged.

"We don't have to. But I— Wait. Did you hear that?" She shaded her eyes with one hand and peered theatrically around the kitchen. Eli, Neha, and Lisa looked, too, afraid that a monster had gotten in somehow. Court just grinned.

Shorty was eyeing Amy suspiciously.

"I don't see anything," said Amy at last, "but I definitely hear something. I can't be sure, but it may be stalking you."

"We're a party, Amy! Whatever it is, it's stalking all of us."

Amy rested her chin on her fists.

"You're probably right. Still, if I was an Invisible Stalker, I'd go after the weakest link. And ever since your brush with super tetanus, you've been looking kind of pale, Shorty."

Now Court's friends were grinning, too.

"You're blackmailing me," said Shorty.

"I'm doing you a favor. It's harder for an Invisible Stalker to murder you if you're suddenly called away on an errand. In fact, if you take Eli, Lisa, and Neha home, I can pretty much guarantee you'll live."

Shorty stood up, bumping his head on the orange-and-gold stained glass lamp that hung over the table. Rubbing his head, he looked at the kids.

"There's just three of you?" he asked.

"And two bikes," said Neha.

He gave an aggrieved sigh.

"The things I do to survive," he said.

"Yeah," said Eli. "We know what you mean."

28

Crud

I can't remember the last time I saw such a surge of creativity in this classroom!" said Mrs. Benton.

It was usual for ARC kids to gather in small clusters to talk about common interests or work on their upcoming projects. But Court thought Mrs. Benton was missing the forest for the trees. Today kids weren't so much clustered as huddled, and there were definitely more empty seats than usual.

Kelly was over in the reading corner, frantically flipping through encyclopedias. Her best friend, Adriana, was sitting next to her, patting her on the back.

"Whatever it was, it's gone now, right?"

"But it could come back! It was a black shadow, and it had claws . . . I have to figure out what it was. Help me look!"

At one of the tables, a kid named Jeff had hijacked some game sets donated by a local inventor and was using their clear plastic tubes and rubber connectors to make an enormous crystalline structure.

"That's fascinating, Jeff," said Mrs. Benton. "What do you call it?"

"A prototype containment system," said Jeff grimly.

But the art area was the busiest. Kids were drawing monsters, kids were sculpting them with clay . . . and their friends were weighing in while they worked.

"The thing that attacked Jay and me was less like a gorilla and more like a really evil sloth," said a girl named Mindy. "His mom didn't believe us. She said it must have been a dog that bit him. But he got a lot of stitches, so she let him stay home."

Angela had been running a business out of her backpack all year, selling little puffball critters with googly eyes and big felt feet—Weepuls, they were called. Now she was laying them out in formation on the table.

"I was here," she told the kid next to her, "and there were five of them over here. Only they had teeth. Big ones."

The ARC class was having a monster-motivated Renaissance.

Court and Eli were hunkered down by a window, watching the school grounds for signs of movement while Neha recounted how she'd escaped by the skin of her teeth the night before.

"Y'all are getting really good at 'That Was Close,'" said Court approvingly.

"Thanks. But we need to talk after school. There are things we can't do here," said Neha.

"Yeah, I think even Mrs. Benton would draw the line at us building weapons in class," Court agreed.

"So, your house, then," said Eli. She rolled her eyes at him, but he was right.

Across the room, Mindy was standing on a chair and sketching out the shape of the evil sloth in the air with her hands.

". . . huge, seriously . . . ," she said.

"You'll need rides home," said Court. "Shorty probably won't drive y'all twice."

Neha had a solution.

"If I tell my parents we're working on that group project, they'll take me anywhere," she said.

Eli nodded. "Momma will, too."

A shadow loomed over them, and they flinched, but it wasn't a monster. It was Scott. They flinched again.

Scott rubbed his hands together.

"We're meeting at Court's house?" he said, trying on a smile. "Great! I was gonna say it was about time we got started."

They stared.

"Uh, on our group project?" he said, in response to their confusion. "That's what you were talking about, right? What time should I get dropped off?"

He smiled again, gradually widening his grin as he watched for a reaction, as if he were doing a science experiment. Court decided to put him out of his misery.

"Six is good," she said, and Eli and Neha deflated slightly on either side of her.

"Great!" Scott said through his unnatural grin. "See you then!"

He walked away.

Eli and Neha turned to look at Court.

"It'll be okay. Having Scott there helps our cover story, right?"

Silence.

Court sighed.

"I'll make donuts."

▲ ▼ ▲

By the time the other kids knocked on the door, Court had set a batch of cinnamon cake donuts to cool on the Castles' counter.

As usual, there was an epic D&D game in progress at the kitchen table.

"Joshie!" yelled Court. "Answer the door!"

She was scrubbing the dishes, because any Castle who didn't clean up after making donuts got grounded from donut making for a week. Court couldn't risk it. There was a constant tournament at the Castles' to see who could make the perfect donut, and the best way to lose was to be unable to play.

Nobody was willing to yield at the D&D table tonight, either.

"Shorty, how are you going to escape your attacker without rupturing the tunnel wall and letting boiling water in?" asked Amy.

"Fog Mode," said Shorty, slapping the table for emphasis.

"You're sure that's what you want to do?" asked Amy, holding the dice aloft warningly.

"Well, not when you say it like that," said Shorty in dismay.

"Hey, if the *guys're* okay with it," said Amy, looking around.

"Did you just make a geyser joke? Not cool," said Wig.

A snicker went around the table.

The doorbell began to ring, interrupting the Mikes' complaining.

"Joshie, get the door, or no donuts!" repeated Court.

He must have, because Scott and Eli came slouching into the kitchen, doing their best to ignore each other even though they were standing a foot apart.

"Hey, fellas," said Court. She tossed Eli a towel, figuring he'd been here enough times to stop being company. "Can you dry?"

Scott didn't offer to help—he didn't talk, either. He kept glancing over his shoulder at the kitchen door, as though it might crash open without warning. It took about five minutes of that for Court to start feeling twitchy as a cat.

A sudden uproar from the table made Scott jump about a foot in the air. Eli stifled a laugh.

"Don't worry, Scott," said Court. "They're only violent on paper."

She had jumped a bit, too, but only because Scott was keying her up.

"What are you going to do?" Amy asked Wig, whose curly hair bobbed as he leaned over to scoop up one of the dice.

"I am going to cast Sticks to Snakes," he said, and the reaction was immediate.

"Who are you, Wig, Saint Patrick?" asked Shorty. "That spell is ridiculous!"

"It's only ridiculous if it fails, Shorty," said Wig.

"What kind of names are Shorty and Wig?" Scott muttered to Court.

"They're actually both named Mike," she said. "That's just how we tell them apart. Come on."

She loaded some donuts onto a plate and grabbed a pizza box out of the fresh stack on the counter. "Hey!" said Amy, looking over. "Don't take all the olive!"

"Like anyone's going to eat it but you and me," scoffed Court. Then Neha arrived at the front door, and all four of them headed upstairs.

Joshie was in Court's room, playing with her Nerf hoop and ball.

"Go play in your own room," she said, before remembering why he wasn't.

"My room's too full," he complained.

Scott raised his eyebrows. "Full of what?"

Joshie started to open his mouth, but Court stepped up behind him and clamped her hand over it, quick. The last thing she needed was Joshie telling Scott his room was full of giant roadrunners and Snorkelchorts.

"Laundry," she said. "His room's a pit. Go get pizza, Joshie."

As soon as she let go of him, he took off running.

"Sleekit came in through Joshie's window," said Neha in her ear as they went to sit down. "She'll keep the other Creeps quiet."

Court hoped so.

Scott was still lurking by the door, even though Court had dragged multiple beanbags in from all over the house.

"Mr. Gabler, can you please join the rest of the class?" asked Court, exactly the way Mrs. Benton would say it. It was so perfect that even Scott grinned a little. He came and sat down, but no one said anything.

"So," said Court after an uncomfortable silence in which a loud thump and giggling Snorkelchorts could clearly be heard, "we're supposed to be looking for the place where all our interests overlap."

"She ought to let us work alone," said Eli. "Groups of four aren't all going to have the same passion."

"But they can work together toward a common goal," said Scott, fidgeting.

"Yeah, you say that, but things only work out with you if everyone's focused on your goal," said Eli.

A bit of Scott's usual cockiness returned, and he scoffed at Eli.

"You don't have enough evidence to make that determination," he said.

"One word. *Zork*," said Neha, and Court figured whatever truce there might have been between them was broken—but to Court's surprise, Scott tried to patch things up.

"You and me have things in common," he said. "The stuff I saw you drawing the other day, the pulleys and stuff? That was really cool."

"But you also make fun of me for the other stuff I like," said Neha. "You do it to Eli, too."

"Why are you defending him? You don't have to hang out with him. You could grow up to be an engineer. You'd be all right if you'd get your head out of the clouds."

Whoa, thought Court.

"I'm an artist," said Neha. Her eyebrows were about to jump off her face and attack him.

"Your little doodles are cute, but there's no way that's why you're in ARC," said Scott.

Neha stood up. "What is *that* supposed to mean?"

"Hey," said Court, "can y'all simmer down for a second?"

"Court, are you listening to this guy?" Eli asked in a disbelieving tone. Out of the corner of her eye, Court could see him trying to catch her attention, so he could make sure she understood just how big a jerk Scott was being. Court got it, but she didn't dare glance away from the much bigger problem that she had just noticed.

"I hear him," she said, "and he makes about as much sense as a screen door on a submarine. But I think we should all look at Neha."

Everyone froze.

A minute ago, Neha's blue beanbag chair had been sitting next to what Court had taken for an empty pink one.

Then she'd remembered they didn't own a pink one.

It was a transparent pink blob. It was alive. It was currently twice their height. And it was towering over Neha, silent and glistening.

Neha tilted her head to look up at the arrested wave of it. Its funnel-shaped mouth was open wide and positioned directly over her face.

"Don't . . . don't eat her," said Scott, finally getting up out of his chair. "Please?"

He was holding his hands up in a peacemaking sort of way. Court had never seen Scott try to soothe anybody before. It was almost weirder than the blob. The monster lifted its . . . head, she guessed, to look at Scott.

"But she was going to pound you," sloshed the blobby mouth.

People wanting to pound Scott was a pretty normal state of affairs, but Court figured now was a bad time to bring that up.

"We were just talking," said Scott. "I'm okay. Slooow down. Chill out."

The blob rippled, then subsided into a much smaller, rounder shape. Neha immediately leaped over to Court's side of the room.

"What is that thing?" she demanded.

Scott sighed. "You don't know, either? Crud."

29

Schmooze

As it turned out, Eli did know what it was . . . sort of.

"It's a strawberry Jell-O monster," he muttered.

"Do what?" said Court.

Eli snuck a look at Scott like he was waiting to be made fun of. Instead, Scott was looking at him with slowly dawning horror.

"I used to tell Lisa that strawberry Jell-O was alive. I'd bump the table so it would jiggle without me touching it, to freak her out. I mean, it's a lot bigger than I remember, but it's the same general idea."

"How is your sister not scarred for life?" asked Court.

Scott had a different bone to pick.

"This is all *your* fault?" Scott exclaimed. "*You* made all these monsters?"

Court made a ringing noise, then held out her hand with her thumb and pinky extended.

"Clue phone, Scott," she said sweetly. "It's for you."

But Scott was still staring at Eli.

"Is this because I picked on your writing?"

"Yes," said Eli. "It is totally all about you."

"Scott . . . ," Neha asked from a safe distance, "how did you two . . . meet?"

"It ate me," said Scott.

The blob rippled, but it was unclear whether it was embarrassed or laughing. Neha stared at it. Even though she'd just narrowly escaped death, all she could think about was how upset her mother would be to see a blob on someone's carpet. That and how she didn't have nearly good enough paints to capture its transparent orchid color.

"It ate you?" repeated Eli, and Neha could tell his monster-movie brain was pondering things that would never occur to her. He was definitely not thinking of orchids.

"How exactly did you survive?" Court asked Scott.

"Maybe he didn't," said Eli. "Maybe he's a pod person now, and that's why he was being so normal when he got here. He has to remind himself to be his everyday jerkface self."

"That hurts, Eli," said Scott.

"Really?" asked Eli.

"No."

"I think it's really him," Neha said, rolling her eyes.

"Let's circle back around to my question . . . ," said Court.

Neha agreed they needed answers. Since Scott obviously wasn't being digested right now, the blob was probably hungry. Unless Scott had fed it Jay, which was possible. Jay had been out sick today.

Scott blushed carnation pink and wouldn't answer. Naturally, Neha thought, when they finally wanted him to talk, he stopped.

Eli looked from Scott to the blob. "When you say it ate you, you mean you—"

"I was fully inside it, yes."

"Suspended in the blob."

"That seems self-evident."

"Here's what I figure," said Court. "He peed his pants, and the monster yucked him up in disgust."

"What? No!"

"You vomited?" Neha suggested.

"No!"

"He screamed," said the blob. It slid forward. Its face undulated, and two pink eyestalks unrolled and extended. Black eyes blinked at their tips. Its mouth rippled again.

"I was going to eat him, but he was so frightened. The screaming was adorable. Also it tickled."

It was sort of soft around the face, so its *r*'s were closer to *w*'s, but it was still really well-spoken for a blob.

"Sooo," said Eli, "you sicked him up because he was too cute to eat?"

"Basically," said the blob. "But his life expectancy is not good. He is constantly trying to die."

"He's a face looking for a fist," Neha agreed. She hadn't forgotten what Scott was talking about when they were interrupted.

"Please do not fist him in the face," said the blob. "I want to keep him."

The idea of anyone wanting to keep Scott was clearly ludicrous to everyone in the room. Neha saw Eli and Court twitching, but no one actually busted out laughing, which was good.

"I'm Neha," she said. "Thank you for not eating me. What's your name . . . sir?"

"I'm technically a unary species," it said.

"I . . . will look that up later," she said. "What's your name?"

"Schmooze," said Eli. "I named it Schmooze."

There was a pause.

"Well," said Court, "I think we have our class project. Good meeting, everyone!"

"Are you kidding me?" asked Scott. "We can't make Schmooze our class project!"

"Why not?" asked Eli. "We can say it's a non-Newtonian fluid we invented."

"See," Neha added, "Eli pays attention in science."

They high-fived each other.

A noise attracted her attention. Schmooze, whose mouth appeared to have migrated downward, was eating one of the real beanbag chairs. There were Styrofoam beads everywhere.

"Hey!" said Court. "Cut that out!"

"You got off easy," said Scott. "It ate my moon chair, too."

Schmooze hoovered its way across the room, sucking up stray pellets, then looked mournfully at Scott.

"I said I was sorry," it said. If eyestalks could be remorseful, Schmooze's were.

"I know," said Scott, "but eating Court's stuff isn't an improvement. And you ate half the food in my house an hour ago."

"I'm still hungry," said Schmooze.

"Are you sure you don't want to eat Scott?" Neha asked.

"Look at him," said Schmooze.

They did. He had the collar of his Izod shirt flipped up as if he was a detective on *Miami Vice*, and in that moment Eli absolutely wanted Schmooze to eat him.

"You know," Neha said, "the best way to keep Scott uneaten is to help us deal with the Howler."

"The Howler is uneasy to deal with."

"But you know it. You were part of its . . ." Was there a collective noun for a group of monsters? ". . . mob?"

"I followed the crowd," said Schmooze. "But only because they were all moving toward food."

Neha decided not to ask what Schmooze had eaten before they met it. She didn't want to know. But she did have another question.

"Will the other monsters notice you're gone?"

"Even if they did," said Eli, "they don't know where we live."

Downstairs, the doorbell rang.

"Somebody get that!" yelled Amy.

"They're going to figure it out eventually," said Court. "If they can smell worth a darn, the rain last night is the only reason Neha got away."

The doorbell rang again.

"Court!" Amy shouted again.

"I'm coming!" said Court.

"Schmooze," said Neha, "if you really like Scott, you should help us!"

Then Court looked around.

"Where did Scott go?"

"Uh-oh," said Schmooze, and oozed with remarkable speed toward the stairs. They rushed out onto the landing just in time to see Scott turning the doorknob.

"Scott, check the peephole!" Court shouted, but it was too late.

Or it would have been, if it weren't for Schmooze.

Before Scott could actually open the door, Schmooze had him wrapped in a gelatinous pink straitjacket. Slowly, it slid backward across the floor, taking Scott with it.

"What?" asked Scott irritably.

Neha stepped carefully onto the thin trail of ooze on the parquet floor. She locked the deadbolt and peered through the peephole the way Scott should have done in the first place.

"What do you see?" Court asked.

All Neha saw was a wide-angle view of Court's scruffy front yard.

Then a big, maize-colored eyeball mashed up against the peephole on the other side.

"Yikes!" she said, jumping backward, just about wiping out in the slime.

"What is it?" asked Eli.

"I don't know, but it's got yellow eyes and it doesn't wear glasses. And it's tall."

The door rattled.

They all backed slowly away, Schmooze still oozing in reverse. But the shaking door had most of Neha's attention.

"What're you guys looking at?" asked Joshie from the top of the stairs.

"Go in Mama and Daddy's room," said Court. "Lock the door."

Joshie looked from them to the rattling knob. He backed away down the upstairs hallway.

The banging was getting worse.

"It's a really strong door," Court said. "It'll hold."

Neha had the urge to knock on wood, but the closest wood was the door, so that seemed like something she should not do.

"I don't know why you're all fixated on the front door," said Scott, who must've been trying out for the Unwelcome Information Olympics. "The whole back of the house is windows."

As if he'd called it to them, something thumped against the glass.

30

Who Can It Be Now?

Usually Court thought their view was real pretty, but she was about to up and change her mind. There were furry, winged things plastering themselves against the windows one by one. They put her in mind of manta rays more than bats, but they had those whirling blade mouths like Blatt, the slug Neha'd exploded. Court had a bone to pick with Eli's imagination.

That was when she heard the creaking of one of the skylights on the sloped ceiling of the family room. She couldn't recall the last time her family had opened them, mostly because once they did they never remembered to shut them, and a rainstorm in the house was really only funny the first time. Now, one of them levered upward, and something dark and furry sidled through the gap.

They needed weapons.

"Neha!" Court yelled. "Grab one of those!" She pointed to the fireplace tools. Neha's eyes widened, but by now it was clear Court was someone who knew how to bash things, so she lunged for them. She got the poker and passed Eli the shovel. Scott reached for the fireplace tongs, eyes still fixed on the flopping, wriggling thing working its way in through the skylight. There was nothing left for Court, but that was all right. The kitchen and the garage were behind her. This was her house, and if the monsters thought they were going to get one up on Court, they had another think coming. For a start, she grabbed the tool the Castles used to open the skylights in the first place, a big pole with a hook on the end.

The furry thing had made it through the gap. It fell, landing with an ungainly whump on the floor. Everyone stood frozen for a split second. Then the thing scuttled on its rippling, furry edges toward Neha's feet. She jumped backward and whacked it with the poker. The other kids looked on in horror, and they were taken by surprise when three more of the furry manta-bats rained down from the skylights. One of them landed on Scott, who was standing directly underneath, but before he could even scream Schmooze sucked it off him, and Court saw its mouth whirring uselessly inside the blob as it writhed. Then another bat dropped in front of her. A blue streak flashed through the air, headed straight for it. It was one of the Serpenteens.

"Zeb!" Court shouted, panicking. "Get out of here!"

Instead he buried his tiny baby fangs in the manta-bat. Across the room, Luna and Archie were doing the same. Zeb's bat flailed, squealed, and then collapsed, knocked out or dead. Zeb rippled through the air, tiny and deadly, in search of more prey.

Scott saw him and raised the fireplace tongs.

"Not the snakes!" cried Court. "The snakes are friendlies!"

Scott lowered the tongs, startled.

If there were more bats than they could handle they'd get chewed to bits no matter what they did, but the bats weren't

Court's biggest worry. She was fretting about that eye Neha had seen through the peephole.

A shadow stooped outside the sliding-glass door, but before she could see what it was, a manta-bat came at her mouth-first. Court hefted the skylight tool. As offensive weapons went, it didn't look real effective. The hook at the end was rounded, after all.

It wasn't until the manta-bat swallowed half of it that things got good. At Court's end, there was a crank. And Court knew how to spin it really fast, though that was a story for another time.

The results were even more satisfying than ceiling-fan spin art.

The little stinker went flying off the end of the rod and smacked into the floor-to-ceiling chimney with a painful thwap. It landed on the hearth and didn't move again. All around her, the others were whacking and bashing their own attackers, and at the edge of her vision she could see a shadow skulking around the pool. She rushed for the wall and turned the ceiling fan up as high as it would go. It hung from a long pole that was attached to the peaked ceiling, and when it really got cranking, the whole thing wobbled like an old record in a jukebox. But that was nothing compared to what happened when another manta-bat fell through the skylight and hit the blades full on. It got slingshotted into the wall with a nasty splat, then oozed down toward the floor. Startled, another one launched itself upward and met the same fate.

The remaining manta-bats lifted a fold at one end of their floppy bodies, sort of like what you get if you make a peak in a folded bandanna. Court heard their mouths whirring in distress.

"Don't like that, do you?" she shouted, feeling full of beans for a minute. Then Scott, in his latest attempt at getting himself and everyone else killed, approached a cluster of bats.

"It seems like it would be in everyone's best interests if you'd negotiate," he said, holding his hearth tongs out in front of him as if he might lay them down. "Don't you think it's time to talk?"

They all jerked their head folds in his direction. The whirring ramped up to a scream. Court didn't think of them as particularly fast moving, but they absolutely launched at Scott. To his credit, he managed to hit one with the tongs like he was bunting a softball, but it's almost impossible to bunt something hard enough to knock it unconscious.

Neha, on the other hand, smacked a manta-bat into next week with the poker.

"Whoa!" Court was impressed.

"Tennis lessons!" she said, beaming, then ducked to avoid the third manta-bat. It ought to have hit Scott full in the face, but instead Schmooze unfurled outward like a sticky sail, and the manta-bat slapped right into it. Schmooze curled back in on itself, and Court realized the remains of the first manta-bat were skeletal and almost gone already. She shuddered. Good thing Scott was so darn adorable when he screamed.

The door to the kitchen swung open, and Amy stuck her head out, frowning fiercely.

"What are you doing out here? No one can hear the DM. You know what happens when no one can hear the DM?"

"Diplomacy?" asked Court, a bit out of breath.

"Diplomacy."

When other people said that word, it meant they wanted to resolve things peacefully. When Amy did, it meant "I hit it with my axe."

"What are you fighting in this game, anyway?" she asked, looking around at all of them brandishing the hearth tools.

"Buncha bats with garbage disposals for mouths," Court said. Another manta-bat got flung off the ceiling fan blades and thwapped against the wall. It slid down and joined the pile on the floor.

"Using those?" Amy asked, raising an eyebrow.

Court was feeling a little bit picked on.

"They were the closest weapons," she said as bats whirled around them.

"What you need is an Area of Effect defense," said Amy.

"I don't speak D&D, so you're gonna have to spell that out for me," Court said, turning to swing her pole at the flapping monstrosity that was headed her way.

"Swarms will just dodge if you try to whack them," explained Amy. "Use something that affects the area they're in. A fireball, or an ice storm, or something."

She paused.

"Not a real fireball, though."

"Of course not!" said Court. This was what she, Joshie, and Amy always said whenever anyone accused them of anything, so Amy stared beadily at her for a few more seconds, just in case.

"All right, then," she finally said. "If you try fire and it doesn't work, you're not using enough of it. Cool?"

"Cool."

She went back into the kitchen, and an idea came to Court so suddenly that she followed her sister without thinking. The swinging door about decked her in the face. Behind her, she heard shouts of alarm as the bats renewed their assault, but she was already skidding to her knees in front of the kitchen sink. One of the Mikes was telling Amy what he'd rolled while she was gone, and Court was on her way back out before Amy noticed she was there.

Neha was standing over yet another bashed bat, so Court addressed her first. "Go in the bathroom and get the fire extinguisher."

"Why do you have a fire extinguisher in the—" she started to ask, but Court frowned at her ferociously and she went without another word.

"Eli!" Court said. "There's another one under the couch!"

"Why?"

It would take too long to list the reasons.

"Just get it!"

Court called the Serpenteens, and they came, wreathing her head and shoulders and hissing at anything that came her way.

In the time it took to gather safety equipment so they could use it for all the wrong reasons, more bats made their way into the house. There was an ominous creak overhead, and Court glanced up to confirm a theory she'd developed the last time she and Joshie tried rock climbing on the fireplace.

The fan was not load-bearing.

It was wobbling to a halt under an enormous load of bats. Some slipped off, but there were always more coming. Then something Court had been expecting for a while finally happened. One of the mantas remembered to chew as it was falling, and shredded right through a fan blade on its way down.

Off-balance, the fan pole vibrated alarmingly, and the fan sped back up, flinging manta-bats across the room. The nasty, flopping, flapping, furry things were everywhere. They chewed gashes in the couch in two places, and a hole in the carpet, too.

It's happening again, thought Court. She couldn't let the monsters trash her house the way they'd trashed the family business.

"Ready?" she yelled.

They were.

"Pull the pin out of the handle, point the hose, and spray!"

She blasted the nearest manta-bat with her fire extinguisher.

Court had to hand it to Amy: she knew what she was talking about. Every bat in range flailed all over the place trying to get away. One of them aimed its snarling, whirring blades at Court, and she sprayed it right in the mouth. To her shock and delight, the circle of teeth ground to a halt.

Across the room, Eli had sprayed his shoes and was only now getting on board with fire extinguisher usage, but Neha sprayed one of the bats on the ground, then came close enough to kick it in its now-brittle mouth. Its teeth shattered as it made a high, keening noise of pain. Neha's eyes glinted fiercely.

"Can't we lure them outside somehow?" Scott asked. Court didn't know what he was worried about. All he was doing was ducking so Schmooze could eat them. Besides, Court couldn't see any way to get the bats out of the house without opening a door. Which was a shame, because now that the kids were on the attack, some of the bats were trying to get back out through the skylight . . . and others, she realized all of a sudden, were flopping toward the fireplace, as if they could smell the fresh air.

"Look at that!" she said, pointing, and Scott headed for the fireplace. He leaned over, one hand on the brick, and tried to open the glass doors, but they were jammed.

Another blade from the fan whickered through the air as Court sprinted over to yank the hearth doors open herself. A second later, she remembered to reach in and open the flue, something she'd learned the hard way one day when she'd pretended she was camping. She whipped backward just in time. A manta-bat sliced off most of her braid as it went by, like some kind of Weed Whacker.

"Whoa!" said Court, reaching for the rough ends of her newly-shorn hair. Then the bats went up the chimney in a gust of chattering evil.

"Yes!" said Eli as Scott slammed the fireplace doors shut again.

Neha cheered.

Court let out a huge sigh of relief.

That was when the sliding-glass door opened.

31

Burning Down the House

Eli watched in horror as a monster he'd dubbed the Lichenthrope stooped to fit through the doorway, blinking an enormous, round, yellow eye. As soon as the creature was in the house, its head flicked in Eli's direction, way faster than anything so darn big ought to have moved.

It was covered with matted green-and-brown hair and half-moon flaps that resembled fungus. Eli had designed it so that it could lie down in the forest and be undetectable until you walked right over top of it.

That was not the most disturbing thing about this monster.

Worse by far was the round, lipless hole in the middle of its face, which showcased a full mouth of flat teeth. It flexed as Eli watched. The creature reached down, grabbed a manta-bat off a pile of dead and injured ones, and stuffed it, wriggling, into its face-hole. It chewed, reflectively, as the manta tail flailed. There was a crunch.

Neha came up beside him, looking down at the fire extinguisher in her hands. She didn't seem to have spotted their new problem yet. "This thing wasn't as hard to use as I thought it would be!"

"Have you got anything left in there?" Eli asked.

"Yeah, I think so."

"Good. Next time you point it?"

"Yeah?"

"Point it *up*."

Neha slowly raised her gaze.

The monster sucked the manta-bat tail into its mouth as if it was a piece of spaghetti.

"Ohhhh . . . ," she said.

They opened fire.

The plant creature didn't take as much damage as the bats had. The Lichen curled, and so did its mossy hair. The ends turned black. In spite of this, the Lichenthrope showed no sign of doing two crucial things: fleeing or dying.

It popped another manta-bat into its mouth and then reached for Eli, who swung his fire extinguisher at its outstretched hand as hard as he could. It hit with a hollow thunk, and the creature pulled back, spraying manta-bat chunks across the room as it screamed.

"Augh!" yelled Neha as gobbets of half-chewed bat hit her.

"Eli!" said Court. "What stops this thing?"

"Not all of them get their own endings," he said. "I make them scary. That's my job."

"You might want to think about programming a back door when you write them, then," Scott said.

"What?"

"Never mind."

The mold monster had stopped shaking its injured fingers. Now it was angry.

"Somebody!" Neha said. "What kills fungus and mold?"

"Super tetanus?" suggested Court.

She vaulted over the couch to get away as Neha took refuge behind an armchair. The monster's arm swept past overhead.

"Scott?" said Court. "Since you seem to know everything, now would be a good time to nerd out and have a really good idea."

"I don't know," he said, "fire, maybe?"

"We don't have fire!" Court said. "We have fire extinguishers."

Eli glanced through the sliding-glass doors in the direction of the pool. He froze. Then he dropped his fire extinguisher with a thunk.

"Court, distract it!" he ordered.

"With what?" she asked, but he was already dashing for the front door.

"Eli, don't—" Neha began, but he didn't listen. As he passed the stairs, Sleekit, who'd apparently heard the commotion and abandoned her babysitting duties, came streaking down the steps, with the Rogue Runners right behind her.

"Keep that thing busy for a minute," he yelled at her, and she chattered an affirmative.

As Eli left the house, the monster spotted the Creeps and made an eager, hungry noise.

Eli raced around the side of the house in the dark. What he was doing was dangerous, and he knew it. There could be ten more monsters waiting out here. But he figured he was taking a calculated risk. The Lichenthrope was about as smart as a box of rocks, and the manta-bats were similarly mindless. This probably wasn't a calculated attack. More likely, the moss monster had been prowling around houses and ringing doorbells the way some kids turned over rocks to see what bugs were underneath.

That meant two things.

First, there might not be any other monsters hanging around.

Second, if he could just keep the Lichenthrope from leaving, the Howler might not find out where Court lived.

Eli tripped and landed flat on his face with a whoosh as the wind was knocked out of him.

When he lifted his head, a manta-bat was gliding straight toward him. It made a tiny sound of glee, then its vortex of a mouth began to spin, faster and faster. Eli's fingers closed on something hard. It was the hockey stick he'd tripped over.

He rolled to the side and hoisted the stick to block the oncoming bat. It hit the handle end with a noise like a woodchipper, grinding its way down the shaft. Before it could reach his fingers, Eli rolled over and slammed what was left of the stick into the side of the house as hard as he could. There was a nasty crunch, and the bat went still.

Eli leaped to his feet and pounded around the back of the house to the patio. Inside, the monster roared squishily. His friends shouted directions to each other, and through the glass he could see that Sleekit was everywhere at once, a purple blur. The Rogue Runners, Pell and Mell, were feinting at the Lichenthrope, plucking tufts of it away as if they were looking for supplies to feather the world's biggest nest.

Eli saw the objects he'd come for, and grabbed them. He crept up behind the monster.

"Hey, what's that smell?" asked Scott.

"I smell it, too," said Neha. Her fire extinguisher was the smallest, and it was sputtering, almost out. "What is that?"

"I think it's gas," said Court.

"Great!" Scott shouted, rolling to one side as the monster tried to step on him. "A farting fungus."

Schmooze put itself between Scott and the Lichenthrope, and

was punched for its trouble. The fungus's fist stuck in Schmooze's blobby body for a second, then the monster pulled it out with a wet glurp.

"Not that kind of gas," said Court, "the kind that explodes! I think the fireplace is turned on!"

How had that happened? Eli peered through the glass at the brick hearth. The key was right where it was supposed to be, sticking out of the—uh-oh.

The truth hit Neha at the same moment.

"Scott, you must have done it," she said. "You were leaning on the fireplace by the key. You turned it by AAAAAUGH! Put me down!"

Eli looked on in horror as the moss monster plucked her up between its thumb and forefinger. Its round, lipless mouth was making sucking noises like she was the best treat it had seen in weeks.

Scott darted for the fireplace.

"Turn it off!" cried Court, slamming the creature with her empty fire extinguisher again and again. Sleekit streaked up the monster's body and attacked the top of its head.

"Which way?"

"Counterclockwise!"

The monster swiped at Sleekit with its free hand, holding Neha higher. Neha kicked it in the eye. It screamed and dropped her. She landed on the couch with a thump.

"Which way is counterclockwise?" Scott asked.

"LEFT!" yelled Neha and Court simultaneously.

Eli dove between the monster's legs and into Court's family room.

"Everybody out of the way!"

He spun around, clicked the lighter in his right hand, and

lit the tiki torch in his left. He swept the flame in a broad arc toward the monster, and the air around the fireplace exploded into flame.

The entire backside of the Lichenthrope went up like dry grass on the Fourth of July. It screamed, slapping at itself. Scott cried out in panic as the monster backed toward him. Schmooze instantly slimed to his rescue, but the shaggy creature was already turning to flee.

Flaming bits of moss started dropping to the carpet as the monster lurched toward the sliding-glass door. They chased after it, stamping out fires so it wouldn't burn the whole house down. It was trying to force its way back through the doorway, but it was panicking, and then Eli realized what was wrong.

It was stuck.

Flames licked up the door frame.

Eli did the only thing he could think of. He grabbed his abandoned fire extinguisher and threw it into the heart of the blaze. It lodged itself in the center of the Lichenthrope's leafy back.

There was a long, desperate pause as Neha tried to spray her own extinguisher and found it empty. Then Eli heard a metallic ticking, like a car engine cooling down.

"Look out!" he shouted. He threw himself back behind the couch as Neha and Court took cover. Scott was staring in horror at the monster, but Schmooze expanded and flattened to form a barrier in front of him.

The fire extinguisher exploded.

A cloud of white enveloped the scene at Court's back door. When it cleared, the monster was outside. Eli could hear it moaning in pain as it headed for the vacant lot.

"Stop it!" he cried, chasing after it. "Don't let it get away!"

"Are you kidding?" asked Scott.

"It knows where Court lives!" he said, rushing out of the house.

Behind him, Court groaned, and he heard her come after him.

Eli still had the tiki torch in his hand. He'd light the Lichenthrope on fire again if he had to. He had passed the pool and was almost close enough to touch it when an enormous shadow rose in the vacant lot, angular and menacing. Eli's sneakers skidded as he reversed direction and landed on his butt in the grass.

"Look out!" cried Court.

The Lichenthrope looked up, maybe expecting help. It was wrong, but it was already too late to run.

The Spider Plant bared an enormous set of fangs none of them had known it had, and plunged them into the monster's moldy neck. The Lichenthrope went limp, and the Spider Plant began to wrap it tightly in spider silk.

"What the heck is that thing?" shouted Scott.

As Court hauled Eli to his feet, Sleekit leaped up onto Neha's shoulder.

"And what is *that* thing?" Scott demanded, pointing at Sleekit. "And what were those giant birds?"

"It's okay, Scott," said Court, slapping him on the back. "Come on in. We'll catch you up."

"You got this?" said Eli to the Spider Plant.

It lifted its mantislike head, cocking it curiously.

"Uh . . . thanks."

The Spider Plant returned to its grisly task, and Eli followed the others with a shudder. He dipped the tiki torch in the pool on his way past, to make sure it was out, and spared a moment to be grateful he'd asked Hairstack to stay home and guard his momma and Lisa.

The family room was not on fire. Trashed, but not on fire.

Nearby, a wounded manta-bat started to wriggle. Eli clubbed it, and it fell still with a squeak. Around the room, the three Serpenteens were dispatching any surviving manta-bats they could find.

Scott was creeping slowly toward the pile that had accumulated against the wall.

"I think they're dead," he said.

"Don't do it!" said Eli, starting forward.

Scott poked one. It whirred, arched, and just about took his arm off. Archie, the monarch-winged Serpenteen, zipped over and delivered a fatal bite just in time.

Eli stormed over to Scott, grabbed his head in both hands, and looked him in the eye.

"Somebody always says 'I think they're dead,'" he said, "and they're *never* dead."

"Well, actually," said Scott, "it could have been a postmortem reflex."

Eli threw up his hands.

"This guy!" he said to them. To Scott he said, "Want to go back over there and check?"

"No!" said Neha and Schmooze simultaneously.

The kitchen door opened, and the four of them spun around to bash whatever was coming. It was Amy again. She stood, open-mouthed, eyebrows raised, surveying the damage. The ceiling fan pole wobbled alarmingly as the remaining three paddles continued to spin. The whole contraption groaned and emitted a horrible smell. Fluff drifted from the hole in the couch, which also had a fan blade embedded in it. Eli sidled over to cover the hole in the carpet with his foot.

Court watched her sister closely to find out if she was going to live or die. Amy pressed the dimmer switch. The fan began to slow. She reached over to touch the ends of Court's halfway sawed-off hair.

"Wow," she said. "That Was Close. The ceiling fan was dangerously defective. Good thing we had all these fire extinguishers."

Court let out a breath. "Yeah. Um. Safety first?"

"Safety first," Amy agreed. She gave the kids a sidelong look. "Payback second."

Court gulped. Amy left the room, and Court turned to her friends.

"So," said Scott, "I think our shared interest should be our mutual survival."

"Yeah," said Eli. "That sounds about right."

32

Won Stories

The fireplace tongs turned out to be useful after all. They were perfect for transferring dead manta-bats into a very large Hefty bag. Manta-bats were heavy, though. Eli held open the trash bag so Neha could use both hands to work the tongs.

Court was up on a ladder, carefully wiping soot off the wall. Sleekit was supervising from the mantel. Scott had found a good use for his attention to detail and was patching the hole in the carpet with a piece Court had snipped out of the matching laundry room rug. Pell and Mell were standing over him, cocking their heads back and forth as they tried to see what he was doing. His hands weren't quite steady, but he was doing his best to chill out about the menagerie of critters living at Court's.

"Try not to walk on this until the glue's dry," he said as he finished. Joshie moved an end table to stand over it, just to be sure.

Eli and Neha finished bagging the bats and dragged the

garbage out the back door, to a spot that wouldn't be easily visible to Court's folks. Schmooze followed them out.

"I think I will simply . . . eat the evidence," it burbled.

They hustled back inside before he got started.

When they returned, Eli sat down on the floor and watched as Neha tried to jam the stuffing back into the couch's new hole.

He was thinking hard.

One of the indignities of middle school was that mutual survival without a class presentation would still result in a failing grade. But that wasn't their biggest problem.

"Survival isn't enough," Eli said.

"It's a start," said Court. Sleekit twined her way from the mantel to the ladder to the floor. Court dropped her Windex bottle for Sleekit to catch, then climbed down the stepladder with a handful of filthy rags.

"I mean it," Eli said. "We have to win, or we're never going to be safe."

"You're right," said Neha, "but I have no idea how we beat the Howler."

She started to pull the fan blade out of the couch.

"Leave it," said Court. "Mama and Daddy won't be as mad about the mess if they're thinking about what could have happened to us."

Sleekit hopped up on the couch next to Neha, who stroked the fur between her rounded ears.

"Sleekit," said Eli, "tell me more about won stories."

"What?" asked Neha.

Eli sat on the floor in front of them, then thought to check under the couch. Relieved to find the space empty, he sat back up.

"The day the Creeps got out of the sketchbook," he said,

"Sleekit told me the Creeps were the heroes of their 'won stories.' What did you mean, Sleekit?"

The otter-weasel sat up and began to groom herself, and for a moment Eli thought she wouldn't answer. She did that sometimes, when she didn't like the question. Then she spoke.

"The first child I ever knew was named Holly," she said. "She was scared to death of snakes. Especially rattlers. Then I came to stay. She never had to be afraid when I was there. I was the snake slayer."

A tiny hiss from above made everyone look up. Zeb's tiny blue form was coiled around the ceiling fan pole. He was fluttering his colorful wings in alarm.

"Not you, Zeb," Sleekit reassured him. "I only slay snakes who bite children."

Eli's shoelaces were wet with fire extinguisher foam. He ran one between his fingers to flatten it. As he did, he thought about the Gargyle, who really did smell like feet, but was also very soft, and had radar for when Eli or Lisa was tired and unhappy. He thought about Frog Boy, who saved tadpoles, and how in Oklahoma you were as likely to find tadpoles in a puddle as a pond, and how it had always made him nervous, because what if the puddle dried up before the tadpoles turned into frogs?

The Creeps showed up because some kid needed them. And they won their stories.

"So all the Creeps have one of these?" he asked. "A won story?"

Sleekit rubbed her head on the couch, then rolled over and regarded him upside down.

"Yep," she said.

He smiled a little. Then he stopped smiling.

"I think maybe the Howler does, too," he said.

Neha sat bolt upright.

"It can't!" she said. "It's evil!"

"Maybe it doesn't matter whether it's good or evil," said Eli. "Something can be awful and still be important."

Amy interrupted the silence that followed when she came in to check their progress. She folded her arms and examined the room.

"Not bad," she admitted. "Vacuum everything but the patched spot. And use some of that Windex on the sliding-glass door, Court. It's disgusting."

Ian stuck his head out of the kitchen.

"Hey, Amy," he said, "does Fish Command work on gigantic, angry crabs?"

"Crabs are arthropods, not fish," said Amy.

Ian wasn't buying this argument.

"They live in the sea. We call them seafood. Cut me some slack, Ames."

"I think that magic trident you found has been humming one too many sea chanteys in your head. A crab is more like a spider than a fish."

"Look. You can either let me use Fish Command, or we can have another talk about accepting Blibdoolpoolp as your goddess and savior."

"No. No more Blibdoolpoolp," said Amy.

"Living weapons are cantankerous, Ames. What can I do? I have to stay on the trident's good side, and the trident wants me to spread the good news about Blibdoolpoolp!"

Ian smiled winningly at her.

Amy was trying to be stern, but Eli could see the grin about to break loose.

"There is no good news about Blibdoolpoolp. She's chaotic evil. If she was lawful evil, maybe we'd have something to discuss—"

Eli's scalp prickled.

"Wait," he interrupted. "What's lawful evil?"

Court, who was slumped on the floor and showed no sign of getting the vacuum, said, "It's when you're a bad guy, but you still pretty much follow the rules."

Amy raised her eyebrows at Court, and Ian dropped his jaw in fake shock.

"What?" said Court. "I pay attention."

Eli's fingers were twitching. He suddenly wished he were at home with his typewriter. "Can you make a contract with someone who's lawful evil?"

"Watch for loopholes," warned Amy. "Lawful evil will find them every time."

"I can do that," he muttered.

"Are you guys ever coming back?" whined Wig from the kitchen.

"We're getting crabby!" said Shorty.

"Stop carping!" said Amy. "I can't help it if you flounder when I'm not there."

There was a chorus of groans from the kitchen.

Amy pointed at Court.

"Vacuum!"

Ian pulled his head back through the swinging door just in time to prevent his own decapitation as Amy left the room.

Neha and Court waited until they were gone, then pounced.

"What was that about?" demanded Neha.

"You have a plan!" accused Court.

"At least one," said Eli. "Possibly two. I have some writing to do."

Neha collapsed on the couch again.

"You already tried to fix this with writing!" she groaned. "It didn't work! And you still haven't tried burning the Howler's story!"

"That's because I don't know where it is!"

Everyone stared at him, including the Creeps.

"I'd burn it if I had it. But I've looked everywhere, and it's gone."

He looked at Scott and voiced a long-held suspicion.

"Do you have it?"

Scott looked genuinely shocked, which was somehow more annoying than anything else he could have done.

"Why would I have it?" .

Neha rolled her eyes. "Because you're constantly playing keep-away with people's stuff on the bus!"

"I'm goofing around!"

"Do you have it or not?"

"No," said Scott, frowning. "I don't take other people's stuff. Not permanently."

Court sighed.

"May as well scrub some bat guts while we argue. My folks'll be home sooner or later." She rolled to her feet, grabbed some newspapers off the stack that had been under the coffee table before they'd moved it, and went to clean the sliding-glass door.

The newspaper was for wiping the door, of course, but Pell and Mell had other ideas. They immediately started tearing it into strips.

"Can y'all stop making a new mess before we finish cleaning up the old one? Joshie!" Court yelled. "Come get your birds!"

Joshie cautiously ventured downstairs and tried to help, but it didn't do much good. The Rogue Runners were using the paper strips to weave a large, elaborate nest, and they promptly shoved Joshie down in the middle of it and began building it around him while he laughed.

"Fine," said Court. "At least they're busy."

"Look," said Eli as Pell and Mell bickered over paper strips, "I'll still burn the story if I find it, but I'm not sure it will matter. We don't even know if the Creeps' stories were ever written down, and they're here. But there is someone who needs a story and doesn't have one."

"Oh yeah?" asked Scott. "Who's that?"

"Us."

Scott blinked. "Us, like . . . me, too?"

Schmooze plastered its pink form against the other side of the sliding-glass door with a squish. In the glow of the pool lights, they could see the shadows of a whole mess of manta-bats inside it, like it was the world's most disgusting Jell-O salad.

"May I come in, please?" it asked.

Court looked at Scott with a grin.

"I'd say you're in this up to your neck," she said.

She let Schmooze in, and he cruised over to Scott. Outside, Eli could see the shadow of the Spider Plant, still and watchful.

"All I'm saying," said Eli, watching the Rogue Runners drag their nest out of the room as Joshie threw paper bits at them from inside, "is I know scary stories, and I don't like our situation right now."

"You mean the one where we keep getting attacked by monsters until we die?" asked Scott.

"I mean the one where we're not the heroes. Scott's right. So far we've been on defense. If we don't change that, we'll end up being the random kids in the monster movie who get eaten. But the heroes of an adventure story usually live, even if there are monsters. I think I should write our story with us as the heroes. And I think we have to fight the Howler."

There was silence.

Neha was the first one to speak up.

"I'm not sure we can win. But you're right, we have to fight back."

Court nodded agreement.

Scott was more hesitant. "Can we try craft and guile before we go straight to direct assault?"

"Definitely," said Eli. "But we'd better be ready for war. We don't have to do this alone, though. If the Howler won't negotiate with us, I have an idea who will."

33

Plot Twist

Is it ready?" asked Eli. "I want to make the copies before everyone comes back from lunch."

"Five more minutes," said Neha. She didn't really need it, but fighting monsters had seriously interfered with her art lately, and it felt so good to draw.

Forest Creeks had been Neha's private hobby. Then the Creeps had moved in, and meeting their needs had turned drawing into the world's weirdest community service. Now she was illustrating her team's tale, a Venn diagram of overlapping stories with the four of them at the center, working as a team to defeat the monsters. The grand finale was a big, unpleasant surprise for the Howler, devised by Eli. They were turning the whole thing into a mini-magazine called a zine, and making copies for the members of the ARC class.

Neha fussed with Sleekit's whiskers on the very last frame until they were good and sassy.

"Okay," she said. "Done."

The intercom on the wall buzzed. Mrs. Benton went over and pressed the button.

"Yes?"

The reply sounded like Schmooze gargling, but Neha could still more or less understand it.

"Please tell Eli Goodman that his sister won't be on the bus today. His mother took her to the sitter's after her dentist appointment."

"I'll let him know," said Mrs. Benton, winking at Eli. He nodded back.

Neha handed him her pages, and he and Court went to the office to make copies. Scott was writing the name of the zine, *Plot Twist*, on the board in bold letters. When he was finished, he pulled the string on the world map, unrolling it to cover the words.

"Ready?" he asked, turning around.

Neha shrugged. "Doing a presentation is less scary after you've fought monsters. Besides, you won't be in the audience to heckle me. That helps."

He grimaced.

"Sorry."

Neha smiled.

"If I'd made a list of terrible punishments for you, being eaten by a monster would have been first on the list," she said. "I think we should call it even."

She took it as a good sign when he laughed. Then Court and Eli came back with the copies.

"Hot off the presses," said Court. "Grab staplers."

▲ ▼ ▲

After half an hour of frenzied assembly, the four of them went to the front of the room to present. ARC class had more empty seats than before, and so did the bus. The kids who were there ranged in appearance from frazzled to downright twitchy.

Neha got down to business.

"Our group's mutual interest turned out to be fighting monsters."

There was a startling absence of laughter, and she definitely had everyone's attention.

"It happens to all of us, right? You're walking home from your friend's house at night, minding your own business, when suddenly something goes bump in the night."

"Sounds more like one of Eli's cruddy stories," sneered Brandon, who'd been frowning at the four of them all morning. Neha could tell he didn't like their truce one bit.

"It does sound like one of my stories!" agreed Eli with a grin. "You could almost say it *was* one of my stories."

His grin faded somewhat as he looked around at the empty seats and nervous kids, and Neha jumped back in.

"We like Eli's stories," she said, "but we didn't want to use one of those for our project, because—"

"Because *everyone dies*," said Brandon, rippling his fingers to fully express his sarcasm.

"All right, Brandon," Mrs. Benton said, and he stopped for the moment.

"He ain't wrong," said Court, and the class chuckled.

"The thing is," continued Neha, "everyone in our group likes scary stories where people get eaten, especially when the people are kind of obnoxious—"

There was nodding at this.

"—but we only like those stories when we feel completely safe. When we feel *un*safe, we want a story about smart kids kicking monsters' butts."

"So," said Eli as the four of them divided copies of *Plot Twist* into stacks and handed them to the kids at the front to pass back, "we made one. Each kid on the team told me their own part of the story, and I wrote it all down."

"I did the art," said Neha.

"And me and Scott did layout and production," said Court.

Neha was pretty pleased with their "killing two manta-bats with one stone" project, which laid the groundwork for defeating the Howler while also saving them from a failing grade. They probably could have gotten away with only making one book, but handing out copies was a way to share the strategies that had kept them alive. Maybe it would help someone else to not get eaten.

As the kids started flipping through their copies, someone knocked on the classroom door.

"You four keep going," said Mrs. Benton. "This is all quite intriguing. I'll be right back."

As soon as the door shut behind her, Brandon started up again.

"So you've concocted this crazy story about a bunch of stuff we know didn't really happen to you, and that's supposed to count as your project?"

"Who says it didn't happen?" asked Court.

Brandon openly scoffed. "Neha exploded a giant snail in Eli's kitchen?"

"No," said Neha, "it was a giant slug."

The class laughed.

"It really exploded?" asked Adriana, who was perking up as she looked at the zine.

Court used her arms to mimic the geyser of slug guts. "Goosh!" she said.

They laughed again.

Kelly held up her copy. It was open to a picture of her protecting her brother while monsters circled around her. At the entrance to the cul-de-sac sat Neha on her bike with a speech bubble over her head that said, "HEY!"

"I didn't realize you were around the night me and my brother were . . . outside after dark," said Kelly. It was as close as she could get to thanking Neha without admitting she'd seen monsters, but Neha still appreciated the way Kelly was backing her story. Kids were looking at Neha, and her cheeks warmed a little bit. She might be good at tennis, but she wasn't someone who got picked first in gym class, like Court. This kind of attention was new.

Brandon had noticed, too, and he didn't seem to like that any more than he liked Scott getting along with them.

"Whatever. Eli's and Neha's presentations are always cruddy," said Brandon. "Welcome to the club, Scott."

"I had fun," said Scott mildly. "I never did anything like this before. It's like *Zork*—"

There was a collective sigh.

"—only instead of choosing the adventure, we got to make one up. When I design my own game someday, I'll know how to write good code *and* a good story."

"And how to kill a bat with a fire extinguisher," said someone in the back, pointing to another page.

"That, too," said Scott with a grin.

Jeff raised his hand. Neha pointed at him.

"In theory, I may have used my dad's Weed Whacker on something that looked a lot like that slug," he said.

Neha blinked.

"Awesome," she said before she thought about it.

"How'd it work?" asked Scott.

"Pretty good. It was super gross. And, like, I lived."

There was a smattering of applause.

"I'm not saying I've seen a monster," said Adriana, "but if I did, it's possible I clubbed it with a croquet mallet."

"That's cool!" said Eli. "We need to make another zine so we can put this stuff in!"

"Whoa," said Kelly, who had flipped to the end. "Look at this—"

"Hey, hey," warned Eli. "Don't spoil it. Let people read!"

That was when Mrs. Benton finally returned with unexpected news.

"Kids," she said, "I'm afraid we're going to have to cut this short. School is closing early. We've got bad weather coming."

34

Off the Bus

P ipe down!" Dwight ordered. "I'm trying to drive!"

"Have we ever seen him succeeding?" muttered Scott. Court snorted.

"Scott," she said, "that was actually funny!"

If Dwight didn't simmer down, he was going to sprain something. He kept trying to look everywhere at once instead of keeping his eyes on the road. It was probably a good thing that half the kids had gotten picked up at school already.

Nobody wanted to see Dwight fired, not even Scott. Up until the last week or so, he was flat out the best bus driver they'd ever had. Rock music, no hollering, and minimal threatening. Now Court figured the only reason he still had a job was because the other options were even worse.

"You doin' all right, Dwight?" Court asked.

"Yeah, yeah, I'm fi— What's that?" he asked, jerking his head and the wheel in the process. Court looked toward the back to see that Brandon had taken some little kid's toy. It was a Popple, one of those plush animals that could be stuffed inside itself to make a ball. He was chest passing it off the ceiling. Court was about ready to pound him, but first she had to make it to the bus stop in one piece.

"It's nothing," Court reassured Dwight as horns honked. "A toy."

"You sure?" he asked, his eyes wide in the huge rearview mirror. A pickup truck turned in front of them up ahead, and he didn't even notice.

"Dwight, drive, man!" exclaimed Eli.

Dwight looked back at the road just in time to avoid the oncoming traffic.

"Brandon, knock it off back there!" he roared, and every last head whipped around.

"What?" asked Brandon defensively, still holding the pink, balled-up plush toy.

"You want a bus suspension? Siddown!" Dwight commanded, and Brandon was so darn shocked that he did. Between his bowl cut and his sulky face, he'd never looked more like a mule.

"Don't make me pull this bus over!" yelled Dwight, and for about five minutes, no one said anything. Court wanted to ask the others what the heck they thought was going on, but she had a feeling it'd be real bad if Dwight heard them discussing the state of his brain.

A note landed in Court's lap, and she knew Neha was worried because she hadn't bothered to do the nifty little trigger fold they all used so there'd be an actual handle to pull to open the note. She unfolded it.

Is it just me, or does it seem like he's hallucinating?

It sure did. He was checking the rear and sideview mirrors again, as though he was in a spy movie and someone was tailing them. But he was also eyeballing anything that made a peep inside the bus. The really mean bus drivers did that. They made impossible rules and then created an entire sport out of catching you. But Dwight wasn't looking at the kids. He was looking between them, under them, and above them.

Court scribbled an additional line and passed the note to Eli. *What if something really is out to get him?*

She found it cute that Eli was their writer but he moved his lips when he read.

He looked up and locked eyes with Court, then passed his note back to Neha. Scott read it over her shoulder.

"But grown-ups can't see them," blurted Scott. Court shrugged and widened her eyes. If anybody had a better explanation, she was all ears. Besides, Dwight barely counted as a grown-up.

Right about then, the Popple sailed past and whacked Dwight upside the head.

It would be fair to say he went to pieces. He made a sound somewhere between a neigh and a shriek, and then every kid screamed with him as he yanked the wheel in panic and the bus went sailing into the center lane. Cars careened past, horns wailing. Then he pulled the wheel again, and they crossed the road the rest of the way into oncoming traffic. Naturally, they screamed again. By the time Dwight finally made it over to the shoulder of the road, Court was betting there were some very wet vinyl seats on their bus.

Dwight leaped to his feet, head swiveling in every direction. When he spotted the Popple, which had rolled down the bus stairs into the well by the door, he turned and pointed directly at Brandon.

"What'd I do?" asked Brandon.

"Off the bus!" Dwight shouted, and this helped most of the

kids wrap their minds around what was going on. In keeping with tradition, the chant began.

"Off the bus. Off the bus. OFF THE BUS. OFF THE BUS."

"Fine!" yelled Brandon. He dragged himself out of his seat and stormed off the bus, kicking the Popple in front of him. There really was no justice for Popples.

The kids sat listening to the butt-chewing that ensued.

"I'm telling you, he's afraid of something," Court said.

"I can't even see them from here," said Scott, craning his neck.

"That's because Dwight has his back against the side of the bus," said Neha.

"Rookie move," said Eli. "Anything with half a brain will get under the bus and grab his ankles."

"Could you not say this stuff where something could hear and get ideas?" said Court.

Neha was looking anxiously out the window at the incoming storm clouds. Dwight must have seen them, too, because he kept his lecture short and quickly herded a red-faced, angry Brandon back onto the bus. Dwight pointed, and Brandon sat in the front row next to a couple of six-year-olds who looked terrified to have him there.

Dwight jammed the pink Popple into the lost-and-found bin that sat next to his seat, then cranked the door shut with a bang. The bus swung out onto the road, and he went back to trying to watch everything at once.

"It doesn't make any sense," said Eli. "Even if he could see them, there've never been any monsters on the bus."

Court immediately started looking for some wood to knock on, but it was already too late for that.

Halfway back, a backpack shot up into the air like it had been fired from a cannon, shedding red-penciled papers everywhere.

"What the heck is that?" cried Jeff, scrambling up until he was standing on his seat. The kids in the rows behind him started screaming, and suddenly half the bus was standing on the benches, holding the seat backs in front of them, frantically looking at the floor of the bus.

Then a round, brown thing that looked . . . remarkably like a balled-up Popple . . . came rolling up the main aisle of the bus.

"WAH!" shrieked Dwight, yanking the steering wheel and unleashing a new round of mayhem. Court spared a single glance at his eyes in the mirror and realized this was exactly what he'd been afraid of. He did it again, and the bus skewed wildly across the road until it was impossible to tell who was screaming at the monsters and who was screaming at impending bus-related doom. The Popple-ball bounced up in the air, uncurled, and landed on four clawed feet. It snarled.

It wasn't a rat, and wasn't a dog, but it was about the size of a pug. It had a ratlike tail and a mouth full of teeth, yellow eyes and woolly-looking fur. More of the critters were bumping their way up to the front over backpacks and Trapper Keepers. The first one leaned over and took a big bite out of the closest seat. It continued to growl while it chewed, making a real interesting WAHRAHWAHRAH sound—which Court might have appreciated if she'd been watching it on television and not from five feet away as the bus lurched back and forth.

"Dwight," said Scott, "you pull over on *that* side!"

He pointed.

"He can't hear you!" said Neha. "He's panicking!"

She was right. He was acting like he could drive away from the monsters, which was impossible because they were on the bus. Some of the yelling had resolved itself into cries of "What is that thing?" and "Hit it!" and "*You* hit it!"

"Dwight!" said Eli, pounding on the back of the seat in front of him to get Dwight's attention. "We need to evacuate the bus!"

The pug-Popple snarled at him. Court stood up and brandished her *Return of the Jedi* lunch box.

"The way Dwight's driving is the only reason they haven't eaten us yet!" said Scott. "Maybe we're better off if we keep moving."

"No way," said Eli. "This bus may as well be a can of tuna right now. We need to get everyone out of here!"

"Dwight!" Court said desperately. "Our folks are gonna call the bus garage again if you don't pull it together!"

He was probably too rattled to care, but it was the only thing Court could think of that might get through to him.

His eyes connected with hers in the mirror, and for an instant he seemed to remember he could lose his job. He slalomed toward the entrance to their neighborhood, losing control of the steering wheel in the process.

With a bang and a crunch, the bus slammed to a halt. Everyone was thrown forward.

There was a hiss of escaping steam, then a terrible silence.

"Everybody okay?" Court yelled as kids started moaning and moving around.

"Yeah," said Scott. His lip was split and he had blood on his teeth.

"He hit a light pole. He had an accident bus," babbled Neha. Court didn't correct her. At this point, "accident bus" seemed right on the nose. The bus must have been a real mess, too, because it was honking over and over as if the horn was broken.

Court realized she could see part of the bus's bumper blocking the door, pinning it shut.

"We can't get out the front," she said. "Come on."

Neha was the first to respond. She slid out of her seat, stepped over a backpack in the aisle, and started pulling the kid in front of her to his feet. It was Brandon. Other kids started clambering over the seats toward the back of the bus.

Then Court saw something that made her freeze.

Eli had fallen out of his seat during the crash. Now he was sitting in the aisle, very quietly, as the Popple monster snarled in his face.

"Help," whispered Eli.

Before Court could do anything, a book-filled red tote bag with a blue Smurf emblazoned on it came crashing down on the monster's head. It collapsed to the floor with a wheeze.

The tote-bag Jedi was Kelly.

"That worked way better than a Wiffle bat," she said, and Neha actually laughed.

Scott wiped his mouth on his sleeve. Court could smell the blood, and she was afraid the rotten little critters—*repugnant Popples*, she thought, because Mrs. Benton made them do Latin roots—could, too. They seemed woozy from the crash, but they were getting over it fast. She could hear them stirring and beginning to growl.

"Off the bus!" she shouted. "Somebody open the back door!"

Jeff, the Weed Whacker kid, was closest.

"We're not allowed," he said. "I'd get kicked off the bus for life."

"Seriously?" asked Court.

He looked over her shoulder at the yowling horde slowly creeping out from under the seats, then turned and started hauling on the bar.

There was a scuffle behind Court, and she swiveled to kick an oncoming Repuggle in the face, hard. That didn't stop it from biting her foot before it went flying. It hurt, so she knew it had gotten through her shoe, but there was no time to check her foot now.

The yowling rose to a fever pitch, and Court realized Dwight had not come with them. Their bus driver was about to get eaten.

Then he rose from the driver's seat, and as he turned Court saw what he had in his shaking hands: a fire extinguisher.

Official weapon of monster hunters everywhere, she thought. She laughed in spite of the pain in her foot. The nasty furballs were prowling closer, leaping from seat back to seat back, skulking up the aisle. With some help from Eli, Jeff was finally able to get the latch disengaged, and the back door swung open with a creak.

"That's so cool," Eli said. Scott turned to look at him in disbelief.

"What?" Eli asked. "Haven't you always wanted to do that?"

Scott started laughing in spite of himself. "You know," he said, "I have."

Eli laughed, too. Then he pointed.

"Go!" he yelled, and kids started jumping. Brandon was out first, followed by a dozen others, but some of the younger ones were too scared to jump. As Court got closer to the edge she realized it must look really high up if you were a little kid. She turned to fight, to give everyone more time to clear out.

Dwight's fire extinguisher started to whoosh. She knew he was trying to help, but he was driving the Repuggles right toward everyone else.

"Scott!" said Eli. "Help me!" Court could hear them bucket-brigading the little kids down to Brandon.

She slammed an evil Repuggle right in the face with her lunch box, sending a prayer of thanks that Amy had packed Campbell's soup today. Court was defending the aisle, but the Repuggles could still get under the seats, and even though half the kids had abandoned their stuff when they ran, the nasty little monsters were still making it through the gaps.

Neha climbed over the seat back beside Court, with the crowbar that normally hung on the bus wall, the one they weren't allowed to touch, in her hands. She knelt on the seat and watched the gap in front of it intently. Court saw a flash of movement three seats up.

"Now!" Court said, and Neha slammed the crowbar down. A Repuggle squealed.

With Dwight at one end and them at the other, they held the Repuggles at bay until everyone else was off the bus. Dwight ran out of foam and whacked the last one with the butt end of his fire extinguisher.

"Yeah!" Court hollered. "Awesome, Dwight!"

He joined them at the back of the bus, stepping over an unconscious Repuggle in the aisle.

"After you," he said.

Court and Neha jumped down, with Dwight right behind them, his ponytail flying in the wind.

35

You Wrote That?

Eli knew what kids were supposed to do when there was something wrong with the bus: line up somewhere out of the way.

Today, it wasn't happening.

All around the "accident bus," kids were charging into battle. Kelly ran past, swinging her Smurf tote bag at a fleeing Repuggle. Adriana, who played soccer, was delivering a series of pretty spectacular kicks to another. Other kids were abandoning the scene altogether; some were fleeing for home, but most were chasing down Repuggles with fire in their eyes and school supplies brandished above their heads.

"Hey, come back!" said Dwight in alarm. "Stay with the bus!"

"I think that ship has sailed," said Court as Eli shouldered past her to give Dwight's midsection a solid shove.

"I can't believe you!" he shouted.

"Hey, what the heck did I do?" asked Dwight.

"Uh, you crashed the bus?" asked Neha in disbelief.

"You stole my story!" said Eli.

A Repuggle who hadn't gotten the memo about losing leaped out of a bus window with a snarl. Neha used the crowbar and her best tennis swing to send it flying.

"How do you know he took it?" she asked.

"Because these monsters were in it," he said. "I called them Pack Rats."

"I call 'em Repuggles," said Court.

Eli grudgingly admitted to himself that he liked Court's name better.

"Man, you wrote that?" Dwight asked over the honking of the bus horn.

"Yeah, and I've been tearing my house apart for a week looking for it so I could burn it!"

"Dude, I'm sorry," Dwight said. "When I found it I checked for a name. I didn't expect it to be a story. I don't do a lot of reading, but I couldn't put that thing down."

Dwight wasn't making it easy to stay angry. Eli tried and failed to stop himself from taking the bait.

"So . . . you liked it?"

"Naw, man, it scared the crud outta me. I've been sleeping with the lights on. I have to leave my bathroom shower curtain open. The curtains over my sliding-glass door are coming down and I don't wanna go over there and fix 'em because something's gonna be out there looking in at me."

It took Eli a minute to answer. He was too busy checking things off his mental list of life goals. Then he remembered he was mad.

"I don't care!" he lied. "I'm sick of you acting like a kid all the time. We're supposed to be the kids!"

"I'm sorry, man. I'll give it back!" said Dwight, sounding more like a kid than ever.

"That's not going to fix it!" Eli began, then shrugged. "Whatever. Do what you want, Dwight."

"Why did you say that?" asked Court. "He can bring it tomorrow."

"He's not going to be here tomorrow," said Scott.

"He is extremely fired," Neha agreed.

Eli nodded. He knew they were right. No one would let Dwight drive a bus now. Which stank, even if Eli was mad at him. Dwight wasn't perfect, but he was the best bus driver they'd ever had, and the whole school knew it.

"It would be too late anyway," said Eli. "The monsters attacked the bus in broad daylight. If we don't do something, we might not be here tomorrow, either."

"Then we'd better get ready to roll," said Court.

"I need to check on Lisa," Eli said. "Just to be on the safe side. My momma had to work, so she left her with Mrs. Harvey."

"That poor kid," said Court.

Eli started walking away, and Court, Neha, and Scott followed. Dwight stood, alone and forlorn, in front of the smashed-up bus. A wounded Repuggle fell out of the back with a squeak.

"You guys can't leave! Where are you going?"

"We're going to kill the Howler," said Eli.

"That big dude in the story? You can't do that!"

Eli looked at his friends. They were dirty, bloody, and ready. Neha still had the crowbar in one hand.

"Somebody has to," said Eli, "and I know one thing: it's not you."

They left Dwight where he was and walked toward Mrs. Harvey's as dark clouds swirled overhead.

▲ ▼ ▲

"I haven't seen her," said Mrs. Harvey as she stubbed out a cigarette in a dirty green ashtray. Her refrigerator was covered with those state-shaped magnets, the kind people bought on vacation, but it was hard to believe she'd ever gone anywhere, because any kid she'd babysat could tell you she spent most of her time sitting in the same kitchen chair, clipping coupons.

Which was why Lisa had been able to give her the slip right before a tornado. Their momma couldn't claim that Mrs. Harvey was more reliable than Eli when she'd lost Lisa, too, but right now that didn't make him feel any better. The monsters were getting bolder and bolder, and now Lisa was who knew where.

"My momma left Lisa for you to look after!"

"And I did. She went out back to play."

"She's not out there now. I checked."

"Then she must have left the yard. Go ask the neighbor kids. It's almost time for dinner anyway."

It was nowhere near the Goodmans' normal dinnertime, but Mrs. Harvey ate early. She scooted back her chrome-and-vinyl chair and shuffled over to the stove. Eli already knew what was coming, and he shuddered. She took one of those precooked chicken breasts out of the oven, the kind with the orange powdered barbeque seasoning, and set it on the stove next to a pot of what appeared to be cream of mushroom soup.

Right there was the reason Eli, Lisa, and the Castle kids had moved heaven and earth to get permission to watch themselves. Cigarette smoke had wrecked Mrs. Harvey's taste buds, or that was the local kids' theory. There was no escaping the disgusting, coupon-motivated messes she fed her charges. Some might argue the monsters were less dangerous.

"If she comes back, keep her inside!" he said. "There's a storm coming!"

"Well, you should just stay here and wait for her, then," reasoned Mrs. Harvey, but the screen door banged behind a departing

Eli before she finished her sentence. He made a beeline for home, but none of the Creeps had seen Lisa. He met his friends in the middle of the street.

"She's not at the Guptas'," said Court as she and Scott reached him.

"I checked the Shotwells'," said Neha, panting from running up and down the steep hill of Eddie's driveway.

They all looked toward the rough fields at the end of the street.

"I get it if you want to stay here," Eli said. "But I have to go look for her."

"Do you even read your own stuff?" asked Neha. "Splitting up is how people—" She stopped as she realized that anything she said about Eli right now could just as easily be true of Lisa.

Scott spoke up. "Look, no place is really safe right now, is it? So going with you isn't more dangerous than anything else we could do."

"Yeah, but we're not ready to fight off monsters," Eli said with a glance at the swirling clouds overhead. "We need supplies and stuff."

"I can grab a few things at my house," said Scott. "I'll get Schmooze, too. You find Lisa, and we'll meet you."

"Wait a second," said Eli. He jogged over and let himself into his garage. He came back with one of Lisa's homemade weapons, the one she called the Whacker! He handed it to Scott.

"Thanks," said Scott, then took off.

Eli, Court, and Neha headed into the scrubby field at the end of the street, and they hadn't looked long when they found a scene that made Eli's heart sink.

Lisa had put up a fight. For three feet the plants along the path were bent or broken, and Eli found her latest favorite weapon, a rope with a stone tied to each end, tangled in goldenrod. Then Neha yelled for him and Court. She'd found the Crackler slumped under a smoldering bush.

"What happened?" Neha asked, putting a hand on the Crackler's shoulder and trying to stay away from his head, which had a lump where someone had hit him.

"The big one, the Howler, it took Lisa. I tried to stop him. Burned it good. But it got her anyway. Snuffed me out in the dirt and gave me a message for you. Said this is what to expect when you toy with monsters, and if you want her, come get her."

The worst part about the trap was how painfully obvious it was. The Howler didn't have to be sneaky. He could walk right up and take Eli's little sister away. All the times Eli's momma had gotten mad at him for getting distracted, this was what she'd been scared of: her baby vanishing. Now it was happening, and Eli thought he might vomit.

"Court," said Neha suddenly, "where are you going?"

Eli looked up to see his usually unflappable freckled friend looking rattled and pale.

"I have to get home. Joshie and Amy are there."

"We can't keep splitting up, not now that we know the Howler's taking people," said Neha. "We'll go with you!"

Eli rose and stepped between them.

"No way," he said. "I don't have time for that. I have to go after Lisa *now*."

"Go where?"

Eli was a storyteller. He knew where the Howler would be.

They'd been planning to confront the Howler on their own terms, but the Howler had outflanked them. They were going to have to do this tonight.

"I'm going," said Court, "but I'll come find you, I swear I will."

She ran toward home.

Eli began searching the bushes as Neha crouched and made eye contact with the Crackler.

"I need you to go to my house and rally all the Creeps. If you find Redwing, send her to scout around the barn, but tell her to be careful."

The Crackler wobbled to his feet. Color returned to his face. The color was fire-engine red, but that was pretty normal for the Crackler.

"Right!" he said, spitting sparks. "I'm on my way."

He lit out for Neha's.

Eli was still rummaging along the trail.

"What are you doing?" asked Neha.

He found what he was looking for and held it up.

"Lisa's slingshot," he said. "We're going to need it."

He turned to look at Neha.

"You could have gone home yourself," he said. "Or gone with Court."

Neha tucked her hair behind her ears.

"I guess you could say we started this," she said. "You with your stories, and me with my art. It seems like we should finish it."

"Yeah," he said. "That sounds right to me."

Overhead, the sky was taking on a greenish tinge. A rustle on the path made them both look up. It was Hairstack, followed by the other Creeps from Eli's house. Hairstack had taken both of Eli's belts and buckled them into one continuous loop, which he wore like a beauty pageant sash across his chest.

"Are you . . . dressed up like Chewbacca?" Eli asked.

"No. Shut up," said Hairstack.

Eli decided not to argue. It wasn't wise to upset a Wookiee.

"Where are you going?" Hairstack asked.

"To fight the Howler and save Lisa," said Eli.

"Are we her only hope?" asked Hairstack.

Eli nodded grimly. "You in?" he asked the Creeps. "It's going to be rough."

Hairstack cracked his knuckles.

"Never tell me the odds," he said.

36

Monster Convention

By the time Court was a block from her house, she knew she'd been right to worry. She could hear the ruckus already. She sprinted the rest of the way, then followed the noise to the backyard.

The Creeps didn't have the luxury of hiding anymore. The Spider Plant was in plain view in the lights of the pool. It was looming over the water, chucking monsters every which way. A school of cootie catchers whirled around the yak beast. Fur was flying as the paper fish delivered a thousand paper cuts. A squat, hairy monster had something black and tentacled stuck to the top of its head, and it was flailing, trying to get it off. Court didn't understand what the tentacle thing was at first. Then it brandished a toothbrush and shoved it up the monster's nose. The Scrubbler!

That was when Court heard a sound that shook her up. It was Joshie.

"Court?" he called. "What should I do?"

The sliding-glass door was wide open, and he was looking out through the screen. Nearby, monsters that weren't getting sling-shotted by Court's giant arachnid pal took note. A few licked their lips. Half a dozen started moseying toward the door.

Court could try to lead them away, but there was no guarantee they'd all follow her.

Amy came to the back door with a broom in her hand.

"What is it, Joshie, a raccoon?" she said. "I'll go take care of it."

Ian hollered an offer of help from the kitchen.

"Not my first rodeo, hon," Amy called back. "That raccoon won't know what hit it."

That tore it. Court grabbed a baseball bat that was lying in the grass and ran for the back door. She burst through the metal gate of the pool fence, whapping a Repuggle out of her way. A five-foot-long salamander with an arrow-shaped head came at her, mouth agape, and she knew a wooden bat was not going to get the job done.

She tore the lid off a bucket of chlorine tablets they kept next to the house, then chucked the whole darn thing at the oncoming amphibian. The bucket landed on its side, sliding, and tablets rushed out of it and into the salamander's mouth.

Court had never seen anything foam up so fast, and she'd once exploded a can of Scrubbing Bubbles. One more thing to be mad at the monsters about: she didn't have time to stay and watch. Instead she waded into the mob at her back door, bat-first.

Between Court whacking everything in sight and the Spider Plant flinging anything she missed, they were able to convince the monsters that were prowling toward her family that they might want to at least back up a bit.

"Stay in!" she shouted to Amy and Joshie, putting her face right up to the screen. "Lock the slider!"

Zeb, Luna, and Archie pressed their noses against the other side, their wings fluttering as they tried to figure out how to get outside.

"Stick with my family," she told them. No way was she taking them out in a storm to fight the Howler. "Bite anything that gets in."

"What are you hitting?" asked Amy, her eyebrows up, eyes frowning. "I heard the bat hit something."

No reason she should start lying now.

"There's a monster convention going on out here," said Court just as the Spider Plant dropped a monster in the pool from about ten feet up. It belly flopped. Amy gasped as she saw the splash. The poisoned salamander, desperate to rinse out its mouth, threw itself in after its buddy. It foamed its way to the bottom.

"Daddy's gonna need to check the pool chemistry," Court told Amy.

"Have you been telling the truth all this time?" Amy asked, her voice shrill.

The monster with the Scrubbler on its head came running at Court, probably because the Scrubbler was covering its eyes. She body slammed him so he wouldn't smash through the screen. The Scrubbler leaped squishily to her shoulder as its victim tripped and ended up in the pool with the others.

"I got it handled," Court said, hoping that was true. "Joshie, you keep an eye out. Y'all stay inside and lock up the house, okay? I'll be back before Mama and Daddy get home."

"I'm not leaving you alone out there!" Amy said.

The clouds chose that minute to dump every drop of rain they'd been holding. The Spider Plant made a complaining little chattering noise and leaned down over Court's shoulder. She reached up to pat the side of its head.

Amy's eyes went wide. Court frowned; then it hit her. Amy couldn't see the Spider Plant, but she could see the rain *on* the Spider Plant, which was almost as good.

"I'm not as alone as I seem," Court said.

Amy nodded. "Okay," she said.

She slid the door shut so fast Court almost forget it was open. Joshie was trying to get closer to the door so he could gawk at some of the monster-vs.-Creep battles raging on the patio, but Amy shoved him back and pulled the drapes.

Good.

Court turned away, only to find an enormous, upside-down arachnid head in her way. She lowered her bat.

"You ready?" she asked.

The Spider Plant nodded.

"Let's do this."

They fought their way back around to the garage, where Court used the keypad to put the door down from the outside. She heard the deadbolt clack on the door to the laundry room as she was doing it, and she crossed her fingers that no monsters were lurking in the garage.

She turned to go for her bike, which she'd left outside the day before, and that was when she hit a serious snag.

The rear tire was half-gone. The other half was being eaten by a trio of manta-bats.

She looked toward the backyard to see a cluster of nightmares watching her with hungry, amused expressions.

Somewhere nearby, Court heard Mixface's play button click.

"Hey, all you kids out there in Radioland! It's time to Beat It!" he said.

Court wasn't sure what to make of her emotions, which were half pride at diverting the monsters' attention from her siblings, and half horror that she'd walked right into their clutches. Hopefully the monsters couldn't see her hands shaking. Still, she was no shrinking violet.

"Where's Eli's sister?" she demanded. She was expecting bared teeth, even a snarl. Instead, one of the monsters spoke.

"She's dangling from the tentacles of a giant squid like the bait she is. But we don't need bait to catch you, do we?"

Ugly laughter rose from the assembled horde.

She turned to run, but some of the monsters had circled around behind the Spider Plant while she was distracted. The Spider Plant drew its legs in closer to her, making a protective cage, and circled. It let out a high-pitched squeal she'd never heard it make before. Court could see what was going to happen before she moved. The Spider Plant would pick her up if it could, but there were too many of them. It couldn't fight them all off before they dragged it down.

"You gotta leave me," she said, trying to get out of the cage of its legs, but it planted a foot in her chest and shoved her back like it was saying *Not a chance.*

Repuggles dashed forward and went after three of its legs. Court slammed one with her bat, then raised it to go after another as the Spider Plant tried desperately to shake the rat-dogs off.

Then a neigh rang out behind them, and a short, beaked monster went flying by. Court whipped around in time to see the Rustlehorse plant her back hooves in the next monster's chest.

Court whacked another Repuggle, then made a run for it. The Scrubbler's short, dripping victim was between her and freedom, but she didn't let that stop her. She jumped as high as she could, planting one sneaker smack on its head, then pushing off. She landed on her belly across the Rustlehorse's back. Half a dozen sets of claws reached for her, and she felt at least one snag in her jeans, but the Spider Plant had freed itself and came plunging into the middle of the crowd, flinging monsters every which way. She dropped the bat and barely got her butt where it was supposed to be before the Rustlehorse's muscles shifted beneath her and the mare leaped forward. They ran toward the storm, toward their friends, with the Spider Plant striding alongside and over them, and a pack of monsters at their heels.

37

Here They All Come

Eli's perspective on monsters was very different now that he was outside in the dark instead of inside behind his typewriter. His writer brain knew exactly when the monsters should attack: the moment he freed his sister and tried to make a run for it. His scared-kid brain, on the other hand, couldn't stop jumping at shadows.

Alongside Eli and Neha (and Scott, who'd met them at the fence) tiptoed an assortment of Creeps from Eli's and Neha's houses—and Schmooze, who didn't tiptoe, but slimed. Eli had temporarily slapped an old rubber Frankenstein mask on Zoop, because she tended to flash with no warning when she was scared. The mask might dim her light enough to prevent her from being a beacon for every monster around. Frog Boy, Sleekit, Swiz, the Treebots . . . almost every Creep from their houses was there, wielding weapons they'd brought with them from Forest Creeks or countermeasures they'd built since. Sleekit, as always, prowled at Neha's side.

Everything was quiet but the wind and the rain. Eli looked everywhere at once, straining his senses for any sign of Lisa, but if she was nearby, she was silent. Then, in the darkness, a slow rumble began to build. It was getting closer. And he didn't think it was the storm.

Eli's feet wanted to run, but he knew they'd never be safe if they did. And over his dead body was he leaving without Lisa. It hurt thinking about her. She was surely scared half to death.

He wasn't prepared for her to come riding in on a giant squid monster, brandishing a lacrosse stick and shouting at the top of her lungs. It was clearly not the squid's idea.

"I don't know who you think you're messing with, but you picked on the wrong girl! You take me to my brother or so help me I'm gonna find out if cutting a worm in half really makes two worms! You think I'm scared? I got no reason to be scared. Nobody's scared of worms! Now, whoa!"

It was a different squid thing than the one from Showplace Pizza. This one didn't have a shell to hide in, so it was just running, which wasn't working. It had way more legs than anything needed, so it was making enough galloping noises to sound like every horse in Tulsa was headed their way. Eli could have told it there was no getting away from Lisa once she was on your back.

Lisa whipped a field hockey stick out of a gym bag slung across her shoulders and hooked the crook around a tentacle, reining the creature to a halt.

"I said *whoa*, mister!"

They looked up at her, slack-jawed.

"You might want to do something, because here they all come," she said. "Some of them might be chasing me, actually."

Uh-oh.

Lisa wheeled her squid mount around to face the way she'd come.

Eli heard something reminiscent of the squid's squishy galloping again. But this was more ominous, and more confusing. There was the thud of hooves, the squish of not-hooves, and a slowly building cacophony of squeals, burbles, and growls. What he wanted more than anything was to grab Lisa and get her out of here, but it didn't matter. There wasn't time.

"Are we surrounded?" Neha asked, looking at him.

He couldn't answer that. He could only say the thing that was bothering him most.

"Where the heck is Court?"

A shrill neigh and the pounding of hooves rose above the clamor of the monsters, and Court came riding in astride the Rustlehorse, with the Spider Plant and the Creeps from her house racing behind her. A cheer rose from the rest of the Creeps.

Then the Howler appeared with a bound.

No creature was scarier than the Howler. It wasn't just that it was toothy, though it was. It wasn't that it was murderous, though it was that, too. It was the glint of humor in its eye that told Eli it knew exactly how scary it was. Every writer, Eli knew, hoped to pen characters that leaped off the page and took on a life of their own. Eli had succeeded beyond his wildest dreams—and most kids' worst nightmares.

In short, he'd created a monster.

The Rustlehorse reared and plunged. As the Howler rounded in front of its army, Court backed the Rustlehorse toward the line of Creeps.

"Sorry I'm late," said Court.

Eli never took his eyes off the Howler. "Joshie and Amy okay?"

"Yeah," she said. "Sorry. I had to be sure."

"I'm just glad you're here now. Miranda was right. We need our action hero."

Out of the corner of his eye, Eli saw Court sit up straighter on the Rustlehorse's back. On her other side, Scott pulled a golf club out of the bag he and Schmooze had brought, then passed it up to her. Swiz handed her a small bag. She opened it, then tilted it to show Eli the glowing orange spheres inside.

"What are those, Swiz?" Eli asked.

"Just some little doodads I whipped up," he said. "I call 'em Orange Sherbet Blasts. Throw 'em and steer clear of where they hit."

Court put the bag in her jacket pocket for easy access.

The Howler pawed at the ground. The line of monsters snorted, rippled, oozed, and prepared to charge.

Next to Eli, Frog Boy adjusted a metal hat he'd made. Eli didn't know what it was for, but it looked complicated. All around them, Creeps brandished weapons and bared their teeth. Eli never would have guessed he'd end up battling his own monsters to save creatures that had sprung from someone else's imagination, but he knew he was on the right side.

He had Lisa's slingshot in his pocket, his dad's old metal baseball bat in his hands, and one final trick up his sleeve. He was as ready as he was going to get.

Problem was, he'd never really thought about how to start a battle before. The Howler seemed to sense his discomfort. It was looking right at him, smiling faintly.

"Well?" it said.

Frog Boy's hat whizzed to life. As its parts began to whirl, Eli realized that Frog Boy had recreated Blatt's drill mouth. Then Hairstack let out a truly spectacular Wookiee yell and ran at the monsters. Eli was scared to death, but he couldn't leave Hairstack out there alone, so he ran behind him, and on all sides of him he could feel others doing the same.

Warring with monsters was not as organized as it seemed in movies and books. Mostly Eli swung his bat and hoped he hit the monsters someplace personal. The noises he heard suggested he was succeeding, as did the fact that he was still alive.

Frog Boy's hat made a woodchipper noise, and Eli couldn't be sure, but he thought Neha might have actually yelled "Thwack!" as she slammed the yak beast with her crowbar. Farther off, Court was hurling Swiz's Sherbet Blasts into the melee, and the orange flares of light and howls of pain were grimly satisfying.

But there were definitely more monsters than Creeps, and slowly, just as they had been when the monsters attacked Forest Creeks, Eli, his friends, and the Creeps were being overwhelmed.

Then something happened that surprised everyone on both sides.

At the opposite side of the field, behind the monsters' front line, a set of headlights flicked on.

Both sides stirred with confusion as they tried to see what the commotion was. But before any of them could do anything, power chords every kid on bus thirty-five knew by heart started blasting at top volume.

Honking, lights flashing, a yellow school bus came blasting through the monster army. The safety bar attached to what was left of the front bumper had become an offensive weapon. It swept a path in front of it, knocking monsters down left and right on the muddy grass. The radio blared:

"It's the eye of the tiger, it's the thrill of the fight . . ."

Through the open side window, Eli could hear Dwight shouting along with the music, his ponytail blowing in the wind.

The Creep army roared.

The Rustlehorse plunged through the monsters, Court clinging to his back, the Spider Plant stalking in his wake. The Spider Plant was dumping monsters into the cow pond, which Lisa and the squid were wading across. Tentacles flailed and monsters howled.

Eli shouted a warning as the Howler rushed Court from the side, terrifyingly fast. The Rustlehorse shied away just in time, but Court still cried out as the tips of the Howler's claws grazed her jeans, slicing the fabric—and her skin, too, Eli worried. Orange balls spilled from her hand as she reached for her leg, and Eli ran to scoop one up before it rolled away into the grass.

He whipped it right at the Howler just as hard as he could. The results were better than anything he could have hoped for. The orange ball stuck to the Howler like glue.

Then it exploded.

The Howler's agonized groan was deafening. The smell of burning fur rose as the Howler rolled on the ground to put out the flames. There was a sudden mad rush from both sides.

Court rallied, and the Rustlehorse stampeded through the middle of the scrum. Court was shouting, directing troops, whipping more exploding fireballs into the crowd, and generally making the monsters sorry she'd ever existed.

Creatures were hanging on to the side of the bus, but they weren't the Howler's minions. Hairstack and a crew of other Creeps were hitching a ride, protecting the bus while also using it to propel themselves through the crowd, fists first. The bus was mowing swaths through the battling creatures.

Above it all, lightning flashed and thunder boomed. When Eli looked up, he saw Redwing fly across the sky and punch a monster smack in the face.

Thudding footsteps behind him made Eli spin around. The Interloper was headed his way, drooling in its eagerness to devour him. Eli yanked Lisa's slingshot from his pocket. He didn't have Lisa's pouch of ball bearings, but he'd grabbed a handful of rocks from one of the street drains they'd passed on their way to the pasture. He loaded it and fired, hitting the Interloper right between the eyes.

The Interloper shook his head and kept coming, which was when Eli remembered that things with antlers were designed with thick skulls so they could head-butt people. He was scrambling out of the way when the bus roared by, flattening the Interloper in the mud.

"Hey!" Eli heard Dwight yell out the bus window. "You guys see that? I think I hit a deer!"

Lisa had set herself up in the cow pond like she was a spider at the center of its web. Her squid mount snatched nearby monsters at her direction, flinging them into the treetops or the wire fence. Eli could hear her imperious little voice shouting, and sometimes laughing, too.

"See? That's what you get when you mess with a *squid rider*!"

Then a wail began to rise over the sounds of the battle. At first, Eli thought someone was injured, but then Court hauled back on the Rustlehorse's mane and turned to shoot him a panicked look across the sea of monsters and Creeps.

She pointed at the sky.

The wailing wasn't coming from anything alive.

All over Tulsa, tornado sirens were blaring a warning.

38

Surprise!

Neha had known the storm was coming, but that hadn't prepared her for the scream of tornado sirens. She turned in a circle, bashing any monster that moved with her crowbar, looking for some solution that would allow her and her friends to take cover without being eaten.

Scott was frighteningly far away. He and Schmooze were defending themselves against half a dozen monsters, which had obviously recognized their old buddy and were taking its defection badly. She could see big globs of Schmooze flying through the air as Scott fought to defend it. She headed that way at a run.

Then she saw the Spider Plant and stopped in her tracks.

The leafy arachnid's fangs were poised, dripping with venom, over the Howler's neck.

Yes, thought Neha. *All of this could be over.*

But the Spider Plant was holding back because the Howler had the Rustlehorse by the throat.

Court had been thrown in the struggle. She was muddy and

scraped up, but as Neha watched she rose gingerly to her feet. She had one of Swiz's fireballs ready to throw, but if she let fly, the Rustlehorse could go up like tinder. The wind whirled and screamed overhead, and the sirens went on and on. Monsters and Creeps alike stilled as they turned to see the outcome of the standoff.

"Neha," said a small voice at her ankle.

It was a green Snorkelchort, one of the many unfamiliar small ones she'd seen since the Creeps evacuated Forest Creeks.

"Hush," she said. "Look."

It tugged her jeans impatiently. She glanced down.

"What is it?" she asked.

"Surprise!" it said.

Through the mud and grass, in a rainbow wave, snorkels erupted from beneath the soil. A low hum emanated from the hundreds of Snorkelchorts who'd been hiding beneath their feet. Instantly, the soil was quicksand. It took the monsters by surprise, but the Creeps, who had a Snorkelchort Safety Committee for a reason, knew what to do. They flew, fled, and even climbed the monsters to get out of the way as the Howler's minions were sucked down into the ground.

The Rustlehorse, on the other hand, was carefully borne aloft on a cushion of air from the pool of Snorkelchorts directly underneath her. The rescue Chorts were much lighter than the monsters, and they paddled to a spot a safe distance from gnashing teeth and flexing claws, wafting the Rustlehorse with them.

The Howler's cohort slimed, strained, scrambled, and pulled, but it didn't do them any good. As suddenly as the humming began it ended, leaving them trapped in the ground up to their necks—or the closest equivalent.

The snorkels vanished back into the earth as suddenly as Whac-A-Moles.

Neha approached the Howler, and she could see her friends doing the same. She scowled at it as it struggled and raged.

In the cow pond, Lisa's squid steed had fared better than the other monsters, but a few of its tentacles had gotten mired in shallow areas. Behind her, Neha could hear Lisa soothing it.

"Think of it this way: it's like the ocean, only it's not moving."

"Howler," said Eli. It looked away from Neha to give Eli its most murderous glare.

"You're not going anywhere," said Eli. "So we might as well sort this out like reasonable people. We want a truce."

Even trapped in the mud with the Spider Plant safely stalking back toward it across the once-again-solid earth, the Howler laughed. Neha might have admired its courage if it hadn't wanted to hurt everything she loved.

"You realize we could kill you right now," said Eli.

"You could try," snarled the Howler.

"Or we could work this out."

"Negotiation is for the weak. Someone has to win," said the Howler. Around them, other monsters growled or hooted agreement.

"No. We can compromise," said Neha.

There was a loud, confused grumble.

"Shhhh!" she said, and to her surprise, they did. "This way, everybody gets something they want."

The Howler grinned. "Yes. A compromise. You surrender, and we will eat these creatures."

"That's you getting exactly what you want," Court said.

"We could eat you, too," said the Howler. It smiled toothily at Court. She tossed a Sherbet Blast idly from hand to hand, and it was clear from its sulky expression that it got the point.

"I had something else in mind," said Eli. "You stay out of Forest Creeks, and out of our neighborhood, too."

"That's not a compromise, either," grumbled the Howler.

Up close, the Howler's head was almost as tall as Neha. She stayed away from its teeth but looked it right in the eye.

"Forest Creeks is mine. You were gate-crashing from the start."

"We weren't the first," he argued, looking defiantly around at the Creeps. He wasn't wrong, but Neha thought he'd missed the point.

"The others introduced themselves and contributed to the community," said Neha.

"We contributed . . . mayhem," said a prickly little creature with a giggle.

"Exactly," Neha agreed.

"We have to eat," said the Howler. Its tone was silky, as if he were patient and reasonable and they simply needed reminding.

"That's what monsters do," said Eli. "No one knows that better than me. But there still need to be rules. If you can't be good, you at least have to be fair."

"Everyone needs to spread out," said Neha firmly.

They all waited while the Howler thought about this.

"Agreed," it said at last, amid cries of protest from its minions. "We won't eat anyone inside the boundaries of Forest Creeks."

Some of the shouting stopped, for obvious reasons. Neha saw Court roll her eyes. Fortunately, the kids were on the same page.

"What you meant to say is you won't hunt in Forest Creeks. Or Walnut Hills," said Eli.

The Howler growled and looked away.

"Because the way you said that implied you could catch prey in our neighborhoods as long as you took it somewhere else to actually eat it. Maybe you didn't realize that."

"Now that you mention it, I can see how that would be confusing," said the Howler.

"So we have an agreement," said Eli.

"We do," said the Howler.

Neha stomped her foot to signal the Chorts. The kids and Creeps hoisted their weapons to the ready and backed away from the Howler. The snorkels popped up a second time, and a milder humming commenced, one that turned the earth to a thicker mud that could be climbed out of. When the monsters had mostly hauled themselves up, the Snorkelchorts popped out of the ground like reverse turnips, and the earth snapped solid.

Immediately, the Howler turned, snatched a wide-eyed purple Chort, and tossed it into its mouth. There was a tiny squeal of surprise, then a pop.

The entire crowd froze.

"Oh," said the Howler, looking at them with a vicious grin. "Did you mean starting now?"

Every Creep bristled, snarled, and took an involuntary step forward. Dwight, whose bus was stuck in mud up past its hubcaps, leaned on the horn.

"Not cool, man!" he yelled out the window, then pulled his head in quickly when some of the monsters noticed. Other monsters were looking around at the Chorts like they were shopping at a corner store. The Chorts piped with fear, then began to hum, and it occurred to Neha to wonder exactly how deep their quicksand could get if they panicked.

In the instant before everything descended into complete chaos, a single voice rang out, silencing the crowd.

"I knew you'd do that," said Eli.

The Howler laughed.

"How could you know?"

Eli didn't answer directly. Instead, he said, "It's a shame. There was a time when you were the best thing I'd ever written."

A murmur began to rise from the assembled crowd of monsters, and the Howler took a hard look at Eli.

"Who are you?" he asked, prowling frighteningly close.

"I'm the Author," said Eli.

Whispers rushed through the assembled monsters like wildfire. The Howler twitched, as if it had the gut instinct to kill Eli for even saying such a thing.

It was possible Eli was quaking in his Adidas, but from where Neha was standing, he looked unshakable.

"I know something else, too. Something you don't know."

"What's that?" The Howler's jaw lolled as he prowled nearer, so close that Eli had to be able to feel the warmth of his creation's breath on his face.

Neha readied her crowbar as if she was up to bat. Court brandished another fireball. Lisa's squid steed reared, and the Spider Plant chattered a warning.

But before any of them had time to act, something shadowy and sinuous slipped between them and stopped behind Eli, its enormous, shaggy head looming over his shoulder. Neha didn't have to look directly at it to know why the Howler's eyes were suddenly as big as dinner plates, or to be certain of the triumph on Eli's face.

"There's a remake."

39

Fouler

It was bigger. It was badder. And this time around, Eli had resolved their little "conflicting worldview" problem.

"What sort of beast are you?" demanded the original Howler.

A hot drop of drool landed on the shoulder of Eli's T-shirt as the remake smiled without speaking. Eli answered for his newest creation.

"I call this one Fouler."

It leaped over Eli, light as a shadow, and attacked.

There was pandemonium as a rainbow wave of Snorkelchorts fled the area. Right behind them came the rest of the Creeps, and some of the monsters, too. The majority ended up clinging to the trees, including Lisa's squid steed, which obligingly held her up so she could get a better view.

"Lisa, move!" Eli hissed. "I can't see!"

Lisa rolled her eyes at him, but she waved a lazy hand at the squid, which in turn rolled the enormous yellow eye facing Eli as it lifted her out of the way.

Below, the remaining monsters had formed a silent, ominous ring around the battle raging by the cow pond. Lightning flashed as the Howler and Fouler slashed and tore at each other.

Monsters scattered as Fouler hurled the Howler across the circle. The Howler slammed into a tree trunk so hard Eli heard the crack and saw the wood split. A few Creeps fell out of the branches and fled a second time. Then the Howler regained its footing and sprang. Monsters cheered, roared, and laughed as the battle raged. The wind and the sirens rose to a scream, as if there were a comet coming their way instead of a tornado.

"Eli!" cried Neha, and pointed.

Eli glanced quickly upward, and another flash of lightning illuminated something even scarier than the Howler: the storm clouds had gone from rolling past to rotating slowly overhead.

Everyone in Eli's tree screamed as the battling monsters crashed into the trunk.

"Hold on!" Eli shouted, and he was weirdly reassured to see the squid steed tighten its grip on his sister.

The branch he was on creaked and groaned, but it held, and Fouler drove the Howler back across the field, slashing at him with wickedly sharp claws that could penetrate even the Howler's matted, shaggy pelt. Fouler was taking damage, too, but even at this distance Eli could tell the Howler was limping on its right front leg. For a moment he felt terrible. The fact that the Howler was a monster didn't stop it from being amazing. Had Eli really imagined it only to let it be destroyed?

As Eli watched, the Howler backed right through the circle of monsters to avoid Fouler—and ducked behind a warthoglike creature Eli had once invented because he needed it to trample somebody in an alley. The Howler shoved it right into Fouler's oncoming claws, and it squealed in agony as it took the attack meant for him.

The squid steed covered Lisa's eyes with the tip of one tentacle, though she tried to push it away.

Any sympathy Eli had left vanished.

The warthog creature collapsed in the mud, and Fouler, Eli's first experiment in lawful evil, was a study in fury. It backed up two steps to give itself enough room, then soared forward, over the unfortunate victim's spasming body, straight for the Howler. The monsters flanking them spun to face the Howler, their teeth and claws bared so they wouldn't be its next shield. There was no time for the Howler to do anything, not even turn tail and flee.

Fouler landed like a lightning strike, with the same accompanying crack, and Eli knew the Howler was finished. Even from his perch, he could see glimpses of Fouler's jaw working as it worried at the Howler's throat. When it stepped back the Howler was still alive, but not for long. It made an effort to rise, then collapsed. Fouler, bloody and victorious, looked around at the assembled monsters, then turned its gaze to Eli. It opened its bloody jaws to speak.

"The treaty will stand." It looked around at its cohort, daring them to disagree.

No one did.

Fouler led the monsters away. They vanished in the darkness.

Eli was frozen for a long minute, staring at the Howler's carcass on the ground, realizing it wasn't the only one. Part of him still thought this wasn't over.

Lisa's squid steed lifted him down from the tree, and he gingerly stepped out into the open. Everything was quiet. Beside him, a blur of red, gold, and black plexed as Redwing bore Neha safely to the ground. Court jumped down, landing with a squelch in the mud. Her jeans were bloody where the Howler had grazed her, but Eli was relieved to see she wasn't limping. They looked at one another.

"You think we're good?" he asked Court.

"I'm cautiously optimistic," she said.

"What about the tornado?" asked Neha.

Lightning flashed, and they scanned the sky for a funnel.

"Do you see anything?" asked Eli.

"No," said Court, shaking her head.

As if they'd gotten tired and were yawning, the tornado sirens wound to a stop. In the quiet that followed, the three of them slowly began to grin.

"Well," said Eli. "All right!"

Court punched his shoulder, and he and Neha high-fived.

A large tentacle set Lisa down beside him.

"That was a pretty good story!" she told him.

He laughed and hugged her, to what was obviously her total disgust. Lisa squirmed out of his arms.

"Not in front of the squid!" she hissed.

Meanwhile, Court had started counting heads. She paused.

"Hey," she said, "anybody seen Scott and Schmooze?"

Neha gave a horrified gasp.

40

Looking Like a True Survivor

They ran down the hill toward the cow pond—or at least they tried. "Running" looked more like picking their way through an obstacle course of debris, though there was a tree down on the barbed-wire fence, which would make it easier to climb over when they needed to.

"See," muttered Eli to the fence, "that's what you get," sounding a lot like Lisa all of a sudden.

"This way!" said Neha, hurrying toward the last place she'd seen Scott and Schmooze, feeling terrible that her help had never come. Sleekit darted in front of her, searching.

At first Neha didn't see them, only a mass of roots where trees had been upended and a scattering of big pink puddles on the ground. Then she realized the puddles were Schmooze.

"Over here!" Neha yelled. She sprinted toward Schmooze, with Eli and Court close behind her. They threw themselves down in the mud.

Scott was lying on his stomach underneath the biggest puddle. It was like looking at him underwater.

"They were surrounded," said Neha. She remembered seeing globs of Schmooze flying through the air, and her stomach did a nasty flip. There had been too many monsters to handle, and Schmooze had done what it always did—put itself between Scott and harm.

"Can he breathe?" asked Eli.

"How?" Neha asked. "We have to get him out of there."

She instinctively tried to move Schmooze, but her hands went right through it. Court tried to slip her fingers under its edges, but that wasn't working, either.

"Schmooze," said Eli. "Schmooze!"

He patted the surface of the blob, the way he might smack the cheek of someone he was trying to wake up. Neha realized what they were going to have to do and shuddered. She turned her body so she was kneeling alongside Schmooze.

"Court," she said, "you take Scott's other arm. Eli, you get his feet."

They both looked at her, shocked.

"We have to," she said. Then she plunged her hands down through the middle of the Schmooze puddle.

Scott emerged covered in slime from head to toe. The puddle reformed, quickly, wetly. Schmooze didn't seem cohesive to Neha, the way it always had before. She was afraid to think about what that meant.

They turned Scott around and put him down on his back.

"I don't see slime in his nose," said Court, checking. "Just dirt."

A whole cloud of it shot out of his nostrils and into Court's eyes as he started coughing. Court turned away.

"I can't rub my eyes!" she said in a panic, and Neha realized her hands were covered with slime. Most of the Creeps were watching, and Neha shooed Snorkelchorts toward the cow pond, then held Court's hands so she couldn't rub her eyes by accident. Tear streaks left clean trails on her dusty face as her eyes began to water.

Beside them, Eli was talking to Scott, helping him sit up.

"Don't look over there," he said.

"Schmooze," Scott choked, scrambling to his knees.

"Scott, don't look," said Eli.

But none of them could help looking. There were streaks of dirt through the puddle where they'd pulled Scott out. It didn't look like anything that had ever been alive.

"Come on, Schmooze," said Scott. "Don't do this."

He was leaning down close to the puddle, and his face was as big a mess as Court's.

The Chorts returned, and one of them carefully sprayed out Court's eyes. Another misunderstood the situation and did the same to Scott, who wasn't expecting it. He burbled through a faceful of water, wiping his eyes on the inside of his shirt and getting himself filthy again in the process. When he was done, he stared blankly at the ground.

"Scott," Neha said, sliding over now that Court no longer needed her. "I'm so sorry."

"Schmooze saved me," said Scott. "I'd have been eaten for sure."

Neha wanted to comfort him, but she wasn't sure what to do. She patted him awkwardly, but he grabbed her arm. She froze, afraid he was upset with her for touching him. Then he pointed.

"Look," he said.

Some of the flat, lifeless puddles had once more risen into spherical shapes.

And they were moving.

They found one another first, joining to form larger globs. Then, as one, they rolled toward the puddle that had covered Scott and rejoined it.

"Ooooooh," muttered a muffled voice, and the edges of the Schmooze pool rippled all the way around, as if its entire form were sighing. It gathered itself into its usual rounded shape. With a ripple, it banished the dirt from its center. Twin bulges traveled up over the top of its head and down on the side facing its friends, then extended to form eyestalks.

"Scott?" it said.

"He's okay, Schmooze," said Neha. "You saved him."

"Of course I did," said Schmooze. "I found him. He belongs to me."

They all waited to see if Scott was going to argue with this.

He shrugged.

"Finders keepers, I guess," he said with a grin. He held up his hand, and Schmooze gave him a globby high five.

Neha gave a huge sigh of relief, then glanced around.

"Are we missing anyone else?" she asked.

"I think everyone's here," said Eli.

The bus was hopelessly stuck. Dwight didn't seem too worried.

"The school will think the storm did it," he said. "I mean, I can't make quicksand, can I? No harm, no foul."

"I'm sorry for yelling at you before," said Eli. "I was wrong. You really came through for us."

Dwight grinned in relief and slapped Eli on the shoulder so hard he almost fell over.

"No duh," he said. "That's what bus drivers do."

"Is it?" asked Scott.

"Shhh," said Neha. "Don't look a gift bus driver in the mouth."

Everyone was banged up and bruised. Some of them were

bleeding. But they were all alive. They started walking home, and Dwight ambled off in the direction of his apartment.

Neha's house was closest, but all the lights were out and the front door was locked. The Prasads didn't have a hidden key. Her mother said there was no such thing as hidden enough.

"What if they went to the police station?" she asked as they walked down the street toward Eli's.

What if they went out in the tornado? she thought, but it was a frightening thought, and she shoved it away.

Eli and Lisa's mom wasn't home, either. No car, no lights. And her car wasn't at the sitter's. Lisa had left most of her courage behind during the tornado. Now she was a tired little kid who wanted her mom. They'd gently suggested to her squid steed that it might be a good idea to lie low for a while, so they took turns carrying Lisa, but she was really heavy. Neha was tripping over her own feet by the time they got to Court's house, and that was where they found three sets of parents, a police car pulled up to the curb, and every light ablaze.

Amy saw them first.

"They're here!" she hollered as they limped up the driveway. Sleekit, who'd been glued to Neha's side, vanished under the nearest car just in case. Eli set Lisa down and put his arm around her. When she let him, it said everything anyone could need to know about their day. Neha stood there looking at them, fiddling with the monster-clawed edges of her shirt. It had been nice having friends in the neighborhood while it lasted, but she was willing to bet they'd never be allowed to see one another outside of school again after this.

Eli's mom came blazing out of the house with the Castles' cordless phone in one hand. She might as well have been Schmooze, the way she wrapped around her kids. Court's and Neha's parents were right behind her. They circled and started checking every-one for bumps, bruises, and missing parts.

"James, can you hear me? I've got them, they're safe," said Mrs. Goodman into the phone. "I'll call you when we're home."

She hung up, gave Scott the phone, and sent him inside with Amy to call his parents.

"I'm okay. I'm okay," Neha said, over and over. "I'm sorry."

"Where on earth were you?" demanded Eli's mom.

"Mrs. Harvey lost Lisa," Eli said. "We went to find her. Then the storm came."

It was true enough.

"Why didn't you come to us?" asked Neha's mother, cupping her face.

"We didn't think there was time," she said, "and there wasn't. The storm came before we could get home. We had to find shelter. If we'd come to get you, Lisa would have been out in the tornado alone."

Her father kissed her head.

"You did the right thing, beta," he said, though his hand shook as he ran it over her hair. "But we are going to have to discuss the rules. We need to know where you are at all times."

Neha gulped.

"Oh, honey," Court's mom said to her, "you scared us half to death. We thought we'd lost you."

Neha wondered what they were even doing home.

"Is the restaurant okay?" Court asked, echoing her thoughts.

The Castles looked at each other.

"Oh no," said Court. "Is it wrecked again?"

Her daddy put a hand on her shoulder.

"It's no more busted up than it was, Coco," he said. "But if you think the restaurant is what really matters to us, you've got the wrong end of the stick. Expect some changes around here."

Looking at the Creeps milling just outside the glow of the driveway lights, Neha didn't see how they could expect anything *but* changes.

"Coco," whispered Eli.

"Shut up," said Court.

Neha smiled.

41

Donuts and Dynasties

Loud pounding on Court's door woke her up.

"Courtney! Come on!"

She groaned and threw her pillow. Somewhere near the door, a Snorkelchort meeped as the pillow landed. The Gargyle rolled over in a flurry of socks, and she scratched his ears. He was a permanent resident at Court's house now. She'd won that battle on the grounds that it already smelled like feet there anyway.

"Fine, then," said Joshie on the other side of the door. "Don't get up. I get to pick the special."

Those were fighting words.

"Joshie, it's my turn!" she yelled. She rolled over and more or less fell out of the top bunk. When she realized she'd accidentally dragged her Miss Piggy sheets with her, she quickly threw them back up there and covered them with her Oklahoma Sooners blanket. Zeb, who was a lot bigger than he used to be, gave a laughing hiss from the foot of the bed.

"Shut up, you," she said. He waved one wing at her to show he wasn't scared.

"So loud," moaned Neha from the bottom bunk.

"Hey, you're the one who was all excited to have a sleepover," Court said, though she'd been looking forward to it, too. Neha had been grounded since their little night of Tornado Tag. The Prasads had cut them some slack and let them have sleepovers at Neha's house, which was how Court had been introduced to Bollywood, but this was the first time Neha had been allowed to stay at Court's. So far they agreed that the Prasads had better movies, and the Castles had better breakfasts.

Speaking of breakfast . . .

"Get up, Neha!"

"I changed my mind," she groaned.

Court laughed.

"No, you didn't. Get up, or I'll put your toothbrush in the bathroom holder."

She sat bolt upright.

"No Scrubbler," she said, fumbling for her overnight bag and her new sketchbook.

They tumbled down the stairs in T-shirts and jeans, Neha still pulling her ponytail through its hair tie. Court was wearing hers short these days, on account of her manta-bat haircut.

"We're ready!" Court called.

"Mama and Daddy left forever ago," said Amy.

"What? We need a ride!" Court said.

Out in the driveway, a horn honked. Sleekit streaked out the front door as Court opened it, winding between their feet.

Their yard and the vacant lot next door were as messy as ever. The mess was a bit more purposeful now, though. There was a warren of Snorkelchort holes. The Cootie Catchers were schooling around . . . catching cooties, presumably. Neighborhood kids hung all over the Spider Plant on a daily basis.

Court loved their yard.

Parked diagonally across the driveway was a delivery van. The windows were down and the radio was blaring. Emblazoned on the side was the logo for the Castles' new business: a big box of breakfast pastries and the words ROYAL DONUTS.

Monsters, it turned out, could occasionally be good things. The folks who owned the whole Showplace Pizza chain had agreed to take the insurance money from the "storm damage" that had happened during the fund-raiser and give Court's parents back their franchise fee. The Castles had promptly opened up a new shop. They liked making donuts way more than they'd ever liked running a pizza parlor, and because donuts were a morning thing, they were home for dinner. They could only afford one van to start, but that was fine. They had big plans and the best donuts in town.

"Get in!" said Dwight.

"New paint job?" Neha asked as she hauled the side door open. "I don't remember the roof being pink."

It rippled, and two eyestalks leaned over the side.

"Good morning!" burbled Schmooze.

"Took you long enough," said Scott. He was grinning, he was friendly, he was still annoying. Court found that kind of comforting.

The girls squeezed in next to Hairstack, who was taking up about half of the backseat. Scott spat out hair as he was smooshed against the far window, and muttered under his breath.

"Who's 'scruffy-looking'?" demanded Hairstack.

Eli was sitting up front, arguing with Sleekit.

"I already called shotgun," he said.

She solved the problem by sitting on him.

Business had been booming at the donut shop, but a fundraiser was good exposure, and it would help pay for Mrs. Barton's summer desert field trip. Not that any of them had signed up. After they'd gotten lost in their own neighborhood, no one was going to trust them to go to Utah. They didn't want to leave the Creeps, anyway. But at least any student who wanted to go would be able to.

They pulled up to the athletic fields at the park and joined Court's parents, who were already setting up their booth. Joshie, predictably, was playing catch with some of his friends, and Sleekit immediately streaked off in search of Lisa.

"We're back!" hollered Dwight as they started unloading the donuts. Eli's momma and Neha's parents were already there, chatting and helping. Scott's were selling hot dogs out of the big wooden concession stand, same as they did every Saturday, so he headed over there, promising to buy one for Hairstack. Schmooze slid off the side of the van and headed over to one of the soccer goals. He thought it was funny to slime his way back and forth through the net.

They'd kept *Plot Twist* going, and ever since they'd started accepting submissions, they'd been noticing new Creeps here and there. Court figured there were probably six for each one she saw. They'd had new monsters to deal with, too. Eli wasn't the only kid with a flair for creepy stories. So far, Fouler was willing to lay down the law to any monster that didn't obey the treaty, but Court kept her eyes peeled when it was her turn to take out the trash. She was getting some pocket money out of it, though. She, Neha, and Lisa had a side gig designing and building monster traps.

Customers were already lining up (for donuts, not traps). Neha was putting the letters on the sidewalk sign while her mom and Court's dad brainstormed a new donut recipe flavored with rosewater and cardamom. Court started arranging donuts in the plastic display cases. Eli's momma came over and squeezed his shoulder while he was stacking boxes of assorted dozens.

"Daddy and I discussed it, and Mrs. Prasad is your new emergency contact while I'm at work," she said. "I'll put her number on the fridge. She says you two are welcome to walk down there anytime."

"I can help you with that math homework you've been struggling with," said Mrs. Prasad, overhearing.

Eli's eyes widened.

"Momma!" he said. "You don't need to be telling people about my math!"

She laughed. "I didn't say a word."

Court looked over at Neha, who was biting her lip.

Mrs. Prasad held up her hands, and it was amazing how much she and Neha looked alike when they were both trying not to laugh.

"All I'm saying is I'm here if you need me," she said before turning to resume her conversation with Court's daddy.

Out on the soccer field, someone scored.

"Yum!" said the goal, which . . . appeared to have eyeballs.

Court dropped a donut by accident.

"If this was a story," Eli mused, "there'd be something creepy hiding under those bleachers."

Halfway up the stands, a little kid screamed. All three of their heads whipped in that direction. They listened hard for a minute, then relaxed.

"You," said Neha to Eli, shaking her head. "Your stories are making us paranoid."

Court made change for a customer. Eli handed over a box of

donuts. Neha, finished with the sign, came to join them. They stood quietly together for a minute.

"It's probably fine," said Eli at last.

"Yeah," Court said slowly.

"Yum!" said the goal again.

Court looked at her friends.

"Maybe we'd better go check."

ACKNOWLEDGMENTS

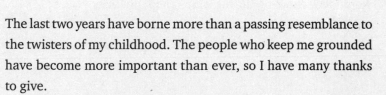

The last two years have borne more than a passing resemblance to the twisters of my childhood. The people who keep me grounded have become more important than ever, so I have many thanks to give.

To Brooks Sherman, my agent: you're a staunch advocate, a tough critic, and a boundless enthusiast. You do wonders for my peace of mind and make an unwieldy disaster of my to-read list. I'm awfully fond of you.

Warm thanks to my editor, Holly West, for our wonderful editorial chats on Google Hangouts and your enthusiasm for my weirdest ideas. I'm so grateful for your encouragement and insight. Many thanks to the entire team at Feiwel and Friends/ Macmillan, including Ilana Worrell, Melanie Sanders, Raymond Colón, Mary Van Akin, Molly Brouillete, and Liz Dresner.

Thank you to the teams at the Bent Agency and Janklow & Nesbit, with particular gratitude to Wendi Gu, and much love to my delightful, collegial agent sibs.

To the writers who whip me into shape and improve my authorly well-being in ways great and small, especially Amy Reichert, Jessica Fair Owens, Supriya Kelkar, Brandon Stenger, Angie Thomas, Becky Albertalli, Celeste Pewter, Melissa Marino, Carla Cullen, Gareth Wronski, Heidi Schulz, Liz Osisek, Nina Moreno, Gail Werner, Devon Greyson, Allison Pang, Sage Blackwood, Hebah Udden, Stephanie Burgis, and Katie Glover.

To the 2014 Pitch Wars mentees, the Pitch Wars Mentor Group, the 2017 Middle Grade Debuts, and the Spooky Middle Grade Crew: thank you for helping me stay connected when life itself begins to feel like an obstacle to connection. Much love as always to the Pitch Wars mentors who took a chance on me, Jaye Robin Brown and Cat Scully; the co-mentor whose team spirit kept me mentoring during a bananapants-busy year, JC Davis; and the mentee whose manuscript provided me with such sweet distraction, Ellen Stonaker. To the many writers who inspire me daily with their craft, advocacy, kindness, and often their bluntness: I love you all.

Because this book is a throwback to my own middle grade years, this seems like the perfect time to thank specific teachers and librarians who exemplified the huge role caring adult mentors can play in kids' lives. Moving as often as I do is an adventure, but over the years, to my regret, I've lost track of people I'd dearly love to thank in person. Perhaps these words will find them. Thank you forever to Miss Garlett, Marion Callahan, Mrs. O'Halloran, and Susan Bishop. Each of you was a confidant and an inspiration. I'd also like to thank three childhood friends I *have* managed to track down, Robin Rozzell Green, Salena Locklin Dixon, and Michelle Pope Surber. Thank you for being wonderful childhood companions and bolstering my optimism by growing up to be remarkable women.

To my students in China, whose chattiness, enthusiasm, and hard work make this planet feel like a much smaller and cozier place, and to their parents: thank you for your everlasting kindness and insight.

To everyone at Coat Check and Provider for keeping me supplied with coffee and workspace, and to the folks at Tyner Pond, for serving up snacks and sympathy in equal measure.

To my fam and my family, two groups that are distinct but overlapping. To all the Heartland and Midwest youth and adult volunteers who've enriched my life and broadened my horizons: thank you for the love, the support, and the memories of late-night editing sessions in strange places. To all my friends far and near who take the time to be a supportive presence, no matter how far away I've moved or how quickly I'm racing in and out of shared spaces—and bless you, Courtney Fishero Bender and Megan Winsted Swazuk, for making so many opportunities possible for our family at a time when my DIY abilities are at a severe deficit. To my parents, Beth, Cathy, Frank, and Joe, my siblings, Chrissie, Jenny, Kate, Matt, and Scott, and my nieces and nephews, Cole, Jack, JD, Natalie, Nathan, and Tracy. You feed my stories in more ways than you know.

To my husband, Bill. I love you and I like you. I'm prouder of us and our family than anything else I've ever done or been part of. And to my children, Will, Evan, and Graeme, you're all brilliant, creative, hilarious, hardworking people. You make being a mom wonderful (and being an author possible)!